I0672678

The Debutante

Worthington Manor, Volume 1

Gemma Frances

Published by Gemma Frances, 2024.

The Debutante

1st Edition

ISBN: 978-1-7635781-2-8 (paperback)

ISBN: 978-1-7635781-3-5 (e-book)

www.gemmafrances.com[1]

@gemma_frances

Cover design by Musrath Humaira Moon

Dedication:

For my parents; for your unconditional love and sacrifice

1.

The layout of the classroom reflected its hierarchy. At the front were the geeks or nerds, eagerly absorbing new knowledge just as a sponge absorbs water - the doctors or lawyers, architects or engineers of the future perhaps, a motley crew of misfits by their side (they didn't know it yet, but one day when their school days were over, this hierarchy would cease to exist - though try telling that to any teenager who longs to fit in).

Occasionally a harassed young teacher might place one of the more disruptive kids at the front to mix things up a bit, but otherwise the bottom tier of school society would give way to the middle tier - the floaters - those very few kids who were neither quite at top of the pecking order nor the bottom - who were gifted with the ability to get along seamlessly with both crowds without being excluded by either. At the back were the most popular kids in class (often interspersed with the most-naughty), for whom fitting in at all costs and maintaining their coveted status was infinitely more important than anything the teacher might have to say.

Issy Worthing fell into the latter camp - you could recognise her by her ironed-straight swathes of blonde hair, willowy frame, and the fact that almost every young girl in that room would have given pretty much anything to swap places with her, even if just for a day, but never more so than today.

There was something so 1990's about a handwritten note, but since Miss Partridge, the English teacher, made a point of confiscating her classes' mobile phones at the start of each lesson (apart from Jack Shaw, who discovered that shoving his phone down his pants was a highly effective deterrent to any confiscation attempts - and not even Miss Partridge was keen to challenge that), the students of class 13B had little choice.

Issy was sat next to her best friend, Mila Stuart, who was almost a carbon copy of Issy except for a perpetually tanned glow that Issy, with her olde English ancestry dating back to William the Conqueror, could not achieve without a bottle, much to her dismay. Miss Partridge was saying something gripping about conjunctive adverbs, as thirty sets of eyes strayed out of the classroom window to the intangible freedom beyond, where the school-field was grazed with daisies and dandelions and a soft, early-summer sun, when a pen flew like a miniature missile and landed at Issy's feet.

Miss Partridge raised her eyebrows but didn't skip a beat, and as Issy bent down to retrieve the pen, she noticed with some excitement - by far the most exciting thing to have happened to her that day, anyway - that wrapped around it was a slip of lined paper. Hastily, she unwrapped the note and set it on her lap, then reached towards the occupant of the desk behind her to return the pen to its owner, a frisson of anticipation running through her as Chad Connor locked his smooth, dark eyes onto hers and winked.

Mila gripped her arm. Unfolding the paper, Issy laid it on her desk so they could both see, careful not to draw the attention of Miss Partridge.

They may have just been three seemingly innocuous little words, but to Issy, they were way more than that: *Be my date?*

She gasped. She'd just assumed that Steph Sutton, with the impressive curves she did her utmost to flaunt insofar as uniform restrictions would permit, would be Chad's obvious choice. It was no secret she'd been trying to capture his attention all year. And whilst Issy had always admired Chad from afar - and she was not alone in that - she'd just assumed he was well and truly off the table. Evidently, she was wrong, and in that moment, there was no doubt she was the most fortunate girl in her final year of school.

'O-M-G, what are you gonna say?' Mila's whisper was almost a squeak.

Issy turned over the paper, and in big capital letters wrote one word: 'YES!'

Mila grinned. None of this had gone unnoticed by Steph Sutton, particularly not when she saw Issy wrapping what appeared to be a piece of paper around her pen and deliberately nudging it to the floor with her elbow. She especially didn't miss the look on Chad's face when he leant over to pick it up, nor his grin when he read whatever the note said, nor the slap on the back he got from his best mate, followed by the frantic whispering that passed between the two girls. She had a pretty good idea what it must be about, and she was distinctly unimpressed.

She'd been able to persuade her mum to buy her a fitted, red dress with a low, beaded bodice and high side slit for the prom. She'd harped on about it so much that she'd worn down both her mum's defences *and* her better judgement. All Steph's fantasies for the past three months had been about Chad's reaction when he saw her in the dress - which she was sure he would be unable to resist - and now priggish Issy Worthing, with her ethereal, olde-worlde beauty, formidable lineage, and ancestral stately home, had done the unthinkable by breaking the unwritten rule and stealing him from right under her nose.

Fortunately for Steph, the kerfuffle in the back row hadn't escaped Miss Partridge's attention either. She nudged her glasses back up her nose, as she had a habit of doing.

'A conjunctive adverb can be used to connect the ideas between two sentences, for instance, "Issy Worthing kept talking in class, consequently - *consequently* is the conjunctive adverb in this sentence, you will observe - she was asked to share her exciting news with the rest of us."'

Issy paled.

'Well?' Miss Partridge cleared her throat. 'Since you were studying your piece of paper so intently a moment before, I can only assume you've been taking copious notes throughout our lesson. Perhaps you could be the first to provide an example of a sentence containing a conjunctive adverb for us?'

Chad smirked, and in the opposite corner, Steph Sutton narrowed her eyes in satisfaction. This wasn't over yet.

*

When Issy stepped into the porch of their small, inobtrusive semi after school that afternoon, she knew not even the niggling presence of her younger sisters nor the nagging from her mum could bring her down. She was floating on air and bursting to share her good news. She'd spent the entire bus ride discussing dress options with Mila, and whilst this had been the primary topic of conversation amongst her friends for the past couple of months at least, never had it held as much import as it did when she had the security of a date and Chad's reaction to seeing her in the dress for the very first time to consider. It was imperative to make the best first impression she could.

She was so full of her own thoughts that it took her a few moments to register things were different. She couldn't hear anything for one. Usually, before she'd even opened the porch door, she'd hear the cartoons on the TV in the background, and her sisters, Jasmine and Ella would either be embroiled in a squabble or playing together boisterously. Their mother, Susan, would be busy preparing dinner, yelling at the girls periodically to either stop fighting or keep the noise down so she could hear herself think. The moment Issy walked through the door, she'd be told to either help keep the girls in line, or (and she wasn't sure which was worse), get roped in to chopping up vegetables or setting the table. Then, after dinner, the TV would go off until they'd finished their homework – without doubt the worst part of the school-night routine that their mother was most adamant about maintaining.

After that, the night was theirs. If she and her siblings weren't quarrelling, Issy would usually spend it watching TV or lying in her room texting Mila, or, especially on weekends, heading out to catch up with her friends.

'Hey mum,' she said, as she opened the door between the porch and their living room. 'What's for d-?'

She stopped abruptly. The TV had been muted, and her mum was leant forwards on the couch sobbing, whilst the younger girls sat either side of her, rubbing her back as they looked anxiously at Issy, unsure of what to do. She could see they were relieved she was home – the elder sister ready to take charge and let them off the hook.

Issy was taken aback. Their mother didn't cry – not since their dad had left anyway, and that was a long time ago now.

'Mum... What happened? Are you ok?'

Susan nodded, though it was perfectly obvious she was not ok. 'It's...' she stuttered. 'It's your grandmother... I'm afraid she's... Passed away. A stroke. It was quick, she won't have suffered.'

Issy gasped. Their grandma was quite a remote figure, but even in her seventies a robust one. It was hard to imagine her not simply living forever. She had to; she had a sprawling country estate and acres of land and outbuildings to manage. She was on all the village committees. Issy and her sisters didn't really know her very well. They didn't see her often – as far as Issy was aware, she and their mum didn't get along, though none of them really knew why. Something about Susan shunning their family fortune and title to live a more ordinary life with a more ordinary man, who, to Susan's infinite chagrin, Grandma had turned out to be quite right about in the end.

'Oh, mum. I'm so sorry.'

Her own news forgotten, Issy gestured for her sisters to move aside so she could squeeze in next to their mum. She wrapped her arms around her and hugged her close, which only made Susan sob all the harder. It felt a little awkward at first – Issy and their mum hadn't exactly been getting on themselves lately. But her mum's tears, her vulnerability – something she rarely glimpsed – tugged at her heart.

'Put the kettle on, Jasmine.' Her voice held all the authority of the eldest sibling, even in a whisper. 'Ella, you go and get the chocolate biscuits, the *good* ones, and try and find the takeaway menus – looks like fish and chips is on the cards tonight.' It was their mum's favourite, after all.

The girls put up none of their usual resistance (though for a moment, Ella did look as though she was about to put up a fight about the choice of takeaway, McDonald's being a particularly rare treat), and were willing to defer to Issy just this once.

Issy rested her head against Susan's and breathed in her scent – the most familiar, impossible to articulate, and yet somehow the most instantly comforting scent in the world.

'We'll need to go to Worthington for the funeral of course, to get everything tied up. I'm afraid we'll be there for quite some time.'

Issy raised a perfectly arched eyebrow. Quite some time. 'How long?' she asked, as a sense of foreboding washed over her. Chad. The prom.

'Weeks at least. Months even. There's *a lot* to do. A lot to... consider.'

Susan wiped her eyes with her hands, eyes the same cornflower blue as Issy's, grabbed a tissue, and wiped her nose before dabbing off her excess mascara. It was easier for her to keep her emotions in check when she remained focussed on the practicalities.

'But...'

Susan looked at her sharply, and the familiar tension rose between them.

'But what?'

'Well...' Issy breathed. 'What about my exams? My A Levels? They're pretty important – you're always rambling on about how important they are. And what about the prom?'

Issy felt her frustration rising as she recognised what was at stake. If she'd gotten the exact same news a mere twenty-four hours earlier, before Chad, as much as an extended stay in the middle of nowhere with only her mum and sisters for company would be a total drag, she wouldn't be dragging her feet. But she so, *so* wanted to get dressed up and make her entrance to the prom on Chad's arm.

'Can't you just take the girls with you while I stay here with Dad?'

'I wish I could, Issy, but I can't. I've already asked him. He's swamped with work and working away a lot – you'd end up stuck at home with your stepmother.'

Issy rolled her eyes. A summer with her stepmum was probably the only thing worse than a summer at Worthington Manor. 'But the prom, my exams...'

'I've arranged with the head-teacher for you to sit your exams at the village school.'

'Really?' She sighed.

Jasmine and Ella crept in, placing their humble offerings on the coffee table. Jasmine glared at Issy to remind her this was not the time to be causing a scene. For once Issy was prepared to accept that she was right, but she could sense Chad's attentions slipping away, and an image of the curvaceous Steph Sutton, a satisfied smirk on her face, flashed into mind.

'I can't promise anything,' said Susan. 'The next few weeks are going to be very busy. But I'll do my very best to get you to your prom, ok? And let's not forget, your grandmother, my mum, has just passed away.' She sniffed as tears threatened to overwhelm her once again. 'In the grand scheme of things, I think you'd agree that is more important than any prom.'

Issy couldn't argue with that. She knew she was being incredibly self-absorbed right now. But it was just the timing... Oh, it was unfair. It was so very unfair.

*

Later that night, Issy threw herself onto her bed and considered all the implications of the next few weeks. Missing her last day of Year Thirteen. Not sitting her A Levels at her own school. Not celebrating the end of an era with her own friends, many of whom would be heading off to college or university. Things would never be the same again. Chad.

Somewhere, tangled in amongst these thoughts, were thoughts of her mother and thoughts of her grandmother, who in hindsight she wished she'd been a lot closer to and made more effort with, but growing up you didn't tend to think too much about those sorts of things - you simply took your lead from your parents.

Her phone beeped.

Hey! It was Mila. *Have you heard from Chad? I hear Steph Sutton's nose is out of joint.*

Issy shook her head in irritation. If Steph and Chad weren't together in the first place, which they weren't, then she had no right to be put out. Chad wasn't her property, and she could pretty much take her pick of the guys anyway, so it wasn't like she was missing out. Deftly, Issy fired back a response.

I'm not sure I'm even going to make it to the prom now. My grandma's just died, and I have to go to Worthington Manor. For months. MONTHS! (Tears emoji).

(Super surprised emoji x 3). OMG, I'm so sorry. But what about school? Chad and the prom? Can't you stay here with your dad?

Huh. Thought Issy. Like he would care. *Nope. He's too busy with work, as usual. Looks like I'll have to sit my exams at the village school. Mum's still gonna to try to get me to the prom, though.*

I hope so, Mila fired back. *It wouldn't be the same without you. And we don't want Steph Sutton swooping in to steal your date.*

No, thought Issy, she very much did not want that.

Whatever you do, pinged Mila, *don't give Chad any reason to think things might be off.*

Moments later, her phone beeped again. *Hey babe...* It was Chad, and her heart leapt with equal parts joy and frustration. *Looking forward to the prom x*

Issy sighed, unsure how to respond. She'd arrived home that evening with so much anticipation, but now... What a mess the night had turned out to be.

2.

Though the sky outside was brightest blue and clear of cloud cover, a frosty silence had descended between mother and daughter as their car traversed rolling hills and negotiated narrow country roads canopied by thick trees that filtered the sunlight streaming in through the windows. Jasmine and Ella's spirits could not be dampened, however. If anything, they were fuelled by the novelty of adventure, not to mention the various sweets and snacks they'd been plied with to help them manage the long journey, and their tender age meant they were oblivious to the atmosphere that had enveloped mum and Issy - either that or the frequency of the hostilities between them had dampened any sensitivity they might otherwise have had.

They bounced around as though seated on hot pins, loud and boisterous as they pointed out this and that, as Issy sat stony-faced in the middle wishing she was back home with her friends rather than racing off to spend the summer in the absolute middle of nowhere with only annoying ten and seven-year-olds for company and her ever-disapproving mother.

Her phone beeped a welcome reprieve from the monotony of the trip, and Issy lunged at it.

*So, you couldn't get out of it then, you've still gotta go to Worthington? Only, a group of us are heading out tonight, and **you know who** is going to be there... x*

If only, thought Issy. It was so unfair. Mila was her best friend, and her mum wouldn't even let her come so that she'd have someone her own age to hang out with. Exam revision and all that.

Fat chance, she replied, *Mum's on a mission to ruin my life.*

Bummer. It won't be the same without you, but there's gotta be worse things in life than spending three months living it up as Lady of the Manor.

Issy rolled her eyes. Her friends just didn't get it. They thought it was really cool her family had their own manor, but to Issy it was just her grandmother's house - she'd known no other. Whilst it may be a sprawling stone house dating back to the seventeen-hundreds when one of her great grandfathers had commissioned its build as a country retreat to help his ailing wife, it was also full of a heap of old junk and there was literally nothing to do there, terrible mobile reception (her ancestors had had little need for it, after all), and not a neighbour for miles. Issy knew she would simply *die* of boredom, and whilst all her friends were off having a great time celebrating the end of their A Levels on an extra-long school holiday, she would be stuck in the middle of nowhere with only her two irritating sisters for company.

To make matters worse, Issy was so worried that Chad would tire of waiting around for her and end up asking Steph Sutton to the prom instead. The thought of them together - of Steph all dressed up in some beautiful clingy, sparkly dress with Chad on her arm - was more than Issy could bear. Couldn't her grandmother have held on just a teensy tiny bit longer so that her whole life wasn't ruined by her sudden passing?

'I don't understand why you couldn't have just let me stay home by myself instead of dragging me with you to Grandma's house where there's nothing for me to do. The Wi-Fi sucks - how on earth am I supposed to revise?'

Susan bit her lip. As it happened, there was one *very* good reason she hadn't really wanted to bring Issy along with her, but in the end, she'd had no other option. 'You know why.'

'But I'm eighteen now, remember. Pretty much an adult.'

Susan gave an exasperated sigh. How many times were they going to have to have this conversation? 'Issy, you don't even know how to switch on the washing machine, let alone prepare yourself three meals a day that don't come out of a toaster or the microwave;

or keep a house clean and tidy, or iron your clothes. You have no sense of direction for what on earth it is you're going to do with the rest of your life. Thinking you're an adult and actually *being* one are two very different things. You don't just get to do whatever you like all day, you have responsibilities. Besides,' her mother glared at her, 'there are worse things in life than crappy mobile reception. Instead of being glued to your phone twenty-four-seven, you might learn how to use your imagination, like I did. You could visit a library. Read an actual book. And you'll have your sisters – they love spending time with you.'

'Huh.' Issy glared at her mother in the rear-view mirror. 'They're babies!'

'You're the baby,' said Jasmine.

'You're a big baby!' Ella giggled.

Issy nudged them with her elbows.

'Ouch.'

'Ow! Muuuum, Issy hit me,' Jasmine whined.

'No, I didn't.'

'Yes, you did.'

'You did,' parroted Ella.

Issy was unimpressed. 'Why do we have to stay so long?'

'You know why. Because,' Susan enunciated, 'there's a funeral to organise, an estate to sort, and all your grandma's effects to sift through. Not to mention probate and all that entails. It will take time. And I'm going to need some help looking after the girls.'

'You're gonna use me as your live-in babysitter?'

Susan sighed. 'It's about time you had responsibilities, Issy. I'll have a lot of important matters to attend to. When I was your age, I had a job - I was earning money of my own. You don't realise how lucky you are - in previous generations, children went down the mines, or worked as chimney sweeps, housemaids or servants. In poor families, older daughters practically raised their younger siblings. Thousands suffered to put an end to all that and give women the opportunities we have today - opportunities you don't seem to have any inclination to take up. All I'm asking is that you keep your sisters out of mischief for a couple of hours each day while I sort things out at the manor. And you never know, perhaps you'll make friends in the village. Or find a job.'

'I'm sure I would, if I could be bothered to walk the two-mile round trip every day,' Issy retorted. 'And what would I do with the money I earned anyway, buy a cow?' Issy couldn't imagine how country folk filled their time. There was no Zara or H&M.

'Fresh country air never did anyone any harm. And there's bound to be a bike or two somewhere on the property.'

'A penny farthing?

Susan narrowed her eyes. 'Why don't you think of this as an adventure. Spending the summer holidays in an old country manor would be considered fairly exciting by some, I'm sure.'

Issy sighed. It was exactly what Mila had said - what they obviously all thought. Did nobody get it?

'The boys at school said the manor's haunted,' said Jasmine, her eyes wide. 'I'm gonna stay up really late and see if I can catch a ghost!'

'Whoa!' said Ella, her expression betraying equal measure of fear and awe.

'You'll do no such thing,' said Susan. It was hard enough work getting Ella to sleep at night without Jasmine putting silly ideas in her head.

'There's no such thing as ghosts,' Issy sniffed, with all the worldly knowledge of an eighteen-year-old. 'And even if there was, you'd never be able to *catch* one.'

'Anyway, there's another reason for bringing you here,' said Susan.

'What?'

'Well, now that I've got some time off work, it will be a chance for me and you to spend some time together. A chance for us to reconnect and try to stop fighting so much.'

'Yeh,' Issy glared at her mother through the rear-view mirror, 'depriving me from all my friends for my entire summer holidays while you work all day and I get stuck with these two sounds like a great way of bringing us together. Like that's going to work. I still can't believe you're making me miss my prom.'

'Oh Issy.' Susan shook her head. 'I told you, if I get grandma's affairs sorted in time, I should still be able to get you there.'

But Chad would probably end up going with Stephanie anyway, thought Issy, so what was the point?

Mother and daughter remained silent for the rest of the journey, each lost in their own thoughts whilst Jasmine and Ella made more than enough noise for the four of them.

Susan shook her head. Whilst it was fortunate she only had one more teenage year to endure, somehow it felt like a lifetime. It was evident that as far as Issy was concerned, Mums were from Mars and Teenagers were from Venus (or, perhaps even further away than that - Pluto), but she knew that Issy wouldn't get the reference, and if anything, her saying it out loud would only reinforce how old and out of touch Issy already thought she was.

Thankfully she didn't need to say anything, as the thick brush of woods to their right gave way to a huge wooden gate flanked either side by two stone pillars. If one didn't know the area well, they'd drive straight past it.

'Look!' cried Jasmine, who had just enough fragments of memory of earlier visits to keep her informed as to what to expect. 'We're here!'

'Whoa!' Ella breathed. Though she had been to Worthington Manor before, she had so little recollection of the place, it was as if she was visiting for the very first time.

Susan pulled over on the gravel, turned off the engine, and leapt out of the car to negotiate the gate's lock and chain. She gestured for Issy to help, and with a heavy sigh to indicate she was the most put-upon teen ever, Issy slowly exited the car and helped her mother push open the wooden gate that creaked and groaned in resistance.

'I'll need you to close it behind us too, Issy, do you think you can manage that?'

'It depends. Do we have to do this *every* time we leave the house?'

'I suspect a ride on a penny farthing no longer seems so bad.'

Once the car was through, Issy heaved the gate shut and scrambled over a whining Jasmine's feet on the way in before pulling the car door shut behind her with a belligerent slam. Gravel crunched under-wheel as they inched slowly along the long, twisting driveway to the house, keeping an eye out for any errant deer that might happen to cross their path.

'Look, Mummy!' Ella gasped, as the oak trees finally cleared, revealing the buttermilk façade of Worthington Manor set amidst a backdrop of rolling hills; a façade that was probably no less impressive now than it had been three-hundred years ago, to everyone except Issy, to whom it represented little more than a gilded cage.

The oak doors opened, and a rotund old lady wrapped in an apron dashed out in a flurry, a taller old man in a tweed suit and flat cap trundling behind her with the hint of a smile playing about his mouth.

'Good afternoon, Lady Worthing,' said the housekeeper, spontaneously abandoning formality to pull Susan into a hug. 'It's been too long since your last visit!'

'Susan, please.' Their mother's voice was stern, but the affection in her eyes was evident as she embraced the old Mrs Lamb.

'I'm terribly sorry about your mum.'

'I'm sorry too.' Susan's composure wobbled slightly. 'I wish I'd been there...' She sniffed. 'But I'm glad she had both of you until the very end. I'll always be very grateful for that.'

The girls looked upon this interaction with interest, even Issy, despite her best efforts to convey a casual disinterest in absolutely everything, as teens are obliged to do. Though the strained relationship between Issy's mum and grandmother had robbed them of the opportunity to become close, Issy was quite sure she'd never observed such easy affection between mother and grandmother than she had between her mother and these two elderly household employees. There was something vaguely intriguing about it as she wondered why that might be the case, and it suddenly struck her that her mother was actually a whole person beyond simply being her mum. The concept was a novel one.

'Edward,' said Mrs Lamb with a flap of her hands, 'what are you doing there, bumbling about? The suitcases! Heavens!'

Susan acknowledged the old man with a smile, and at his wife's bidding, he immediately set about unloading their car.

'My, haven't your girls grown,' said Mrs Lamb approvingly, and the two youngest beamed their widest smiles at her in response. They couldn't help but be drawn to this grandmotherly old lady. 'And your eldest,' she gestured at Issy, 'what a beauty! Just like you were when you were that age.'

'Only slightly less agreeable.' Susan laughed as Issy's sulky expression did nothing to contradict her.

'Now, do either of you girls like cake?' Mrs Lamb peered at each of them in turn.

Jasmine's eyes widened. 'Are you kidding? We love cake!'

Ella nodded enthusiastically, and whilst Issy shrugged as though she could take it or leave it, secretly, she didn't want to miss out on a slice.

'We like ghosts too,' said Jasmine. 'Do you think we'll find any during our stay?'

'Oh,' said Mrs Lamb, 'don't let my husband hear you mention ghosts - he'll talk your ear off.'

'Ghosts, you said, lass?' Mr Lamb dragged a pair of suitcases across the gravel with a huff and a puff before lowering his voice conspiratorially, with a pointed glance in Issy's direction, 'I think you'll find the most surprising thing about Worthington Manor are the things that *disappear* by night, not the things that appear.'

Issy wondered what on earth he meant. Perhaps he was referring to their Great, Great, Great Grandmother Worthing, who had disappeared all those years ago? Otherwise, she concluded that the only thing Mr Lamb had lost was his marbles.

'Mr Lamb, please!' Susan implored him, 'I would like my girls' to sleep tonight.'

Mr Lamb simply winked at her. After all, it felt like only yesterday that Susan had demanded he share all his best ghost stories with her when she was a girl. Jasmine and Ella followed him into the hall, hanging onto his every word.

'Come, my dear,' said Mrs Lamb to Susan, 'the kettle is still hot. Let's have a cuppa and a chinwag like old times. You too, if you like, Issy. It looks as though your sisters are nicely occupied for the time being.'

She winked, and Issy understood the subtext: 'You're off the hook, for now.' However reluctant she was to find anything to like about her enforced stay at Worthington Manor, Issy couldn't help but take a liking to the old Mrs Lamb.

3.

The study was timeless, and Susan breathed it in, hopeful that even the faintest trace of her mother's perfume might linger in the upholstery. It was exactly how it had been when her mother was still alive, just as for her mother, it was exactly how it had been when her grandfather was still alive. The rosewood bureau, the swivel chair – a novelty of its time, her mother's typewriter - even the dim light that filtered in from the window upon dancing dust motes, just as she remembered. For a study, the light was never quite adequate.

Mrs Lamb was already at the desk, rifling through its drawers.

'Susan!'

She seemed startled and Susan frowned. Surely Mrs Lamb realised this was the first place she'd come to make a start on the estate's affairs?

'You look just like my youngest when she's caught doing something she shouldn't.'

'Do I?' Mrs Lamb closed a drawer then placed a pile of paperwork onto the desk – Susan recognised them instantly. They were scribed in ink. 'I... I was just looking for the deeds – I thought you might need them.'

Susan raised an eyebrow. There was something odd about Mrs Lamb's manner that she couldn't quite put her finger on. She was flustered, and Susan had to remind herself that she had lost not only her employer, but her dear friend and companion these past fifty years. Mrs Lamb and her mother had grown old together - now she was grieving whilst trying to manage an estate that would be no easy feat for a woman half her age. Mrs Lamb always was the stoic type - that's what had made it so easy for Susan to confide in her growing up. No matter how big the problem, nothing had ever seemed to phase her. Not like her mother...

She sighed.

THE DEBUTANTE

'I'll leave you be,' said Mrs Lamb gently, one arm behind her back, concealing what she held in her hand as she edged out of the room.

She needn't have worried however, for Susan was too preoccupied by her own thoughts and the mammoth task before her to notice.

As soon as Mrs Lamb was out of the room, she began frantically throwing open drawers and filing cabinets, searching for the key. She was able to find the key chain easily enough, the one that contained a key for every lock on the property – but though she checked multiple times, the one she needed was missing, and a discomfiting sense of foreboding blended into her grief.

*

The next morning, Issy stretched out on the four-poster single bed of one of the family suites. It had a colour palette of rose and gold and was immaculately preserved with some modern touches – the most essential of course, being a well-sprung mattress, electric lighting, and a radiator – one of those cast-iron ones. The manner was always freezing, so their mother had avoided overnight stays if she could. The last time they'd stayed over was when their grandfather had died several years ago, and it had been so cold in this very room, with the wind whistling in through the mullioned windows, that Issy had gone to bed with her dressing gown and gloves on as well as her pyjamas, lost beneath a pile of blankets. Even then her breath had still come out as a cloud.

There was a washstand opposite – more ornamental than it was useful, a blackened fireplace with a stand of utensils that looked as though they were last used just yesterday by some poor servant or other, and a writing desk. Issy opened the heavy drapes and peered out across the vast, dawn-streaked landscape of their land. There was a wide stretch of formal lawn with stone steps leading to a walled garden that Mr Lamb spent a good deal of time tending (perhaps a tad more time than Mrs Lamb would prefer), then beyond was a shallow stream and acres of sprawling fields that reached a full two miles into the village of Worthington. The horizon was splashed with peaches and rose, and Issy spotted a single deer grazing alone, close to the woods.

It was still very early, and the house creaked and groaned its way into daytime like an old man with a sore back. Issy wondered what on earth she would do all day. It was too early to text Mila, and she had struggled to sleep in the cold, unfamiliar environment of her grandmother's home. As much as she didn't want to be there right now, a part of her was sad they hadn't come more often and spent more time getting to know their grandmother. Now it was too late, and what had passed could not be undone.

Perhaps Mrs Lamb might be up already, she wondered, recalling hot English breakfasts on cold winter mornings in the great kitchen. She was hungry. She pulled on her fluffiest dressing gown – an essential even at the height of summer – and a pair of slippers her mum had insisted upon that she'd never be caught dead wearing back home. She was just about to head downstairs when her eye was drawn to a silver box upon the washstand. It glittered, caught in a shaft of rising sunlight. Issy had never noticed it before. In fact, she didn't remember noticing it when she'd gone to bed the previous night. She dismissed the notion as ridiculous, otherwise she was no worse than her sisters who'd been too scared to sleep in separate room, then had committed to staying up as long as they could together in the vain hopes of spotting a ghost.

The box was so delicate and pretty that Issy couldn't resist taking a closer look. Inside was a folded piece of paper imprinted with their family's crest. Her eyes widened when she lifted it out to reveal a key so large it filled the entirety of its black, silky interior. The key was heavy and cool in her hand, and Issy wondered which lock of the vast property it could possibly belong to. It would take forever to find out! Intrigued, she unfolded the paper and read:

THE DEBUTANTE

Dearest Isabelle,
Oh, what it is to be a girl on the cusp of womanhood, the future a
blank canvas upon which to create the most beautiful art. I remember
those days well – those days of dances and courtships, romance and
adventure! The door to your childhood is closing fast, just as a new door
is about to open, and here, dear girl, is the key. Use it wisely.
All my love, sweet Issy,
Granny.
~LW~

Issy gasped. Whatever could it mean? She tucked the note back into the box and slipped the key into her pocket. She resolved to find out... Somehow.

*

'Catch any ghosts then, lasses?' Mr Lamb grinned as Jasmine and Ella made their late appearance at the breakfast table, both bleary-eyed and with tangled hair.

Just as Issy hoped, Mrs Lamb had laid out quite a spread – there was fresh fruit, pastries, porridge and toast spread thickly with jam made from the berries that grew wildly on their land, topped off with a hot breakfast of anything a hungry belly could hope for. Steam streamed out of the teapot, and Susan gratefully poured herself a measure into a delicate porcelain cup.

The girls exchanged a look. 'Actually, we *do* think we heard something,' said Jasmine. 'It was coming from the direction of Issy's room. But we were both too scared to go out and check.'

'Really,' said Issy, rolling her eyes.

At the opposite end of the breakfast table, Susan raised her eyebrows in an expression of distaste for the direction the conversation had taken.

'Oh yes,' said Ella. 'A... A sort of creaking sound.'

Ella tried to make mimic the sound and Jasmine laughed. 'It was nothing like that. It was more like this...'

Issy raised her eyebrows. The jewellery box. The note. The key. 'Well actually,' she began, tentatively. 'I did find something in my room this morning that I'm sure wasn't there when I went to bed last night...'

The girls gasped. 'We told you so!' said Jasmine.

Susan eyed them wearily, but when Issy met Mrs Lamb's eye, she gave a barely perceptible shake of her head. *She knows something,* thought Issy.

'What was it?' asked Ella, almost too scared to find out the answer.

'Well,' Issy continued carefully, 'it was quite possibly the biggest spider I have ever seen in my life! It sprang out from the curtains when I pulled them open and scampered under my bed.'

'Huh!' said Jasmine. 'That's not scary at all.'

'It is a little bit,' said Ella. 'How big?'

'Enough,' said Susan, setting down her knife and fork and dabbing at her mouth with a napkin. 'All this talk of spooks and spiders is putting me off my breakfast. Now, I'm going to be very busy today so you lot will have to amuse yourselves. There are three rules I expect you to follow during our stay here. Help Mr and Mrs Lamb whenever they need it; make sure you two girls stay together as far as possible – try to get plenty of fresh air but do not leave the manor grounds without permission and either Issy or another adult with you; and, most importantly, I do not, under any circumstances, want either of you going into the attic. There is a lot of old junk up there and one of you could get hurt, and it would be very hard for any of us to hear you from all the way down here.' She gestured up at the ceiling. 'Ok?'

'Ok,' said the girls, and Issy nodded, a myriad of thoughts running through her mind.

'Issy?'

'Yes,' Issy snapped, with a glance at Mrs Lamb, who exhaled in something akin to relief.

'Good.'

'Isn't that how great, great, great grandma Worthing disappeared, anyway?' asked Jasmine. 'When she went up into the attic?'

Ella gasped.

'Enough,' said Susan. 'Remember what I said. This is not a suitable conversation for the breakfast table.'

But at the far side of the table, just out of view, Mr Lamb nodded in spite of himself.

'You have a meeting with the head teacher at the village school at eleven this morning to organise your exams, Issy,' said Susan. 'I can drive you if you're happy for me to be there, otherwise I'm sure Mr Lamb will be able to find you a bike and you can make your own way there so that I can get on with things.'

'I'll make my own way,' said Issy with uncharacteristic enthusiasm. She needed time to think, for things at Worthington Manor had suddenly become that little bit more interesting than she could ever have anticipated.

*

The village school was tiny, and still had separate entrances for boys and girls carved into the stonework above the doors. The primary school, assembly hall and offices were housed in the main building, but the high school dwarfed it all in its comparatively bleak-looking prefab located out the back. Mrs Bright's footsteps echoed upon the parquet flooring as Issy struggled to keep pace and dust motes danced in their path. It was like stepping back in time, as if the scent of chalk still lingered in the air, and it wasn't hard to imagine a staid old school-master striding down the halls in a formal suit with his windy moustache and menacing cane.

'I think you'll find the examination process here much the same as what you'll have become accustomed to during your mock exams, so whilst it's not exactly ideal, sitting your exams here shouldn't be too disruptive for you,' Mrs Bright reassured her. 'I'm aware it's something of a sensitive time for you and your family, but the most important thing you can do to give yourself the best chance of success is to utilise the next few weeks to revise. You're welcome to use our resources, and I've arranged for Georgie Stevens to give you a tour of our school. He'll take you to the library to set up an account if there are any books you'd like to borrow. Ah, here he is.'

Issy found it hard to concentrate as Mrs Bright droned on about the importance of revision, which was practically all she'd heard about from every single one of her teachers for the entire academic year. It wasn't revision she was thinking about right now of course, but the note from her grandmother and an imaginary run-through in her mind's eye of searching the entire manor to find the correct lock. She suspected Mrs Lamb would know a thing or two about it and resolved to ask her next time they found themselves alone together. So focused on these thoughts was she, that she didn't even notice Georgie regarding her with some distaste as she and Mrs Bright approached him.

'It was a pleasure to meet you, Isabelle,' Mrs Bright continued, 'but now I must go to a meeting. Please give my best wishes and sympathies to your mother. Your grandmother was quite a woman - we all thought so. I used to play bridge with her on Thursday nights, WI on Saturdays, and she was president of the PTA, of course. Oh, and I realise you may not be here that long, but you'd be very welcome to attend our little end of year celebration if you wanted to. I'll leave it to Georgie to tell you more about it. See you soon!'

THE DEBUTANTE

Mrs Bright disappeared back from whence she'd came, leaving an invisible cloud of musky perfume in her wake, and Issy and Georgie regarded one another awkwardly. It was awkward on Georgie's part, because Issy was almost exactly what he imagined the youngest lady of the manor might be - posh, proud, infinitely stuck-up, and not at all the sort of person he appreciated being forced to spend time with, no matter how pretty she was. Awkward for Issy on the other hand, because Georgie was nothing at all like the boys back home - in fact, he was so broad and muscular he was barely a boy at all - he was already a man.

'Hello,' said Georgie with a curt nod.

'Hi,' said Issy, with an embarrassingly bashful smile as she looked into eyes as green as the rolling hills their little village was nestled into. What was wrong with her? She had Chad. Well, for now.

'Best follow me then.'

Georgie turned on his heel with a stride so powerful, Issy struggled to keep up. He showed her the examination hall where she'd be expected to line up on the day her exams began, the study, and finally the library, but he barely so much as glanced in her direction until she heard a wolf whistle.

'This your prom date then, Georgie? She's a stunner.'

Though Issy coloured, she couldn't help but beam primly at the owner of the voice - another equally strapping young lad who was more man than boy, only he was as dark as Georgie was fair and far more prone to easy laughter, unlike Georgie.

'Definitely not my date,' said Georgie, a little too quickly for Issy's liking. 'I'm sure she's much too good for the likes of me, who only mows her lawn every weekend and helps old Mr Lamb take care of the place for her. No. This is the new Lady of the Manor, Isabelle Worthing, and if she knows what's best for her round here, she'll stick to her own prom at her own private boarding school, wherever that is.'

Isabelle was taken aback. 'I do not go to boarding school. Do you work at the manor?'

'Yes, not that I'd expect *you* to know. I work for Mr Lamb, under your late grandmother. Mr Lamb *sees* me, not like your kind.'

'My kind?' Issy had had a relatively ordinary upbringing despite her family's privileged background. In fact, part of the conflict between Issy's mother and grandmother had related to her grandmother's insistence that Susan should do everything the right way - attend boarding school, find a suitable husband, produce an heir (not a *male* heir necessarily, fortunately for a mother of three girls, things had moved on by then). The way things had always been done. But Susan had been determined to do quite the opposite on all counts, so there'd been no boarding school for Issy or her siblings.

'Never mind him,' said the other lad. 'Ructions between his family and yours go way back.' He grinned. 'It's about time they got over it, really. And the old Mrs Worthing wasn't bad at all, in the end.'

Georgie shrugged.

'Well, I'm Sammy,' he grinned, 'and if you're still here at prom, you're welcome to come along with us and we'll introduce you to a few people.'

'Thanks,' said Issy, 'but I should be back home by then.' She narrowed her eyes at Georgie. 'Anyway, I have my own prom to go to, and my own date to go with.'

See how he likes that, she thought. Georgie didn't bother her at all. *Not at all.*

And though Georgie's expression was impossible to read, it seemed the feeling was mutual.

4.

With increasing trepidation, Susan climbed the servant's staircase to the very top of the manor where wind whistled through the windowpanes and the décor became increasingly simple. She shivered and hugged her cardigan closer. It was eerie, for no-one ever came up there, and she'd quickly learned as a child that no matter how loud you yelled, no-one down below could hear you. Not for the first time, she hoped the girls' explorations wouldn't extend to this part of the manor, and cursed the circumstances that had prevented her from leaving Issy at home where she belonged.

At the end of the hallway, a velvet curtain revealed a narrow staircase leading up to the attic. The door was locked, and the wood was so solid there was no getting in. Perhaps her mother had finally realised that no good could ever come from what lay beyond its threshold. She exhaled, her relief palpable, and hurried towards the main house before Mrs Lamb or the children could miss her.

Mr Lamb, who was busy bringing in his spoils from the kitchen garden with eyes as bright and merry as his hands were full, took one look at her pale face and winked.

*

It was in low spirits that Issy returned to the manor house that afternoon, and though the sunlight cast a dazzling glow upon the mullioned windows and the sweeping grass of the formal lawns, her temper could not be dampened. Mr Lamb was tending to the vegetable garden, and he gave her a cheery nod as she made for the back entrance into the kitchen on the off chance she might catch Mrs Lamb, but Mrs Lamb was nowhere to be seen and she was longing to ask her what she knew about the key. She was certain she knew *something*.

Her mother was in the study, distracted and tense, and her siblings were noisy and fraught in the informal lounge. The room was too large to be adequately lit by the floor length-windows, where swathes of fabric sapped the light. If Issy had her way she would remove the curtains altogether, otherwise the place looked as dreary as she felt. She threw herself upon the chaise longue, then her mother bustled in.

'I hope your meeting with the school went well, Issy,' she said. 'I have to go into the village to get some paperwork signed off for the funeral preparations. Can you watch the girls for me until I get back? I should be about an hour, maybe two.'

Issy rolled her eyes. 'Do I have to? This place sucks. Everyone is horrible.'

'Not quite everyone,' said Susan. 'Mr and Mrs Lamb have been nothing but nice to us since we arrived.'

'I didn't mean them.'

She was thinking of Georgie, of course, and fervently wished she was back home with her friends, getting sorted for the prom, spending time with Chad... Everything was up in the air, and it was all her mother's fault. Issy didn't need to be here with her and the girls.

'Please don't make this more difficult for me that it is already, Issy.' Susan sighed. 'You can either take care of the girls, get on with some revision, or go and ask Mr or Mrs Lamb to give you a task to do. I'm not having you at a loose end all day.'

Issy rolled her eyes. 'Fine. But don't expect me to entertain them.'

'As if I would. Thank you. You never know, you might just enjoy yourself. The girls adore you, you know.'

'No, we don't,' said Jasmine, who until then had given absolutely no indication whatsoever that she had been listening. 'She's boring. All she does is play on her phone and yell at us.'

'Right, girls, I'll be back soon. Be good for Mr and Mrs Lamb and your sister, and whatever you do, DO NOT, UNDER ANY CIRCUMSTANCES, GO INTO THE ATTIC.'

Susan swept out of the room in a flurry of paperwork, and Issy's phone beeped. The girls rolled their eyes and continued with whatever game it was they were playing - Issy didn't much care.

How's it going? It was Mila.

She contemplated telling Mila about the letter and the key, which she still had in her pocket, but thought the better of it. She'd wait until she had something more to tell. *Ok, I guess. I visited the village school today.*

Oh really? Were there any hot guys there?

Issy pushed the image of Georgie and his forest-green eyes out of her mind. He may be hot, but he was also a bit of an ass. *Not really.*

Damn. Anyway, guess what - Jack Dunn has asked me to the prom! He's to die for, I'm so excited! Mum has already ordered my dress. I'll send you a pic when I get it, but it's blush pink, with so many sequins that it weighs a ton.

Jack was Chad's best friend, and Issy felt a twinge of envy as she was reminded for the second time that day of all the reasons why she didn't want to be in Worthington.

That's great, she replied instead. *I'm so excited for you!*

Chad's been asking after you. You should send him a text. Keep yourself fresh in his mind - you don't want him to forget about you. Not with Steph flaunting herself at him at every given opportunity...

I bet, huffed Issy. *I will. Gotta go. Mum wants me to watch the girls while she goes into town.*

Drag. Speak soon x

Issy sighed. It seemed as though her friend's lives were moving forwards whilst hers was stuck in a very long, boring limbo. She texted Chad, but there was no response. He was probably busy.

As if to prove the point, Ella appeared before her, bright eyed and breathless from all the running around she and Jasmine had been doing that morning. 'Issy! Issy, will you play hide and seek with us?'

'I'm too busy.' Issy pulled her gaze away from her mobile phone with some reluctance.

'*Please?*' Ella eyes were round and pleading in such a way that it was far harder than it should be to say no.

The key felt heavy and cool in Issy's pocket, and the ghost of an idea formed. Mr and Mrs Lamb were too busy to monitor them too closely, and their mother wouldn't be back for some time...

'Ok.' She shrugged, as if their request was neither here nor there to her. 'Count to a hundred, and I'll go hide.'

And to her sisters' great surprise and excitement, Issy sprang from the sofa and made for the main stairwell. She knew exactly where she was going to try first.

*

Issy's explorations brought her to the very top floor of her grandmother's dilapidated old manor, the one place, the *only* place, her mother had told her she was absolutely forbidden to go. She didn't really know why, but like most of the fun things her mother didn't want Issy or her siblings to do it was probably deemed *too dangerous*. There was little light in the hallway because the higher up she'd gotten the smaller the windows had become, panes of missing glass allowing cool air to whistle through, and the floorboards themselves were bare and creaked underfoot. The décor was minimal - no family portraits, no tapestries, nothing but bare, whitewashed walls. It was a remnant of a bygone era, when the money spent on lavish interiors extended only to the rooms habited by the family that had lived and entertained there, with little care for the comfort of those they employed to help keep the place up and running.

The doors to the left leading to the servant's quarters had revealed nothing more exciting than disused bed frames and cracked old wash basins, but it was the velvet curtain closing off the far end of the hall that caught Issy's eye. Intrigued, she bit her bottom lip as she debated whether or not to heed her mother's wishes and re-join her siblings before they noticed she was missing, or, at the very least, take a little peek behind the curtain to satisfy her curiosity as to what lay beyond.

It was with some trepidation that she approached, because they'd all heard the tale about great, great, great grandmother Worthing, who had once entered the attic, never to be seen again. Issy was old enough to know this was all fancy, so no matter how eerie the place seemed, she assured herself it was just a load of rubbish and nothing she need concern herself with. Stories were often embellished and distorted with the passing of the time, and she didn't doubt that the purpose of this particular tale was more to deter her and her sisters from entering the attic than to protect her from sharing the unknown fate of the young Lady Isabelle, for which there was probably a perfectly rational explanation that had somehow gotten lost in the fabric of time.

The velvet was so threadbare that parts of it almost disintegrated in her hand. Ever so gently Issy pushed back what was left, revealing a narrow, gloomy staircase with plain wooden treads worn down by the footsteps of maids and servants that had walked the manor in lifetimes past. With a quick glance over her shoulder to make sure no-one was coming, she pulled the curtain closed behind her to make it look as though she had never been there. Then, taking a deep breath, she fumbled for the handrail and negotiated her way up the stairs, a slender figure cloaked in darkness.

There was a sturdy door at the top. Grasping for the handle, it wouldn't budge. She felt for the key and it gave a satisfying clunk as she turned it in the lock. After pushing forwards with her full weight, the door gave way with a creak so loud, Issy was sure she could be heard from three floors down. Trembling, she took a step forward. As her eyes adjusted, she could make out shapes in the darkness, of blankets and throws cast haphazardly over old items until they resembled a gaggle of apparitions. Though loathe to admit it she was afraid, and she wondered if her family's ever-dwindling fortune had been able to stretch to installing a light in the attic. Fortunately they had, and with the flick of a switch, a solitary light sprang into muted life.

Issy exhaled with relief then stepped forwards. The attic was vast. It towered high in the centre before tapering steeply downwards on each side, running the length and breadth of the building. The dust was thick, as though the place hadn't been disturbed in decades except for the wildlife that now inhabited the place, with unfamiliar rustling sounds and squeaks occasionally piercing the silence. It was no doubt teeming with rats and mice, bats and insects, if the piles of droppings were anything to go by. She grimaced. If her grandmother hadn't even bothered to venture up here, then perhaps she really shouldn't either.

But then she spotted a pile of magazines alongside an old dressing table, and before she knew it, as she flicked through the pages advertising the latest Edwardian fashions that were unutterably different to anything she herself had ever owned, she became so absorbed in unearthing the attic's treasures and imagining the lives of the last people to have used them that she lost all track of time.

Issy discovered all manner of things, from luggage chests to jewellery, broaches to bed frames. There was a roll-top bath with golden feet, and a massive bureau from which the original Lord Worthing must have once conducted his affairs. She was just thinking that she had better make an appearance back downstairs, when a chest engraved with her missing great, great,

great-grandmother's interlocking initials caught her eye. Undoing the latch, it took all of her strength to lift and push back the solid lid.

Inside was a decorative hand mirror, a well-thumbed book entitled the *Etiquette of Good Society* by Lady Gertrude Elizabeth Campbell, a charming porcelain doll, a selection of silver hair pins, some undergarments including a lace-up corset, a pair of long silk gloves, and an exquisite tiered dress that had obviously once been white, but was now yellowed and coarse. Though she knew she shouldn't, that she was handling an item that essentially belonged in a museum, there was a part of Issy that longed to put on the dress and see what she would look like wearing it. In fact, after a moment's hesitation, she simply couldn't resist. She knew that if her mother caught her, she'd be grounded for at least a month, but what did it matter? There was nothing to do there anyway.

Leaving on her leggings for extra warmth, she stripped off her jumper and carefully pulled the dress out of the chest. The yards of fabric made it heavy, but after a lot of tugging she had the dress bunched up on the floor and ready to step into. Shivering, she held onto an obliging table as she stepped one foot in at a time then poked her arms through the short, capped sleeves, the tight bodice rough against her bare skin.

She'd already uncovered a mirror, and now she stood before it, peering through the grime at her reflection. How she wished she could see the dress as it must have once been. It fell in layers of delicate white lace with a long trail that imbibed her with a sense of femininity and importance. The bodice pinched in beneath her bust with a silk sash and cut low across the bosom accentuating breasts that Issy had always bemoaned for being too flat compared to her friends. She almost didn't recognise herself - she looked less like a girl, and more like a woman. If only Chad could see her now.

She was just reaching into the chest to pick out a pair of gloves to complete the look when she heard a rustling sound close by. Too close.

'Hello?' She tried to sound braver than she felt.

There was another rustle, closer now.

'Jasmine, is that you?'

Silence.

'If it's you, Jas, then you'd better not tell mum I was up here, otherwise I'll tell her that you were up here too and we'll both be in trouble.'

All at once, a large, winged creature came flying haphazardly out of the darkness towards her, flapping its great wings as it jutted aimlessly from one side of the attic to the other. Just when Issy thought it had disappeared back into the eaves, it swooped by her for a second time, so close she felt a rush of air against her face as it soared past.

'What on earth?'

She shrieked and tried to crouch down under the table. But as she twisted and lunged, her movements inhibited by the confines of the dress, she tripped over its train. Suddenly she was falling down and down, her unanswered screams and deafening heartbeat ringing in her ears as she toppled backwards into the chest, the lid slamming closed on top of her until panic overwhelmed her and everything went black.

'Isabelle, dear, are you quite alright? Why, you are as white as a sheet! Mary, loosen that corset at once.'

When a dazed and confused Issy finally came to, it was to find half a dozen eyes staring at her above where she lay sprawled on the floor before a full-length mirror and an open chest engraved with the initials *IW.*

'What happened?' she asked as she peered all about her, astonished. Raising a hand to her head, she winced at the emerging lump.

The bedroom was elegantly decorated in muted tones of rose and gold. She had no doubt it was her very own bedroom at the manor that she had woken up in only that morning, which seemed so long ago now. The same four-poster bed, the same mullioned window overlooking miles of rolling countryside, the same fireplace and washstand. A doll, the very same doll that Issy had found inside the chest, lay on top of the bedcovers.

'Hush, Isabelle, it will be alright. Quick, Mary, you can see she is quite unwell. Please relieve her at once. Let's help her up to standing.'

And before Issy could understand what was happening, two sets of arms reached under shoulders to lift her, and the next thing she knew she was standing before the very same mirror she had stood at in the attic, as a lady's maid unlaced her dress and freed her from the confines of her corset, enabling her to gulp in vast lungfuls of air for the first time in what felt like forever.

'Ah, the colour is returning to her cheeks already.'

Issy slumped into the nearby chair, where a glass of water was promptly placed into her hand. Dazed, she sipped it slowly, and for the first time looked into the concerned eyes of a pale-faced girl with rosy cheeks and long wavy hair hanging loosely to her waist. Though her features were plain, her eyes conveyed an appealing sincerity and warmth. To the right stood a much younger girl; slim, with long red hair, the same grey-blue eyes, and a petulant set to her mouth.

'Everything exciting happens to Isabelle,' said the younger girl. 'Nothing exciting ever happens to me. Oh, I wish I could come to court! Instead, I have to stay here with Great Aunt Cassandra, and she is never kind to me.'

'Nonsense, Lottie. Aunt Cassandra favours you above us all - she always brings you the best gifts. And Isabelle is the eldest so it's her time to come out, just as it will be my turn next year and then yours too, soon enough. Think, we are three sisters, and with Isabelle carrying all of the Worthing beauty, our hopes rest almost entirely upon her to find a suitable husband to ensure the continued good fortunes of our family. You see it is a burden that our dear sister must carry. You must learn to count your blessings.'

It was evident that Lottie had no thought of doing any such thing. 'But it isn't faaair, Flora. I wish I could go to parties! Miss Browning said I can dance The Two Step better than either of you, and my French is coming on quicker than yours did too, Issy.'

Flora rolled her eyes. 'You should learn to hold your tongue. You know as well as I do that Isabelle is not there for the parties and merriments, she is there to attract the attention of Lord Eltham.'

Issy paled. 'Who?'

'Oh, Issy, you really did suffer quite the knock to the head, didn't you, dear?'

'Lord Eltham is one of the richest men in the land,' Lottie parroted, 'after King Edward, of course,' she added as an afterthought, and Flora couldn't help but smile at that. 'Though I did overhear Mama say he is one of the most disagreeable men in her acquaintance. When I am eighteen, I shall not allow myself to be forced to marry such a man.'

'Lottie!' Flora admonished her. 'You should be very grateful you are not promised to old Uncle Arthur, like our poor cousin. Anyway, Lord Eltham is nowhere near as rich as King Edward, and it is terribly rude to refer to him as disagreeable. What would you know of such things? He may be somewhat aloof, yes, but it is a great responsibility that now rests upon his shoulders since his elder brother's unexpected death. He is now sole heir to the Eltham fortune, and he must act and marry accordingly, though he was never raised to be such.'

Issy's eyes widened as she listened to the sister's quarrel. She didn't know what to do or say. She had no idea what was happening or how she had found herself there. It was as though she'd stumbled onto a movie set, but instead of being a passive observer, her companions demanded interaction. She was just about to say something when the door opened and in walked an older woman with a stern expression upon her face, greying hair knotted atop her head, her dress rustling as she strode into the room. Her back was ramrod straight, chin up, shoulders square.

The lady's maid immediately dipped into a curtsey. 'Milady,' she said.

'Found it!' announced the older lady, wielding an intricate silver hair pin studded with jewels. 'I knew I had set it aside somewhere. This is what I wore when I was presented at Queen Victoria's court as a girl, and now you will wear it too.'

'Mama!' Flustered by her entrance, the other two girls straightened up immediately.

'Heavens, stand up at once, Isabelle. And Mary, pack away her gown for London in the morning - we cannot afford it to get crumpled.'

'Isabelle fainted, Mother,' said Flora. 'She suffered quite a knock to the head.'

'What?' The older lady peered at Isabelle and placed a cursory hand upon her brow. 'Hmm, you do look pale. I insist that you go to bed and rest immediately. Mary will bring you a tray later. We simply cannot afford you to become unwell so close to the start of the season.'

With that, the older lady was gone. London? The season? Thought Issy. Whatever did it all mean?

'Goodnight, sister,' said Flora, pressing a kiss upon Issy's cheek. 'I hope you feel much better in the morning. Lottie and I must go to dinner with Miss Browning. But oh! Isabelle, you looked so wonderful in your debutante gown! I must admit I was quite envious. I am not sure how poor Lord Eltham will be able to help himself from falling in love with you.'

'Huh,' said Lottie petulantly, placing a dutiful kiss upon Issy's cheek. 'When I am older I shall dance and dance all night long and *never* marry. Goodnight, Issy.'

The two sisters exited the room, and after helping Issy into a nightgown and into bed and lighting a candle for her, Mary exited with them, promising to bring her up a tray of dinner from the kitchen.

Alone at last, Issy watched the last of the daylight fade beyond a rolling green landscape that was at once alien and familiar, just like the bedroom she now found herself in, and the unexpected chill in the air brought her breath out in cloudy bursts. The only thing that convinced her this was not a dream was the black leggings she'd discovered she was still wearing beneath her layers of undergarments. Bewildered, she sat up against a mountain of cushions and wondered what on earth had just happened to her, and how she would ever get home. One thing was certain, if she ever did get back to her family, she was bound to be in a whole heap of trouble when her mother found out about all this.

5.

When Susan returned to the manor later that afternoon, she could sense the panic in the air before she'd so much as uttered a word to anyone, and somehow, she immediately just knew.

'Mummy, we lost Issy,' said Ella apologetically.

'We were playing hide and seek, but we couldn't find her,' said Jasmine. 'It's been ages now. I think she's disappeared - like Lady Worthing did.'

Ella's eyes were wide.

Mr Lamb shifted uncomfortably in his seat, and the dutiful Mrs Lamb, who had obviously been responsible for fulfilling her late mistress' wishes insofar as Lucinda Worthing's eldest granddaughter was concerned, could scarcely make eye contact with her because she already knew her views on the whole thing – she'd made them very clear long ago. It was evident from the girls' pale and guilty faces however, that they did not know, that they really thought Issy might be gone – especially with the tall tales old Mr Lamb had been keeping them up at night with, and it was no easy task to reassure them and settle them off to bed.

It was getting late when Susan was finally able to retrace Issy's steps up to the attic where she found exactly what she'd expected to find – the door unlocked, a solitary light casting its dim glow upon the vast, dusty interior, and her ancestor's trunk thrown open and the dress gone. She crumpled to the floor and cried. She cried for the daughter she loved so dearly but was terrified she might lose, and she cried for the hopeful young girl she had once been, until she too had stepped into that trunk and her life had never been the same again.

'Susan, dear...' It was Mrs Lamb.

'How could you?' said Susan. 'How could you let her go?'

'It was what your mother wanted,' Mrs Lamb replied simply.

'What about what I want, does nobody care about that?'

'*What about what Issy wants?*' *said Mrs Lamb, gently pressing a palm upon Susan's back in a gesture of comfort, just as she had done many times before when she'd been a young girl growing up. 'She is grown now, Susan. How about we let her decide for herself, just like you once did, and your mother and all those Worthing women before you?*'

Susan sighed. Mrs Lamb needn't remind her because she had never forgotten. How could she forget her own 'season'? And how could she ever forget William?

*

She thought she'd never fall asleep but somehow she did, and the next morning Issy awoke to a sound she couldn't quite place, like metal scraping against a rough surface. When she opened her eyes, she was astonished to find herself in the very same room in which she had fallen asleep - she'd assumed she had just suffered a nasty concussion. Opposite, a young girl of perhaps eleven or twelve dressed in an over-darned black dress had crept in to stoke a fire, her cheeks flushed from the exertion. Issy felt a pang of empathy that a girl as young as her own sister obviously had no choice but to work so terribly hard, with so little, just to survive. Learning of her family's history and being confronted by the reality of it was really quite different, and her heart ached.

The girl jumped when she realised that Issy was staring right at her. 'I'm terribly sorry, Miss, I didn't mean to disturb you.' She bit her lip, as though afraid of what Issy might say or do next.

'Hey, no problem,' Issy reassured her. 'And thank you.'

The girl's eyes widened in horror, and Issy couldn't think what she might have said or done to have caused offence. She dipped into a curtsey and couldn't scurry out of the door fast enough.

Next the housemaid, Mary, entered, her manner brusque and efficient. She set a breakfast tray to one side, before pulling open the curtains to reveal the pale lemon light of morning, a determined dew still clinging onto the grass of the formal lawns.

'Good morning, Miss Worthing, I see you are already risen. Perhaps you are feeling better?'

Issy, afraid of making another faux pas, merely nodded.

'Lady Worthing said you are to breakfast in bed this morning, then join your sisters for luncheon before departing for Worthington this afternoon, then onwards to London on the morrow. I do hope your head does not pain you too much today, for you have quite the journey ahead of you.'

'I feel much better,' said Issy carefully. She'd come to the conclusion that the less said the better.

'I am glad to hear it. I shall relay this news to Lady Worthing at once, she will be most pleased. She is anxious there should be no delay, for Lord and Lady Brampton have a busy itinerary planned and are expecting you. I will return very soon to help you dress and see that your trunk is loaded onto the carriage.'

Issy nodded, scared to speak lest she give cause to the servants to suspect her as an imposter.

As soon as she was alone, she leapt from the bed. She simply couldn't risk leaving Worthington Manor to travel with these strangers, because if she did, how would she ever get home? Though the smells emanating from the breakfast tray were very enticing, Issy knew she didn't have time to waste. Her eyes fell upon her great grandmother's trunk, stuffed to the brim with the belongings she would obviously require for the trip. If Mary or Mama caught her removing them, she was certain she would find herself in a great deal of trouble. But if she didn't, she might remain stuck in the past forever, with no way of getting back to her own mother and sisters, who were surely worried sick.

Resolved there was no other option, Issy quickly began removing items from the trunk. On the very top was the same book of etiquette she had found in the attic, only now it appeared as good as new. Intrigued, she would have liked to read more, but she knew that Mary would be back soon. Pulling out the debutante gown, she laid it on the bed as neatly as she could manage. Then, when she had made just enough space available to enable her to climb into the trunk, she did so, pulling the lid closed on top of her until everything went black.

Issy waited, but nothing happened. It looked as though she was stuck for the time being. She could see no way out of her situation, and after having spent so much time wishing her family would just leave her alone, now she wanted nothing more than to find her way back to them. She just had no idea how, or if it was even possible. Not a full day had passed, yet it felt like a lifetime. She missed them all, even Jasmine. It was hopeless. She bit her lip and sobbed.

All at once the bedroom door opened. 'Isabelle! Isabelle, where are you?'

It was Mama's voice, and Issy's heart sank. She could hear the rustling of her dress and the shuffling of her footsteps, which came to an abrupt halt right next to the chest before the lid was torn open, and Mama peered down at her, aghast to find her in there.

'Isabelle Worthing, what in Heaven's name are you doing?'

Issy blanched, and her eyes landed on the doll with the ringlets that was lying haphazardly on her bed. 'I... I was just looking for my doll, Mama, and somehow I tripped over my nightdress and fell into the trunk.'

Mama softened so slightly it was barely perceptible. She nodded and reached out a hand to help pull Issy out of the trunk.

'Very well. You may bring Dolly if you wish, but you must ensure Papa does not find out – he will say you are too old now for such childish fancy. But remember, I was once a girl on the brink of womanhood too, dear. The carriage is ready, and it is almost time to say goodbye to your sisters.'

Issy gasped. If she went to London with Mama, what if there was no way back and she was stuck in the past forever? 'Mama, perhaps we might, erm... delay just a little while? My head....'

Mama raised an eyebrow. Reaching out a hand, she cupped Issy's cheek in a rare gesture of affection. 'Truly, Isabelle, you have nothing to fear. It is a fine match your Papa and I have designed for you - a very fine match.' She set herself about replacing the dress in the trunk, placing Dolly gently on top before closing and locking its lid, then tying back the curtains and straightening up the bedding. 'As you are aware, the season waits for no-one. If you do not make your debut this year, then you cannot marry this year. And if you cannot marry, Lord Eltham will marry somebody else. And that would be most unfortunate indeed. Your father will not hear of it. It would also postpone your sister's debut.'

'But..,' Issy continued, desperately, 'Lottie said that Lord Eltham is...' She tried to recall the term. 'Most disagreeable.'

Mama smiled. 'Did she indeed? And who is she to speak of such things at only ten years old? Better a disagreeable husband, Isabelle, than a poor one, you mark my words. You can be agreeable enough for the both of you, and you may find he is not so bad once you become better acquainted. Now, no more stalling. I will see to it that Mary comes up to dress you immediately. Please hurry up and eat something. The carriage is waiting.'

The bedroom door opened. 'Ah, Mary, there you are, just in time. See to it that Miss Worthing is downstairs on the hour. I will have Samson collect the trunk.'

'Yes, milady,' Mary dipped as Mama bustled out of the room, her skirts swishing behind her.

Though she tried her best not to, Issy could have cried at the hopelessness of the situation and as thoughts of her own mother and sisters consumed her, so very different from this family. Even though she found herself in the exact same house she had left behind less than twenty-four hours ago, she had never felt more alone, or so very far away from home.

*

Issy said barely a word the entire, hair-raising coach journey. She spoke little in fear of saying the wrong thing, and her apparent change in demeanour was not lost on her mother, who, if she happened to look up and make eye contact with her, she'd find peering at her suspiciously. Mama spoke enough for both of them, of society gossip and family matters, dancing and courtship; and Papa barely glanced up from his newspaper except to remind Issy of her duty to the family, as the carriage lurched on rough, uneven roads until her head and bottom ached. The corset squeezing at her ribcage only made everything worse, and she wondered how on earth Mama and all those other women of the era could bear it.

Issy hadn't missed the date on Papa's newspaper – February 1904, and King Edward was on the throne. She wished she'd paid greater attention to her history lessons in school – but the only things to jump out from her memory were the Women's Suffrage movement, the sinking of the Titanic, and the looming of the Great War. She wasn't sure why she was surprised, since the laws of the world she'd known before had been well and truly turned on their heads, to find herself in mid-winter rather than summer – but it looked as though in that respect as well as in many others she was set to be left with more questions than answers.

It seemed a miracle they made it to their destination in one piece at all, an interminable journey that took almost a full week, with stops at various inns to refresh themselves and change horses and spend cold, sleepless nights. Issy swore she would never take the convenience of car travel for granted again. Very occasionally they might pass a motor car on the road, especially on the approach to London, and Papa would admire it and declare his intention of buying one; and Mama would say don't be ridiculous they were a waste of money for such a fad would never take off, and Issy would find it hard not to leap in and let her know she was quite, quite wrong about that.

The carriage came to an abrupt halt before a smart, three-storey townhouse, and Papa exited first to assist Mama and Issy down in turn. The distance to the curb was steep and Issy panicked as she alighted, afraid her long dress would get caught in the wheels as the coachman did his best to keep the horses steady. Never before had she appreciated how dangerous coach travel could be, it certainly wasn't evident in all the historical dramas she'd watched on TV with her mum. Nor had she appreciated how interminably boring a long journey could be without a screen to occupy her.

Comparative to the peace and beauty of Worthington; London was bustling, dirty and bleak, and carried in the air an unpleasant odour Issy couldn't quite place but she was sure was made worse by the waste of what looked like a thousand horses. About her was a hive of noise and activity, with beggars, paupers and gentry forced to pass shoulder to shoulder on narrow streets, yet to all intents and purposes still worlds apart. It was icy cold and dull, and Issy could hardly wait to get inside before a fire. At the top of a set of stone steps stood a portly old pair, and beyond them a number of servants bustled back and forth to bring in their luggage as though invisible, and Issy bit back the urge to thank them.

'Welcome,' said Lady Brampton, a formidable woman of considerable width who lacked the height to balance it out, emphasised all the more as she hunched over her walking stick, one hand on the small of her back. 'Do come in and make yourselves at home. Luncheon will be served in the parlour – you must be ravenous! My, Isabelle, what a beauty you have become. I'm sure all the most eligible young men will be lining up around the corner for you after your debut next week!'

Issy hesitated, and Lady Brampton regarded her expectantly. When Issy failed to come up with a suitable response, Mama's disapproval was evident.

'Oh, you mustn't mind, Isabelle,' said Mama, a little flustered. 'She had a nasty fall before we left and suffered quite the knock to the head. She has been a little out of sorts eve since, but I'm sure the excitement and merriments will soon bring her back to herself.'

'I see,' said Lady Brampton, and her eyes of violet-blue held such a sharp intensity about them it was as though she could see directly into Issy's own mind, a notion she found most unsettling.

Issy needn't have worried however, as Mama diverted the conversation as quickly as she was able, and before she knew it, Papa was deep in conversation with Lord Brampton about his new motor car, and the ladies were bustled into the parlour where they were presented with quite a spread. There were centrepieces of trussed-up roasted pig and bird, and whilst the rest of her party exclaimed over the food, the vegetarian in Issy recoiled.

She was ushered into a chair by a servant, where she had no option but to sit ramrod straight, her skirts gathering at her ankles, as she came face to face with the confusing myriad of cups, cutlery, plates and glasses set out with precision before her.

A servant began piling her plate with slices of meat, and before she could help herself, Issy said, 'Oh, I can't eat that, sorry, I'm a veget-'

The room fell silent, and Mama's mouth dropped open as Papa, his be-whiskered face turning puce, regarded her with barely contained fury. It was only the fact they were in polite company that prevented him from exploding.

Issy bit her lip. 'That is, erm, I mean to say, that's absolutely lovely, thank you.'

She fumbled her way through the rest of the luncheon, an unnecessarily complicated and uncomfortable affair as her corset failed to expand with the amount of food she was expected to eat. The adults talked around her as though she wasn't even there, and Issy thought that she had never felt more like a child in her life than she did at that moment. But soon enough Lord Brampton invited Papa for a drive of his motor car, an invitation he couldn't resist of course, and Lady Brampton, Mama and Issy retired to the drawing room for tea and cake. Issy allowed herself to breathe a sigh of relief – surely it wouldn't be long before she could go to her room and have a little break from pretending to be someone she wasn't all day?

Mama excused herself to go to the ladies' room, and Issy felt cast adrift without her there to fill in the silence. Lady Brampton directed a maid to brew them a fresh pot of tea, and the moment the door closed behind her, she fixed Issy in her penetrative violet gaze.

'Who are you?' Lady Brampton asked her directly.

'I'm sorry?' said Issy.

'I said,' continued Lady Brampton, unperturbed, 'who *are* you? For we both know you are not Miss Isabelle Worthing of Worthington Manor.'

6.

Susan had no idea where she was. All she knew was that it was cold and dark, and there was a frightful sort of wailing noise coming from the village that pierced her sore head. It reminded her of something she had once heard on the monitor in school – an air raid siren, that was it.

'Oww,' she cried, rubbing at the emerging bump.

'Oh, Elizabeth, must you always be so clumsy? You are a young woman now. Sit up and stop making a fuss. That was one of your father's finest brandies, and that was your great grandmother's debutante dress. We shall have to get someone to fix that, though who, when we barely have any servants left, is anyone's guess.'

There was a smashed bottle on the floor, and Susan realised that the damp she could feel about her shoulders must be the liquid from inside. She sat up, as surprised to find that she was in a cellar where there were rows and rows of bottles reaching as far as the eye could see, as she was to discover the company she was with – for whilst they all claimed to know her, she was definitely not Elizabeth, and these were definitely not her parents or siblings, and everyone appeared to be dressed for some sort of vintage tea party.

'Never mind that, Mary. There are plenty more where that came from, as you can see.'

'Yes, and I suppose it won't be long before they take all this from us too, as if they haven't taken enough from us already – the army will probably drink their way through it all in a week.'

'There's no use worrying about that – we are fortunate to have gotten all the way to 1944 and yet our home has not been bulldozed or requisitioned for the war effort when many similar properties have.'

'No, but there is talk of them turning it into a hospital – imagine! A hospital, in here, with injured men everywhere and all manner of bodily fluids staining our beautiful home – and it would hardly be appropriate for our daughters to be exposed to all those soldiers.'

'Well, let's just hope it is nothing more than talk, for thus far talk is all it has been. And if we must contribute to the war effort, would it really be so bad for us to do our bit?'

'Your father did his bit for our country during the Great War,' said Mary, 'and look how that turned out. No, we must get Elizabeth married and removed from here as soon as possible. It's the only way.'

'You know as well as I do that there are no suitable men left near Worthington, Mary.'

'There is. There's Hugo Harding. He's looking to remove his offices to the country until the danger in London passes.'

'Hugo Harding? At his age? With our daughter? Not a chance!'

'I have already taken the liberty of inviting him to tea Saturday next.'

'You haven't!'

'I have. For honestly, Ruben, look around you – there is barely a man left in sight, and who knows how long this darned war will last? Who could be better for our daughter than the owner of a building society?'

'Well, if you insist,' said Ruben doubtfully, though it was clear even to Susan that he was not at all happy about it. 'She can at least meet him and see what she thinks. I suppose that can't hurt.'

'Yes,' said Mary, unperturbed, 'though I fail to see why it is so important what she thinks about it – we had no choice at that age, and it's not as though there are any better options available around here.'

'Leave it be, then, Mary – I have acquiesced, haven't I? Elizabeth dear, did the glass hurt you, are you cut?'

'No,' said Susan, her dazed voice barely a whisper, 'just a little bump, is all.'

There was a deep humming noise overhead, and instinctively Susan crept closer to the others and covered her ears with her hands to block out the foreboding sound, wondering as she did so how on earth this had happened to her, and how she was ever going to find her way back home.

*

'Actually,' said Issy as steadily as she could, though she was trembling before the great Lady Brampton's enquiring gaze, 'I'm afraid I *am* Miss Isabelle Worthing of Worthington Manor - Issy for short. Only...' she trailed off. What was the use? How could she even begin to explain?

'Only?'

Issy didn't know what to say, so she said nothing at all. She felt a little breathless in the tight bodice of her dress and hoped she wouldn't faint. But if she did, perhaps the act of losing consciousness would somehow transport her back home? She hardly dared hope.

'Only,' Lady Brampton spoke for her, 'you're of a different time. Am I right?'

Issy gasped. 'But... How could-'

She waved a dismissive hand. 'Never mind that,' said Lady Brampton. 'I think I understand perfectly well what is happening here.'

'You do?' Issy was not convinced.

'Indeed, I do, dear girl. I do, because it happened to me too.'

Just then the door opened and in walked Mama, looking enquiringly from one to the other, as a maid carrying a tray of tea scurried in to set it out on the low table between them. Beside it was a beautiful selection of pastries and cream cakes laid out on a variety of glassware and China set upon doilies that reminded Issy of her grandmother and Mrs Lamb's afternoon teas.

'Is anything amiss here, Monica?'

'No, Edith. In fact, Isabelle was just telling me how excited she is for the opening dance of the season, and how she may benefit from a little extra tutoring and practice to ensure her coordination has not been too badly impacted by her recent fall. She is keen to make the best first impression she is able, which is admirable. I shall see to it that she comes under regular instruction here, commencing tomorrow morning. Isn't that right, Isabelle?'

Issy's mind was a tangled knot of questions, but there was nothing she could do but acquiesce.

'My daughter dances beautifully already, Monica,' said Mama, 'but if you think it would help, then of course I will support it.' It was evident that whilst Mama could not see the point of the whole thing, she was too relieved to hear of her daughter expressing an interest in something normal again to argue the point.

'Well then, that settles it,' said Lady Brampton. 'The sooner she gets some rest, the sooner we can begin. Isabelle, perhaps you would like to settle into your room now, and I will come up before dinner to discuss the timetable? I'm afraid we don't have much time before the ball.'

'Yes, Lady Brampton,' said Issy.

'Excellent, that's the spirit! Delia,' she addressed her maid, 'show Miss Worthing to her room.'

Delia curtsied, and Issy followed her out of the drawing room as though in a dream from which she could not awaken. As she exited, she heard Mama say to Lady Brampton, 'Do you think I should call a doctor? I don't understand the child. She was most excited about her debut, but now...' and Lady Brampton replied, 'Not at all, Edith. It's nothing other than nerves that have gotten to the girl, that's all. We've all been there. Say not a word of it to Lord Worthing. Simply leave it to me, and I'll keep her so busy she doesn't have time to dwell. Then before you know it the charms of the season will overtake her, and everything will turn out well.' 'If you think so,' said Mama, though she had sounded as unconvinced as Issy, who couldn't help but wish she had a little of this unusual woman's optimism to carry her through this strange journey she now found herself on.

*

It felt like an eternity before there was a knock on the bedroom door and in walked Lady Brampton herself, unannounced. Already Issy had been stripped from her travelling clothes, bathed, and dressed in a slightly looser tea dress that she was grateful for, and provided with ink and paper should she wish to write to Flora and Lottie back at the manor. Her trunk had been unpacked into the wardrobe, and her every comfort and convenience had been carefully considered. Even Dolly lay in wait for her on top of her pillow.

Issy had become slowly accustomed to having little to no say in the direction of her days, for every aspect of her routine was determined for her by Mama or the other adults around her, and Issy realised how powerless the young women of days gone by were - even the well-off ones. She couldn't even dress or bathe in private. She longed for her mobile phone to text her mum or Mila - anyone who knew her and truly cared. She missed them greatly – even her sisters - and determined she was going to show them just how much, if she ever found her way home.

Lady Brampton took a seat opposite her on the window seat. 'Well.'

Issy smiled awkwardly.

'Are you quite comfortable here? Do you have everything you need? Has Delia been attentive?'

'Very much so,' said Issy. She had no complaints about the smart little attic room she found herself in, with its dormer window overlooking the hustle and bustle of the street below.

'It's ok, you needn't stand on ceremony with me. You can be quite yourself.'

Issy smiled politely, but she didn't think even this robust older lady was ready for a young woman of the next millennium, when so much of what she knew had changed. 'I have so many questions...'

'Me too,' said Lady Brampton. 'Shall we start with the obvious one? Who are you?'

'I'm Miss Isabelle Worthing of Worthington Manor. I was named after my Great Great Great Grandmother, who... well, she disappeared in 1905, shortly after the birth of her first child. I've come from the year 2024.'

'2024!' Lady Brampton exclaimed. 'I cannot begin to imagine that far ahead. But 1904... I remember that year. It was an unusually cold winter, and I was sick, very sick -practically on my deathbed - and right before the season too. My mother was beside herself. Then somehow I ended up here, in the year 1868, at the start of the season of a previous Lady Worthing. And now it seems that I have become Lady Monica Brampton, and you, my dear girl, have become me.'

Issy tried to process this information, to make sense of it. She found she couldn't. 'But why?'

Lady Brampton shook her head. 'I've asked myself that many, many times over the years, and I have never happened upon a suitable answer. Sometimes we must content ourselves to live knowing we are part of something much greater than we can ever imagine, where the laws and rules of existence are not known to us, and as challenging as it can be, to learn to accept it.'

'But I want to go home.' Issy's eyes brimmed with unshed tears. She was tired of pretending.

'Of course you do, child, of course you do. But you must wait until after the season. You are not the first and you will not be the last, and it always comes down to the season. The season is key.'

Issy thought about the key to the attic that had led her here. The key that was left by her own grandmother - had she too, experienced something like this as a girl? Travelled back in time along the family line?

'Didn't you long to go home?' Issy asked. 'I know *I* do. This time is so very different from my own. I could never fit in here.'

Lady Brampton's eyes misted over. 'For me, 1868 was not that different to 1904. But I fell in love with a man of this time, you see, with Lord Brampton. In my time, my husband... Well, when I recovered from my illness to join the season Lord Eltham was already taken, and unfortunately I married a man who was... Let's just say he did not care much for women. I was afraid of him. My son was not my property - as heir he was my husband's property, to be raised to uphold the family name. One night my husband had been drinking heavily. He came for me and I fled to the attic - I thought he would never find me there, but he did. He hit me, and somehow I ended up back here as though I had never left. I had no wish to return to my own time, except to see my son.'

She sniffed. 'I would dearly love to have brought him back here with me, but could think of no way of doing so without creating suspicion - and to do so would mean losing everything I had, followed by a life of poverty for my son and I. I knew no matter how my husband had been to *me*, my son would be safe and well provided for by him in *his* time, so I could not do it.'

Issy could feel Lady Brampton's pain, and reached into her memory to see if she could recall any information whatsoever about her great, great grandfather. She knew her mum had met him, that he'd still been alive when she was a baby. She knew he had smoked a pipe and wore thick-rimmed glasses, and that he was mad into racing horses and liked to eat sweet liquorice after dinner. If only she'd been closer to her own grandmother, she could have found out so much more.

'He lived a long life,' said Issy. 'I believe he and my great, great grandmother were very happy together. They had four children, including my great grandmother.'

Lady Brampton smiled. 'It is my great hope to live long enough to meet one of his daughters, to feel that little bit closer to him and learn more about him. For it is always the eldest daughter this curse, or blessing, or whatever we shall call it, afflicts. Which brings me to the rules.'

'Rules?'

'Yes, there are rules. Do not interfere with the course of time. Do not bring disgrace upon the family name, and do not tell anyone - and I mean anyone - the truth about who you are. These are times when women like us can be committed to an asylum on a man's say so - a time of suspicion and fear of the unknown. Once there were witch hunts, so you cannot be too careful - you must try your utmost to blend in. It will be hard, but your very life and future freedom may depend upon it. That is why your classes will commence first thing tomorrow morning and you have no option but to try your very best. If you can dance, draw, sew and paint, and sing well enough and play the pianoforte, you'll be fine.'

Issy almost laughed aloud at the outrageousness of the situation. She could do none of those things - she'd done ballet as a child of course, but she was very rusty on that front. There was no way she could do this. It was obvious to everyone, even Mama, that she was some sort of imposter. Not even Lady Brampton could imagine how drastically life had altered between her time and Issy's.

'And if you can't, then at the very least we must get you through your debut without incident and secure you a husband whilst we work on those other matters.'

'But my exams...'

'Exams?'

'Yes, to finish my education I must first complete my exams.'

'Education, for a woman? But what on earth for? You will marry and have children, surely?'

'Yes,' said Issy, 'I hope so, but also plan to have a career, so first I must finish my education.' Issy had no idea what her career was going to be, but it was the first time she'd realised she truly wanted one.

'A career?' Lady Brampton was aghast. 'Have we lost *all* of our money? Are we *working* class?'

'It's a bit more complicated than that,' said Issy with a grin, and she explained to Lady Brampton that girls like her could attend university and enjoy many of the same opportunities as boys, and that the class system was not at all as it had once been, and that people with stately homes like theirs had to find a way to monetise them in order to keep them.

'But how do I get to go home?' Issy asked once again.

'I believe you must recreate whatever scenario brought you here to begin with,' said Lady Brampton, after a pause. 'And from memory, time doesn't pass the same while you're here.'

Issy thought about it, went over in her head for the thousandth time the moments leading up to her fall back in time. 'It was the dress,' she said. 'I had taken off my clothes to try on a dress I found in an attic - your debutante dress, and when I put it on, I was startled by a swooping bat. I fell into your chest and woke up here, with my leggings still on underneath.'

'Do you still have the, what do you call them, leggings?'

'I do.'

'Then I suggest you put them on along with the dress then get into the chest and see what happens. But I beg you – please wait until after your debut.'

Issy bit her lip before nodding, though in her heart she was caught between wanting to get into the chest the moment Lady Brampton left the room, and not wanting to further disrupt the fabric of time in fear of the consequences. 'But,' said Issy as a thought came to her, 'wouldn't you like me to get engaged to someone else for you?'

'Oh, Issy,' said Lady Brampton. 'Absolutely not, not even to Lord Eltham, because to do so would take my dear boy away from me forever - and then you yourself, and therefore I too... Well, we would cease to exist.'

Issy nodded. It was hopeless.

'I will leave you to sleep. I know this is a lot to take in. It really is a pleasure to meet a grandchild of mine, the blood of my sweet boy.' Lady Brampton kissed her cheek and made to leave.

'Why do *you* think we're here?' Issy asked her. Of all the questions their situation inspired, this is the one that played on her mind most - that and how to get home.

Lady Brampton paused. 'I have had a great deal of time to consider this, and there are any number of scenarios. I'm aware of a young woman who once brought great shame to our family and almost cost us our reputation and our fortune - she was saved by a love-match, fortunately, but her father swore that no other female child would ever have cause to blot the family name. It's easy to throw something special away when you do not realise its worth, but when you have an opportunity like this you learn the true value of family and you learn to love them and care about what happens to them through all their trials and tribulations. Perhaps it's because of that.'

'Or maybe it's because you got sick?' Issy suggested. 'Didn't many children of your day get sick and die young? Maybe I'm here to stop that from happening to you?'

'I had not thought of that,' said Lady Brampton. 'It's just the way it is - the way it has always been. Is it not the same in your time?'

'No, said Issy, 'we are expected to live well into our eighties, if not to a hundred nowadays. There have been many medical advances - we have vaccines, and the death of a child is rare - in our part of the world, anyway.'

'Then perhaps you are right, Issy, though in truth I think we shall never know. I no longer try to make sense of it, I simply accept it. Now, I will make excuses with your parents and have a tray brought up for you. Try to get some rest because you will need it - tomorrow the real hard work begins and there is a lot depending upon it.'

Issy could see that the conversation was closed for the evening, but as she settled into bed that night, her head was filled with many more questions than answers, and a great sense of anxiety for the responsibilities coming her way that she could not evade, and the confidence her great grandmother was placing on her to pull it all off. Suddenly, looking after her sisters for her mum, finding a Saturday job, and choosing a career to study towards seemed minor in comparison to what was expected of her in Edwardian England.

7.

Her mother had told her later that all the first daughters of the Worthing line had travelled back in time to participate in the 'season', where the expectation was that they'd find a suitable match to prosper the family name. Lucinda Worthing had travelled back to the late eighteenth century where she'd apparently had no difficulties in securing the hand of the handsome and wealthy young bachelor that had been picked out for her, and by all accounts she'd enjoyed every moment of her success.

In the summer of 1944 however, the season had distinctly lost its bloom. Most of the eligible men were already at war, and of the ones left behind, whilst Hugo Harding may have been the heir to a fortune at a time when most of the old families had already lost theirs, he was also twenty years her senior, in just conveniently poor enough health to avoid conscription, and his bumbling attentions set her teeth on edge. Susan didn't care what anybody said, there was absolutely no way she was going to agree to marry him, and she was sure that the 17-year-old grandmother she had returned as - Elizabeth Worthing - would thank her for it too.

That was why she found herself at the village hall, answering the government's call for anyone who was fit and able to sign up to the war effort, with a view as much towards minimising any further encounters with Mr Harding as to doing her bit. Her (great-grand) parents had no idea – she would just have to wear their reaction when she got home, because there was no getting out of it now – she'd already signed the contract and would be starting that night, which just so happened to be when Mr Harding was next due to pay them a call.

'You'll be paired up with another trainee under a more experienced warden to begin with,' said the officer, an older man, who by the looks of all the adornments to his uniform had served in the Great War but was unable to serve beyond the home front during this one. He traced a

finger down his list then peered at her over his glasses. 'You'll be paired with young William Manning. Mr Rogers will expect you both here at seven. Do not be late.' He snapped shut his book and pointed to the door behind him. 'Uniform is through that way. Next!' he yelled, and Susan knew she was dismissed.

She could barely contain the spring in her step as she walked back to Worthington Manor through lush, unspoiled fields beneath a vast sky of such crisp blue, it was difficult to believe there was really a war going on at all – until she got home that was, and Lady Mary waged enough war for the Germans towards her all by herself.

*

Issy was so nervous she could have done with some of Mama's smelling salts. The instruction she'd been given on dance and deportment had been so intensive, and the stakes were so high, she knew she couldn't afford to make even the smallest mistake. To do so would risk bringing great shame to her family, and that was something Mama and Papa and, of course, Lady Brampton, would find intolerable. She had also studiously devoured her little book of etiquette every evening after dinner, overwhelmed by the complexity and rigidity of the social expectations of the era. She knew her mother would wish she could apply herself to her A Level revision with such zeal, but there was rather less dependent upon that, wasn't there? The entire course of her family's history, for one.

'My, Issy, you are a vision,' said Mama, as she pushed the silver jewelled hairpin she had worn at her own debut many years ago into Issy's hair as the finishing touch - a finishing touch that competed with the requisite three white feathers already adorning her head, causing Issy to wonder how she'd ever fit into Lord Brampton's motor car. The Edwardian era was certainly extra.

Issy stood in the tiled entrance hall ready to leave, with her back straight, her head held high just as she was taught, and her breathing even despite the tight lacing of her corset, as the adults in their company gazed upon her approvingly. Her dark blonde hair that usually hung down in ringlets had been intricately knotted upon her head just like Mama's as a mark of her transition into womanhood - no longer would her locks hang long and loose in company. She was dressed in her debutante gown complete with long sleeved gloves feeling unusually elegant and feminine - more so than her modern clothes had ever allowed. In spite of her reservations about her own performance, she couldn't help but feel excited about what the day might bring.

'She reminds me of you at her age, if you don't mind me saying so, milady,' remarked Mary, her mother's maid who had joined them on their trip.

'I don't think Lord Eltham stands a chance,' said Mama in approval.

Papa eyed Issy shrewdly. 'He'd better not,' he stated, and the subtext was not lost on Issy. She must not screw this up.

'Shall we, ladies?' said Lord Brampton affably. The motor car was ready, and Lord and Lady Brampton would be accompanying them to Buckingham Palace for the afternoon. He linked arms with his wife, Papa and Mama did the same, and when Lady Brampton turned to lock eyes with Issy, she gave her a little wink.

The day was young, the sky as stone grey as the townhouses around them, and the air bitingly fresh. Issy breathed as deeply as her undergarments would allow, and despite the dreary day, the afternoon still held a whisper of promise and adventure. Perhaps this was the adventure her late grandmother had referenced in her letter? She would soon find out. She could scarcely believe that the *season* - what she had learned comprised of several months of garden parties, balls, theatre shows and sporting and charity events - would begin with a curtsey before King Edward VII himself!

The ladies were assisted into Lord Brampton's motor car by the gentlemen, each dressed in their finery, with Mama gathering up Issy's train (the prescribed three-yards, measured exactly) so that it didn't touch the ground and get spoiled. With a nod, the chauffeur was off, and it was obvious to everyone how much Papa in particular enjoyed the ride.

*

No amount of instruction could have prepared Issy for the spectacle that followed as their car crept in procession through the famed tree-lined sanctum of central London along The Mall to the palace. Fortunately, their car was not too far from the front of a seemingly endless row of cars and carriages containing hundreds of other anxious young debutantes accompanied by their fussing mothers - many aged only in their thirties themselves - or staid chaperones.

Issy clutched her royal invitation close to her breast and snacked surreptitiously on a handful of nuts, which was all Mama would allow lest she get bloated and spoil the good impression she was determined she would make. Issy felt like telling Mama that her corset was laced so tightly, her body simply wouldn't allow her to become bloated anyway, so she needn't worry and just let her eat the damn nuts already. But that simply wouldn't do.

Most disturbing of all was that she and all the other debutantes were, quite literally, a spectacle. It seemed that all the men in London had turned out to lock eyes on the production line of young women and marvel at their looks under the guise of marvelling at their costumes. With their array of elaborately feathered or flowered hats carrying either a bouquet, fan, or parasol (or in some cases, all three), each with a string of pearls tied about their neck - anything more fancy was considered too vulgar until they were formally 'out' in society - the debutantes must have been quite a sight to behold, especially for the poorest amongst the crowd who could no more dream of touching the fabric they wore than of owning it.

The attention was overwhelming to Issy, but some of the more extroverted young ladies among them waved at the crowds to great appreciation and uproar, only to be admonished by those accompanying them. Some of the more determined men among weren't content to simply watch from afar - some even went so far as to tap on the car windows, or in some instances, rather disturbingly - to try to open the door to get a better look. Was this how Taylor Swift felt, Issy wondered? If so, one thing was for sure - fame was not for her. Should she stop posting videos of herself on social media, lest she go viral?

It was with more than a little relief that the rain held off and they managed to avoid the car-trespassers and reach the relative peace and safety of the West Portico - a sort of stone covered entrance wide enough to accommodate a car, where a lady could step out onto a red carpet without having her outfit ruined by the elements. It was surreal to Issy, as though she were in some sort of childhood dream, to present her invitation to a guard then be led inside the palace itself and up a wide sweeping staircase to a private dressing area where she and all the other debutantes could put the finishing touches to their look at a row of full-length mirrors, before lining up one by one to be presented before royalty.

Mama pinched Issy's cheeks until they glowed red, and with a furtive glance to make sure no-one was watching, she pressed the tiniest bit of rose-coloured tint to her lips then quickly slipped the small pot back into her purse.

'You are very fortunate, Isabelle, that you will be presented to King Edward himself. There is nothing worse than going to the trouble of being presented into society - a once in a lifetime event - only to have the King tire and leave another member of the royal family in his place.'

'Did Queen Victoria tire when you were presented, Mama?'

'Of course not,' said Mama, her face taking on something of a wistful expression. 'Your grandmother saw to that - we made very good time. Quickly now, let's take our place in the line.'

Contrary to what you might expect upon setting eyes upon the row of smart and properly young women dressed in demure white, there was something of a less than graceful clamour to secure the best place in the line, and it was evident that Mama had been through all of this before because, utilising her parasol as a deterrent, she was quite determined not to back down and relinquish their coveted spot near the front. It reminded of Issy of queueing for the rides at Disney with her mother and sisters - whilst the context was as different as one could possibly imagine, the adrenaline rush was just the same.

'It is almost our turn, Isabelle,' whispered Mama, with a polite nod at the palace guard. 'Remember, someone will assist you with your train. You must dip as low to the ground as possible without falling over before the King and all the other members of the royal family, whilst also retaining as much elegance and poise as gravity will allow. Do not drop your fan - hold onto it for dear life.'

'Yes, Mama,' said Issy meekly. If it was her own mother speaking, she'd have said for crying out loud, stop telling me, I already know! But this was 1904, and she had to suppress such outrageous retorts that might have perhaps earned her the strap from her father, lady or not. In fact, she had to suppress her very being in order to fit in here at all, and in that respect she wondered if she was actually all that different from any other female in the room.

'Here we go.' Mama nudged her forwards. 'It's your turn.'

'King Edward,' announced the Lord Chamberlain, 'I present to you Miss Isabelle Violet Worthing, daughter of Lord Worthing of Eastshire; accompanied by her mother, Lady Edith Grace Worthing.'

This very moment was one that Issy had rehearsed at least a hundred times under Lady Brampton's watchful eye. *Must. Not. Screw. This. Up.* she repeated to herself as she pasted a chaste smile upon her mouth and forced her body to propel itself forward before an eagerly waiting crowd. Ahead of her was a dais upon which sat the formidable King upon his throne, his bright red suit embroidered with gold, with a bejewelled Queen Alexandra of Denmark by his side, both surrounded by several other officials and high-ranking members of the royal family. She had to curtsey to each of them in turn, after first making her curtsey to the King himself.

Keeping her breathing as even as she was able, Issy's dress felt heavy and cumbersome as she walked, like walking through sand in a dream. But this was evident to no-one but her - to everyone else she glided along the red carpet like a swan across a lake. She was grateful of the ballet training of her formative years, which allowed her to dip into the lowest curtsey her body could possibly allow, and the King - who was much older than she'd imagined and whose beard and moustache lent him a very stern air - gave her the faintest nod of approval that signalled she could consider herself presented and go on her way. It was hard to believe that so much fuss was made over such a small moment in time.

If anyone thought that the dipping down was the hardest part, they were quite wrong about that. Getting back up again without dropping her fan, tripping over her train, or falling over altogether was a million times harder, and Issy wasn't quite sure she'd be able to pull it off, not once but five times. Thankfully she did, and it was with some relief and elation that she glided backwards out of the ballroom, careful to never turn her back on her King, her part done with for now. There were several other unfortunate young ladies that day who would not carry off the duty quite so successfully and would suffer the inevitable subsequent public humiliation, but the King had seen it all and was careful to keep his face impassive, and Issy didn't get to see any of it - if she had it might have allayed her nerves after all the horror stories her tutor had utilised to scare her into submission.

And so Issy had made her formal debut into society, and after all the preparations and hours of waiting for only a moment of King Edward's time and attention, that single poignant moment had taken Issy from schoolgirl to woman in the eyes of all society.

'Wonderful! She was wonderful!' Lady Brampton enthused, as Mama and Issy re-joined their party afterwards for champagne and canapes. Issy was ravenous, but she was not permitted to eat as much as her appetite demanded and had to content herself with a miniature something or other as often as the waiters brought a tray around. Only the champagne flowed freely, and all that champagne on an empty stomach made her feel slightly tipsy, and the adrenaline from the day's events fuelled the sensation further.

Papa gave her a nod, which was as much of a compliment as it seemed he was capable of giving, then he and Lord Brampton embroiled themselves in conversation with old friends, and the ladies did not see them again until the close of the event.

'Of course, she was wonderful,' Mama retorted. 'She did not have to dip quite so far as we did - after all, King Edward is head and shoulders in height above the late Queen Victoria, God rest her soul.'

The latter was said in a whisper, and Lady Brampton laughed – she too had made her own debut before Queen Victoria many years ago, had kissed the hand of royalty, and could absolutely relate.

'It is all so different nowadays. To think,' Mama continued, 'there's talk of presenting the girls at garden parties next - imagine, in this climate! Where do they think we are - the Mediterranean? We are lucky to have had Isabelle presented when we did.'

'I fear that one day this tradition will die out altogether- all the best ones do,' said Lady Brampton. 'Anyway, hush Edith, dear, before we get locked in the Tower for treason. Though you are not far wrong.'

'So, what happens now?' asked Issy, who had been too nervous to think far beyond the curtsey. She was enjoying the rare freedom to indulge in as much champagne as she pleased, something her own mother would never approve of, even though back home at least one of their friends managed to produce a bottle of something forbidden every weekend for them to share between half a dozen people then pretend to be tipsy from.

'Now you will get your likeness taken,' said Mama.

'*Another* queue?' Issy sighed, as she stared wistfully at the retreating waiter carrying with him a retreating tray of food. Her feet were sore from her narrow-buttoned shoes, and she longed to sit down.

'Another queue,' Mama confirmed. 'Your appetite can wait.'

'But-'

'No buts, Isabelle. Come along.'

Issy could have laughed at how long it took to take a photograph in 1904, had she not been quite so hungry, tired, and ready to go 'home.' But a couple of mornings later it seemed the effort had paid off, because Lady Brampton and Mama lost no time in telling her at breakfast that that very photograph had made the front page of *Society and the Season*, in which she had been dubbed 'Debutante of the Year' due to her *faultless combination of beauty and poise, innocence and grace.*

Mama was delighted, Lady Brampton was proud, and even Papa gave her another of his nods.

'Let's hope Lady Eltham is reading this,' said Mama astutely.

'Oh, I'm sure she is,' Lady Brampton affirmed. 'What with the eldest Miss Eltham due out in a couple of years, I am certain of it.'

'You will be the talk of London now, Isabelle, and a flurry of invitations are sure to follow. Everyone who's anyone will want you at their party.'

Mama smiled. And Lady Brampton was not far wrong, because the invitations began rolling in the very next day. The first was to invite them all to a grand ball that would kickstart the season in which anyone who was anyone would attend, including of course, Lord Eltham himself. Though Lady Brampton had her sights set on another match for Isabelle, Issy couldn't help but wonder about the character of this man her parents were so determined she should marry. Fortunately for her, she wouldn't have long to wait to find out.

8.

Susan shivered, as much from excitement and nerves about what the night would hold as from the cool evening air that brushed against her cheeks as she cycled towards the village dressed in her heavy, black ARP uniform with her cumbersome gas mask strapped over her shoulder. Her mother had refused to allow her father to drive her there once she'd found out what she'd done.

Lady Mary had assumed that the reality of her riding out alone at night might be enough to deter their sheltered and privileged daughter from pursuing her latest course of action – but what she had not counted on was that Susan was actually an independent young woman of the nineties who had cycled into Worthington unaccompanied a million times, and she was quite determined not to spend another moment in Mr Harding's company if she didn't have to. Fortunately, her father was quite impressed by her pluck, and she'd barely gotten beyond the manor's gate when she'd heard his motor car crunching upon the gravel behind her.

'You must promise to go easy on your mother, Elizabeth, dear,' he said as he drew to a stop directly outside of the village hall, pausing thoughtfully to exhale the smoke from his post-dinner pipe. 'Your mother and I are old enough to recall there is never a more uncertain time than wartime. She is trying to find some certainty for you now, because she wants what is best for you. We both do.'

Then please don't make your daughter marry that horrid man, thought Susan privately, but all she did was plant a dutiful kiss upon his cheek, for she could not help but take a liking to the kindly Ruben Worthing, though she resolved to withhold judgement on his choice of wife. For now.

'Ooo, recruiting the hoity toity now too, are we?' remarked a tall and lean young man with chestnut hair, hazel eyes, and a smattering of *freckles across his nose and cheeks. Susan assumed he must be William Manning.*

'Mind your manners, lad,' warned the older gentleman. 'She's from Worthington Manor.'

'Is she now? Doesn't look like a toff to me.'

'Who does in these uniforms?'

'That's correct, Mr Rogers,' said Susan. 'In this uniform, we are all the same.'

'Me and a lady - the same? I never thought I'd hear the like!' William fell into fits of laughter, which the elder gentleman's stern gaze only seemed to encourage. 'Wait 'til I tell me ma I've spent the night with a lady – she'll have kittens!'

Mr Rogers shook his head, as though quite at a loss as to how best to manage his unruly charge. Susan knew she should be offended, but she wasn't. There was something about the young man's animated face, warm smile, and sparkling eyes that instantly set her at ease. She could tell he was just teasing, and besides, in her opinion, when she was wearing her uniform, they were all the same and she hoped to be treated as such.

'Elizabeth Worthing,' said Susan, extending a hand to Mr Rogers, who shook it as though scarcely able to believe it himself. 'Reporting to duty, Sir.' Next, she turned towards the young man with the chestnut hair. She could feel his eyes assessing her. 'That's Lady Worthing to you,' she grinned, her eyes merry. It didn't take long for Willliam to realise that she too was just teasing.

'Pleasure to meet you, Lady Worthing. The name's William, but you can call me Will. Will Manning.' He extended a hand towards hers, and she noticed as she took it that his fingers were marked with grey smudges. 'Charcoal,' he said, by way of an explanation. 'I like to draw.'

And when he grasped her hand, and Susan's eyes locked onto his and he smiled his cheeky, lopsided smile, she couldn't help but feel a surge of warmth rushing through her, even though it was no warmer inside the village hall than it was outside.

*

To the great envy of the wallflowers lining the ballroom, there wasn't a single blank space left on Issy's dance card. To Mama's glee, her first dance would be with none other than the eligible Lord Eltham. Learning how to curtsey had been one thing, but learning the intricacies of Edwardian dance had been quite another altogether, and Issy felt sick with nerves. It didn't matter if she looked the part in her gown of loose folds of tulle laid over palest blue satin - if ever she was to be exposed as an imposter, surely a couple of dances would be all it would take?

'I can't do this.'

'Nonsense,' said Lady Brampton. 'You didn't think you could curtsey to the King, and not only did you succeed, but you were dubbed debutante of the year! There is a not another young lady in this room who wouldn't give their best parasol to switch places with you right now. You did that, Isabelle, and you can do this too. You must.'

Issy gulped. She glanced at Papa, who narrowed his eyes. She knew that whatever he was thinking, it would involve a curt reminder of the word 'duty.' She glanced at Mama, who peered at her and Lady Brampton as though she wished to be privy to a conversation that might offer some insight into why the Issy of the last couple of weeks was quite unlike the Isabelle of before, and how concerned she ought to be about that, and what she could do to get her back. If only Issy knew.

The band struck up a waltz, and the eligible (and not quite so eligible) young men of their company strode across the room to claim their intended partners. Couples slotted into any available space on the dance floor, to the great delight of the mothers and relatives looking on at them in approval, each determined to outdo the other in securing the best possible match for their sons and daughters. With his thick dark hair, lean build and molten dark eyes, Lord Eltham was easily the handsomest among them, but, as Issy was to find out, looks were unfortunately about as far as his appeal stretched.

He did not smile as he offered Issy his cool hand and led her to the dance floor, where he cupped her stiffly in his arms. In fact, he barely spoke a word at all. He might have hoped that Issy would be disappointed, but she had long since realised that in her situation the less said the better lest she reveal the truth about herself, so she was actually quite relieved. She was so focussed on getting the dance moves correct that she didn't have time to give the matter much thought.

Lord Eltham guided her backwards in a circle about the room, the gowns of elegant young ladies forming bright bursts of colour to the watchful bystanders.

'So, you have your sights set on the Eltham fortune then?' said Lord Eltham, eventually.

'I beg your pardon?' Issy had learned enough about Edwardian society to recognise that such a line of enquiry was not at all respectable or befitting to the activity they were engaged in.

'Well,' he persisted, 'do you?'

Issy paused. 'I do not,' she said honestly.

'Huh.'

'But I must confess,' she continued, 'that my parents do. Though it is neither here nor there to me.'

Pointedly, she directed her gaze to the merry couples surrounding them, smiles upon their flushed faces as young women found themselves in such daring proximity to young men for the very first time, and the men enjoyed the novelty of their experience as much as the women did. Lord Eltham followed her gaze.

'It seems there are many more, shall we say *agreeable* partners in attendance at this ball tonight.'

'Then why did you agree to this dance?'

'You are a good dancer,' Issy begrudgingly admitted, and thought she saw the faintest hint of a smile play about his mouth, which was hidden somewhere beneath a thick moustache which seemed to be the current fashion.

It was true. Where many of the men had faltered and trod awkwardly on the toes of their red-faced partners, Lord Eltham was so graceful he danced well enough for both of them and helped keep Issy in step. She was grateful for that if not for the company. It seemed Lottie had been quite right about him, and she made a mental note to write to her and tell her – for she was certain that's what the real Isabelle would do.

'Anyway,' said Isabelle, 'why did you ask me?'

Lord Eltham paused before stating simply: 'Duty.'

'That's hardly a compliment.'

'I only pay compliments where I feel they're due.'

'I paid *you* one. I believe the only polite thing to do in such circumstances is to reciprocate.' Her little book of etiquette was quite clear in that respect, however it was evident that Lord Eltham had no intention of doing any such thing.

'Why did you accept my invitation, given you seem to have formed such a poor view of me already?'

'Oh no,' Issy refuted, 'I was actually quite prepared to give you the benefit of the doubt, but it seems my initial reservations about your character were correct.'

'Ah,' said Lord Eltham. 'Those rumours about my demeanour unfortunately do not seem to have had the desired effect of deterring social climbing young ladies and their mothers.'

Issy was certain the real Isabelle Worthing would have been flummoxed by this blatant disregard of propriety, but fortunately for him, she wasn't. 'The female attention can't be all bad,' she joked. 'I'm sure most men would find it quite an enjoyable hardship to endure. And are there not many equally respectable young ladies present here tonight, myself included? Which I presume is why we find ourselves in this position, as much as it obviously pains you.'

She risked a glance at Papa, who was watching her keenly. 'But if you must know, I accepted you for the same reason you asked me. *Duty.* Though it does help that you're also rather good at these steps.'

And easy on the eye, Issy thought but did not say, lest she cast even the slightest doubt upon her respectability. Needless to say, they danced the remainder of the dance in silence, and Issy could not help but wonder what Mila would make of the whole thing if she could see her now.

'Well?' asked an enthusiastic Mama, as she returned to her party and a fortifying glass of champagne was thrust into her hand by Lady Brampton.

'Well,' said Issy. 'I'm afraid he is just as I feared.'

'Disagreeable or not,' said Mama, 'you must persevere.'

The ladies were soon interrupted by Countess Astbury of Lady Brampton and Mama's acquaintance, accompanied by a stunning young lady dressed in a gown of finest bottle-green silk with gold embroidery.

'Lady Brampton, Lady Worthing, Miss Worthing, may I introduce my eldest daughter, Miss Alice Astbury. She has been most anxious to meet you Isabelle, since you made your debut. It appears you made quite an impression at court! I'm sure you two ladies will have much in common.'

The three elder ladies were quickly caught up in conversation, leaving Issy and Miss Astbury to regard one another steadily. Miss Astbury made it clear she did not think much of what she saw, and Issy was immediately put in mind of Steph Sutton. She swiftly pushed away thoughts of Chad Connor, of her best friend Mila, and of her home and her family. She must remain focussed on her *duty*.

'I see you have danced with Lord Eltham already,' said Miss Astbury. 'What is he like? I am to dance with him next.' She said it as though the prospect might unsettle Issy, but of course it didn't.

'Well,' said Issy, who could think of nothing especially becoming about Lord Eltham to say, 'he's a very good dancer.'

'Yes, that was apparent. But what of his character?'

'I'm afraid I cannot say,' said Issy. 'We did not talk a great deal.'

Miss Astbury looked upon this as a victory, and she regarded Issy with obvious pity. 'Perhaps you did not make quite such an impression upon him as you did at court. Perhaps he and I might have more in common.'

'Perhaps.' Issy smiled, though she doubted that very much. *Good luck to her,* she thought, for Miss Alice Astbury did not know what she was in for.

The band struck up once again, and Lord Eltham strode across the room to claim Miss Astbury for their dance, who took his arm possessively then had the bad grace to peer back over her shoulder at Issy and smirk. Issy ignored her and wondered what her own next dance partner would be like. An oaf or a bore, she was sure. The precedent was set.

A man strode towards her. He was tall and solid, with tightly curled blonde hair and piercing eyes. His lips were full and pink revealing surprisingly good teeth for the era, false of course, and a mark of money. *New* money in this instance. He beamed at Issy as he approached.

'Miss Worthing,' he said, looking deep into her eyes with his penetrating gaze, a gaze that made Issy feel dizzy and tense all at once.

'Mr Walker,' she replied as steadily as she could manage.

'Now we are introduced, I suppose we had better dance together!'

Issy smiled in spite of herself. She felt warm inside as Mr Walker took her arm in his and led them to their place on the dance floor. His hands were warm and his frame solid as he pressed her close to his chest for the foxtrot - a dance Issy had been dreading due to its complex pacing and steps.

Forward, forward, side, close. Back, back, side, close. Slow, slow, quick, quick, slow. Slow, quick, quick. Issy traced the steps of the dance in her mind as she moved, but something about her proximity to Mr Walker and the sensuous movements and synchronising of their legs and hips caused her thoughts to muddle. To her the dance almost bordered on improper, and she was surprised it was permitted in the Edwardian era at all. But then she thought of the tight lacing of her corset and the low-cut neckline of her dress designed to expose her bosom to all and sundry to the best of its advantage, whilst the rest of her dress was designed to hide as much of her figure as possible, down to her very inoffensive ankles. If nothing else, it was an era of contradictions.

Slow, slow, quick, slow, quick. Whoops. She stepped on his toe and beamed bright red. She was certain that from across the ballroom she saw Miss Astbury sneer.

'Mr Walker, I apologise.' Issy was horrified.

'I don't know what you mean,' he smiled.

As they moved and turned, Issy eased into the dance, relaxing into her proximity with him until eventually their movements blended together seamlessly.

'I see you have danced with Lord Eltham already,' said Mr Walker, 'and I imagine your dance card is too full to dance with me a second time tonight. I suppose I shall have to wait until I am fortunate enough to have our paths to cross again.'

She nodded. It was unfortunate indeed, because how could any subsequent dance partner that evening possibly compare to Mr Walker?

'Are you always this quiet, Miss Worthing?'

'Yes,' said Issy, with this suppressed Edwardian version of herself in mind, who was too busy trying not to fall over. 'I mean no,' she said, as she recalled the real Issy - the Issy from over a century ahead whose life was usually filled with fun, friendship and laughter.

Mr Walker laughed. 'Which is it, then? We have only a couple minutes left for me to find out and now I am most intrigued.'

'It depends on the company,' she replied, carefully.

'Ah, well I saw you dancing with Lord Eltham, and you certainly did not appear to be short of words then. Not like Miss Astbury over there now.'

Issy laughed, and it lit up her face. It was the first time she had really laughed since her step back in time. Mr Walker was right - Miss Astbury and Lord Eltham really did seem to be lost for words.

'Perhaps I am one dance too late for you Miss Worthing,' Mr Walker continued, 'for never before have I seen Lord Eltham quite so animated with a female.'

'Oh no,' said Issy, then instantly regretted it. It was not appropriate for her to encourage a man, and certainly not in public. At least, not a man that Mama and Papa did not approve of anyway. 'I mean,' she faltered, 'Lord Eltham made it quite clear that he is not interested in me. Actually, I'm not sure he is interested in any of the ladies here tonight. He seems to find all of our sex intolerable.'

'You may be quite right about that, Miss Worthing.' Mr Walker regarded Mr Eltham astutely. 'More than you could possibly know.'

Whatever did he mean? Issy wondered. Perhaps Mr Walker and Lord Eltham were already acquainted. Perhaps he knew of a secret love interest of Lord Eltham's, a love so strong that no other could interest him, just as she was certain no other dance partner that evening could arouse her interest like Mr Walker had. She allowed her thoughts to wander. Perhaps it was a poor woman, a commoner whom he could never marry - especially not now that circumstance had forced him to become heir? He had said it himself - his actions that evening were duty bound. What else could excuse his rudeness? For the first time, Issy felt a stab of empathy for Lord Eltham. A small one.

Like all good things, the dance ended, and Mr Walker led Issy back to her party. He gazed into her eyes in such a way that made her feel as though to him she was the only girl in the room, if not the world, and he pressed a kiss upon her gloved hand before disappearing back into the throng. Issy was breathless, and the part of her hand where his lips had touched her still felt warm and moist through her glove.

'Enjoy yourself, Isabelle, but do not neglect your duty,' Mama warned, when Countess Astbury had finally moved on.

'That's him,' whispered Lady Brampton when Mama was out of earshot. Her face was ashen - even the violet of her eyes had paled. 'My husband.'

Issy shook her head, as she absorbed the meaning inherent in Lady Brampton's words. Mr Walker was a drinker. Mr Walker was violent and cruel. He did not respect women. She tried to assimilate this part of his character with the part of him she had just encountered, and failed.

'No,' she said, shaking her head as a wave of heat rushed through her, causing her to feel faint. 'Not him.' Not Mr Walker.

9.

The minimum commitment was three nights a week. Susan worked from dusk to dawn and had the luxury of sleeping all day, unlike poor Will who had to go straight from volunteering as an air raid warden to assisting his father as a labourer on the Worthing's land, for his three brothers had all gone to war, and his mother knew that the moment Will turned eighteen, if this war didn't end soon he would be called up too. No, sleep was a luxury Susan doubted the real Elizabeth would have known she'd had, sheltered as she had been from the ordinary lives of the ordinary people living just a couple of miles beyond the manor's boundary – lives that her ancestors had not wanted to cross paths with unless it was to serve them in some way. No matter how Susan looked at it, it just didn't seem fair that they had so much when so many people had to make do with so little, especially during wartime.

'Oh, look,' said Will, 'it's that darned old Joe letting the side down again. I wonder what his excuse is this time?'

'Oh no.' Susan shook her head. 'Poor Joe, I wonder why he can't just admit that he needs help.'

'Huh, most men would rather get shot by one of Hitler's men than admit that.'

'Then most men are stupid. Ignoring the problem won't make it go away, you know.'

'No need to tell me that, Lady Worthing, you can tell him yourself – see how he takes it.'

Will pushed open the low wooden gate that was bordered each side by overgrown honeysuckle and climbing roses and rapped on the door hard enough to guarantee a swift response. A stout, elderly man with white hair and a squint shuffled to the door.

'Mr Gardener,' said Will, what have we told you about obeying the blackout? There's not just a chink of light – it's like Blackpool bloody

79

illuminations in here. You could singlehandedly signpost Hitler's airmen to the munitions factory if you carry on like this.'

'I just wanted to see your pretty young lady again,' said Mr Gardener with a grin.

'We all do,' said Will, and Susan couldn't help but blush, 'but must you really go to such dangerous lengths to do it? I'm sure her parents would let you drop in at the manor for a spot of tea and cake any time.'

The two men laughed, and Susan rolled her eyes. Will really was incorrigible. 'Come on then, Mr Gardener, we may as well help you while we're here. Though when you'll finally admit defeat and book in an appointment with the eye doctor is anyone's guess - then you won't keep getting all these late knocks on your door.'

'Then we'll all have far less need of our Anderson shelters,' said Will.

'I don't know what you mean.' Mr Gardener stumbled back inside, feeling his way to the sofa whilst Susan set about blocking out every last chink of light. 'There's nothing wrong with my eyes – they've served me well enough these past sixty years.'

'I'm sure there's nothing wrong with them that a strong pair of glasses wouldn't fix so they can serve you for another sixty,' said Susan. 'I'll make you an appointment myself if I have to.'

'No, I won't go to no doctor, not me. I'd know my way around my own house with my eyes closed, anyway.'

'And a darned good thing that is too. Goodnight, Mr Gardener, no doubt we'll be seeing you again tomorrow evening.'

'Until then!' Susan ensured he was comfortable before she could bear to leave him to it, setting a pot of tea within his reach.

'I don't care what he says,' she said, as soon as she and Will were out of earshot. 'With my next allowance I will be purchasing that man a pair of glasses.'

Mr Rogers bumped into them at the end of the cobbled street. 'Everything going alright with your rounds then, you two?'

'Everything seems to be in order here, Sir,' said Will, and Susan nodded.

'Alright then, looks like a pot of tea is in order before we start the night-watch.'

Susan and Will exchanged a grin, for they both knew that despite his best intentions, Mr Rogers would be unlikely to stay awake beyond midnight, earning him the unfortunate nickname of Cinderella. Fortunately, the fate of Worthington did not rely on just the three of them – the village hall was a hub for other volunteers too, from ARP teams to fire and ambulance wardens, policemen, and anyone else willing to lend a hand. Though Worthington itself wasn't considered much of a target, the new munitions factory located just a couple of miles away was, and it would be all too easy for the village to be bombed by mistake if they did not go to such great pains to get the blackout just right.

It was eerie, sitting out on the decking each night beneath the stars of a vast inky sky just waiting for a threat to present itself. If it did, one of them would have to sound the air raid siren, and they weren't allowed to take cover themselves at the first siren that signalled a looming threat, but instead had to first assist the villagers then wait until the second siren which signalled an immediate threat. Susan hoped she'd have no cause to put any of this into practice any time soon.

'Aren't you scared?' she asked Will, pulling her thick woollen blanket more tightly about her shoulders as they watched and waited.

He smiled and shook his head. 'Not me. Fear won't keep our families safe, and it won't help us win this war.'

'Whatever you do,' said Susan urgently, 'please don't sign up.'

'Gee, if it weren't for my ma, I would've lied about my age and signed up ages ago like my brothers, but I promised her I wouldn't – not until at least one of them returns home. Unless I'm called up first, of course.'

He smiled, and his hazel eyes danced in the starlight. He had such an expressive face and warm presence that Susan couldn't help but be drawn to him. A man like Will could not be lost to war, he just couldn't.

'Promise me, too,' she said before she could stop herself, and in an instant the jovial atmosphere between them changed. Will became uncharacteristically serious, and Susan felt acutely aware of her own heartbeat and breathing.

He raised his eyes to hers, and, checking that Mr Rogers was indeed asleep, reached out a hand to brush a loose curl back from her face. 'I promise, Elizabeth,' he said, then he took out his sketchbook and charcoal, and drew her earnest face with eyes that asked more from him than he felt he could give in that moment.

*

A maid poured Issy tea, and she nodded her thanks – she simply could not bring herself to allow such acts of service, however small, to go unacknowledged.

Letters! She sat down to read as she sipped, savouring this more traditional form of correspondence more than she had ever savoured a text message.

Dearest Issy,

I'm sure it must be difficult for you to find time to write to your poor sisters now that you are a true lady, but please consider me (and Lottie's incessant questions about the season and suitors and balls and all manner of things she is too young to concern herself with) and let us know how this letter finds you. As you can guess, Aunt Cassandra bought Lottie the best present - a telescope, can you imagine? Now her head is full of planets and solar systems and all manner of things not befitting a young lady. Mama will be most unimpressed! I must content myself with a new hat, a pair of gloves, and some books (with which I am fortunately well pleased). We look forward to visiting you soon, and (we hope), to hearing some exciting news.

We miss you so,
Flora.

Issy,

Why do you not write? It has been insufferable here without you!
Flora is boring and does everything Aunt Cassandra tells her to. Though
Aunt Cassandra did buy me a telescope and she has been teaching me
how to find Orien's Belt and Ursa Major. I can find them by myself
now!

Miss Browning is as intolerable as ever. She wants us only to paint
and dance and sing. I want to learn! I want to explore! I want more.
I am most envious of you and your London adventures, though I pity
they will come to an end forever when you marry. Is Lord E. as horrid
as we were led to believe? I hope not for your sake.

Anyway, we are to visit you in London soon, then we can have
adventures of our own. Be sure to have lots to tell!

Love,
Lottie.

Issy sat at her writing desk beneath the gable window of her
London townhouse bedroom and smiled. A buttery sun cast a soft
shaft of morning light into the room, and she clutched the letters in
her hand and read them again and again. If only she had the girls
for company, how different this trip would be. She could appreciate
why the occasional receipt of a letter must have been the height
of excitement in this era. She longed to message her own sisters,
Jasmine and Ella, and wondered how the family would be coping
without her. Would they have sent out a search party, she wondered?
Would it have even occurred to either of them to look for her in the
attic? Mrs Lamb had certainly seemed to know something - perhaps
she would have told them where to start looking.

Dipping the nib of her pen in a pot of blue ink, she took a fresh
sheet of writing paper and crafted her reply, careful to keep it in line
with what she assumed to be the real Isabelle's voice.

My dear sisters,

The season has only just begun and already it has been quite the adventure. I have curtsied to the King, danced with several suitors at a fine ball, and lunched with Mama and Lady Brampton more times than I care to count (I have the blisters to prove it!). I have danced and drunk champagne and worn pretty gowns and -

There was a knock at the door and Mary entered.

'A gentleman caller for you, Miss Worthing. Your mother requires you in the drawing room at once.'

Issy was all aflutter. A gentleman caller, already! Who could it be? Mr Walker? Lord Eltham (surely not)? The short and overly keen one who had kept standing on her toes (*please, let it not be him!*)? She had no idea what or who to expect, and she was ashamed to admit that a not too insignificant part of her longed to see Mr Walker again, even if it was wholly against her better judgement.

'Who is it, Mary?'

'I'm not sure, Miss Worthing. Delia answered the door, but your mother sent me up straight away to make sure you're suitably dressed. You look lovely, I think we should go down.'

Issy nodded. 'Give me a moment, please. I'm coming.'

Mary curtsied and exited the room, assuming Issy merely wanted to beautify herself before greeting her gentleman caller, as any young lady would. It was still hard for Issy to get her head around the concept of a grown woman thrice her age curtsying to her - a teenager barely out of the schoolroom!

A gentleman caller! I wonder who it could be? Let's hope it is not a certain Lord E. - as much as I would like to say I have reserved my judgement about him, my worst fears have unfortunately already been confirmed in that regard.

I must close now, but please know you are in my heart and I'm so looking forward to seeing you both in a few weeks' time - if I (and

my poor feet) can survive the onslaught of balls, theatre performances,
sporting events and garden parties... I'm sure there will be lots to tell.
All my love,
Issy.

Issy gave the letter to the housekeeper for posting on her way down. She was wearing a long-sleeved gown of spring green overlaid with white lace, her bottom-length hair piled high and offset with a pair of simple pearl earrings. She still felt naked without a slick of mascara and lip-gloss and would have killed for a tube of tinted moisturiser – or better yet, a bottle of fake tan – but at least the rush down several flights of stairs from bedroom to drawing room had flushed her pale cheeks. Taking a deep breath, she entered the drawing room.

'Lord Eltham, I wasn't expecting to see you again quite so soon.'

Though he looked incredibly debonair in his grey tweed suit, Issy found it hard to hide her disappointment. He didn't look too pleased to be there himself, and she wondered why he had gone to the trouble of coming at all.

'You will see that Lord Eltham has brought you the most beautiful flowers, Isabelle,' said Mama, her voice dripping with approval.

Issy blushed under her pointed gaze. 'Thank you, Lord Eltham, they're stunning.'

And they were. An extravagant bunch of spring flowers in all manner of colours. Issy couldn't imagine someone like Chad Connor ever buying her flowers, and she had to admit there was something delightful about being the recipient of such a simple, age-old gesture.

But there the conversation stilted. Issy had no idea what to say. She'd been certain that she and Lord Eltham had exhausted their entire conversational repertoire at the ball.

'Would you care for some tea, Lord Eltham?' Mama asked.

'Please,' he nodded.

'Certainly, I will return in a moment. I will just let Lady Brampton know you are here. I'm sure she would like to greet you herself.'

Without Mama watching over her every move, Issy felt she could finally exhale.

'As grateful as I am, Lord Eltham, I must admit I thought Miss Astbury may be a more suitable recipient of such a fine bouquet.'

'Miss Astbury?' He raised his molten eyes in surprise. 'I would sooner stick a hat pin in my eye than call on Miss Astbury. She is wealthy, undeniably, but she has too much pretence. There is something... *real* about you that is lacking in so many silly young women these days.'

If she wasn't so offended by the insinuation that all young women were silly, Issy might have laughed at the irony - the only thing real about her was her name.

'Then to what do I owe the honour of your visit, for we both know that we did not exactly see eye to eye at the ball?'

Lord Eltham exhaled as though pained. 'Your mother will return at any moment so I will keep this brief. I'm afraid I am not a flowery or poetic sort of man - even the flowers were my mother's idea, but, Miss Worthing, my business here today is simple. I have come to ask you to enter into a courtship with me, with the intention to ask for your hand in marriage. I have not yet spoken to your father as my mother thought it best to first ascertain your views on the matter.'

Issy was astounded. 'Your business? You intend to ask for my hand in marriage, and refer to it as business?' Did this man have *any* feeling at all? She could see he was exasperated.

'Did you not say yourself that you are duty bound in your choice, as I am?'

Issy shook her head. It was hopeless. How could she explain? She was duty bound to marry - not Lord Eltham, but Mr Walker. As much as she felt she was walking Lady Brampton straight into danger, she had no choice but to do it for her son's sake, even if it meant risking the wrath of Mama and Papa. 'Yes, I suppose I did.'

'Well then, do you really expect a man to make love to you, or shall we manage this situation for what it truly is - a business transaction? A merging of estates and old names? We will each have the satisfaction of accomplishing our duty to our respective families. Is that not what you wanted, or have I misread the situation entirely?'

Issy paused. 'You have misread nothing.'

'Then what is the problem?'

'The problem...' she hesitated a fraction before continuing, 'is Mr Walker.'

'Mr Walker?'

Lord Eltham swept a hand roughly through his hair as he paced across the room, loosening the neck of his tie as he did so.

'I might have guessed. I saw the way you danced with him - Miss Astbury pointed it out. But let me tell you, I know things about Mr Walker that are not befitting for a young lady's ears. You must trust me - a match with him would not only be a grave mistake for you, but it could bring shame and misfortune upon your entire family.'

Issy's eye filled with unshed tears. How on earth could she tell Lord Eltham that she already knew?

'Do you understand what I'm telling you?'

'I do.'

'And yet you will not yield?'

She looked at Lord Eltham, her eyes pleading. 'I'm afraid I cannot.'

'Then you are as a lamb to a wolf, Miss Worthing.'

'I'm sorry, Lord Eltham, for I know your proposal does me a great honour. But wouldn't you rather marry for love?'

'Huh! There can be no wisdom in a love-match if it leads to decisions like yours, and unfortunately not everyone is free to follow their heart – the very concept is nothing more than a fancy.' He said it as though it pained him, and Issy wondered what secret hurt might lie behind the words. 'I'm afraid it is I who is sorry, Miss Worthing - I am sorry *for* you. And now I must bid you good day.'

Mama returned, wearing a hopeful smile that softened her face, as Delia bustled in behind her wheeling a tray of tea alongside a selection of pastries and cakes.

'Good day, Lady Worthing, Miss Worthing, I will show myself out.'

With a curt tip of his hat he was gone, leaving Issy to face Mama's wrath alone. She took a deep breath and prepared herself for the onslaught. Fortunately, she was saved by the ringing of the doorbell. They heard voices in the hallway, and a moment later, Delia opened the door and the fine figure of Mr Walker stepped into the room. Issy couldn't help the fizz of excitement that bubbled within her at the sight of him, with his easy smile and bright, cheerful manner - quite the opposite of Lord Eltham in every respect.

'Mr Walker.'

She curtsied, unable to keep a wide smile from spreading across her face. This did not go unnoticed by Mama, who had no intention of leaving Issy to her own devices with this particular gentleman caller for even a moment.

'Miss Worthing,' he nodded. 'Daffodils,' he said, presenting her with a bright bouquet that looked as though they had been picked by Mr Walker himself. 'My mother could never go past a field of daffodils without picking out a bunch. She always said that daffodils heralded fresh starts and new beginnings.'

'Was that before or after her shift at the factory?' said Mama snidely, in reference to how his parents had met before his father had made their money in industry.

Unperturbed, Mr Walker furrowed his brow as if trying to recall. 'I think it was before.'

'Would you like some tea?' Issy asked before Mama could say anything else.

'Please, I'm parched. I played squash this morning, and I'm ashamed to say that I was sorely beaten. Too much bubbly at the ball, I think.'

Issy grinned and poured them each a cup of tea, offering Mr Walker the platter of pastries to choose from. He took a selection and ate unselfconsciously, clearly undeterred by Mama and her prejudice. Issy didn't doubt he had encountered such a response a great many times before, but she knew enough about Edwardian society to know that ultimately, money talked no matter how it was made, and in that respect if not in any other, Mr Walker was not poles apart from Lord Eltham.

Lady Brampton entered the room. 'Oh, Mr Walker, I did not know you were here.'

'It is not the first time today that I have come second,' said Mr Walker with a grin. 'I happened upon Lord Eltham on my way in, and I see his bouquet quite outshines mine.'

'Nonsense.' Lady Brampton smiled somewhat sadly. 'I always did love daffodils myself.'

It was the reminder Issy needed of Mr Walker's true character, as she wondered just how many bunches of daffodils he had picked for Lady Brampton in those early days of their courtship, before he had changed immeasurably from the man she had fallen in love with.

'These pastries are delicious,' said Mr Walker, brushing away the flakes of pastry that had caught in his moustache. 'You must complement your cook for me. Now, I have business to attend to this afternoon, but I wondered if Miss Worthing would like to accompany me to the theatre next week? I believe *Carmen* is showing and I've heard it is remarkably good.'

Mama hesitated as though trying to come up with a viable excuse. She looked to Lady Brampton for moral support.

'I'd love to,' said Issy.

Mama had little option but to nod in agreement.

'Wonderful. That's settled then. Good day, ladies.'

When the door closed behind him, Mama lost no time in admonishing Issy. 'And what in the world do you think you are doing?' She was so angry that her eyebrows practically met her hairline.

'Oh, Edith, leave her be.' Lady Brampton waved a dismissive hand. 'He has the money, Issy has the name - it is as suitable a match on the face of it as any. You must realise there are many more eligible young men in society than Lord Eltham.'

Mama shook her head. 'Kenneth will not hear of it.'

'It's just the theatre Mr Walker is proposing, not marriage. Lord Eltham seems keen on Issy, I'm sure he will not be deterred by a little competition. Perhaps quite the opposite.'

Issy almost laughed at the absurdity of anyone believing that Lord Eltham's interest in her was genuine or to any degree romantic - she had encountered more romantic rocks in the manor grounds.

'On the contrary, many young ladies aspire to be pursued by a man like Lord Eltham. If Isabelle will not have him now, she may never have him.'

'Well, like I said, perhaps that is ok. If he does not pursue her, then Mr Walker is a viable alternative.'

'And allow new money into our family?' Mama said it as though he would be polluting their very bloodline.

'Why not? There are men out there marrying American heiresses - women of independent means. As we speak, Mrs Pankhurst is trying to win the right for women to vote. Times are changing, Edith, perhaps it is time that we change along with it before we become extinct.'

Isabelle felt like little more than a pawn on a chessboard as Mama and Lady Brampton argued about her future, making it clear she had no real choice in a decision that, if she was the real Isabelle, would impact every facet of her entire life far more than it would ever impact theirs. One thing was for certain, if she ever found her way home, she would never again take for granted her freedom to determine her own destiny - a freedom she hadn't really understood or appreciated she had until now.

10.

Susan must have fallen asleep, because she was jolted awake by William leaping up to his feet, followed by the cries of the other men interspersed with the odd woman as they poured out of the village hall and into the street. At first Susan couldn't see what the commotion was, but then she saw it, just on the horizon, the configuration of enemy aircraft who were getting closer and louder by the second. The air raid siren wailed, and she wasted no time in throwing off her woollen blanket, donning her black helmet and gas mask, and awaiting orders from Mr Rogers.

They ran from house to house, assisting the elderly and those lone women with babies and young children – encouraging them to make use of the Anderson shelters that lay submerged beneath the earth of their back gardens even if it was the last thing they wanted to do in the dead of night. Judging by the ominous roar of the engines as the aircraft made their approach, this was not the time for complacency. Mr Gardener, however, was having none of it.

'Has everybody taken shelter?' Mr Rogers yelled above the din.

'Yes, Sir!' said Will.

'Everyone except Mr Gardener!' Susan yelled. He really was a stubborn old soul.

The second siren sounded, and she knew they were running out of time to take cover themselves. The enemy were already upon them.

'Then I'm afraid he's decided to take his chances,' said Mr Rogers with a mournful shake of his head. 'We must seek cover immediately.'

'But surely we can't leave him?' Susan cried.

'That's orders,' said Mr Rogers. 'Mr Gardener is a grown man, and he has made his decision. We need add no further casualties to our list tonight, for I fear there may be several, and we'll need all hands on deck to respond to them.'

Susan had no choice but to obey. She and Will had tried everything they could think of in the brief window of time they'd had available to get Mr Gardener to safety, but he wouldn't budge.

'What's that?' she asked, pointing to a flash of orange in the sky.

'Golly,' said Will, 'I think it's a doodlebug!'

'Then God help us all,' said Mr Rogers, as he urged them both to their nearest shelter and the bomb spluttered its course across the sky right towards them before suddenly falling silent. The silence was worse than anything, because they all knew that in exactly fifteen seconds it would be followed by an explosion, only nobody could predict the precise location of the impact or the degree of devastation that would follow.

Two miles away, at Worthington Manor, Lord Worthing sprang from his bed. 'Elizabeth!' he yelled, as he heard the unearthly sound of the bomb and knew immediately what it meant.

'Go to her, Ruben!' Lady Worthing cried, her face ashen, as she grabbed her dressing gown and ushered her sleepy younger children down the stairs towards the cellar. 'Bring her back here at once!'

*

It was, of course, positively out of the question that Issy would attend any kind of social event in the company of a male without a chaperone present. In fact, there was little a female of the era could do without a chaperone, whose primary purpose was to ensure a woman's virtue remained intact and her reputation upheld at all costs (and if they could indulge in a little gossip, card-play, and tipple whilst they were at it, more's the better). To be so much as caught outside alone with a man could threaten her reputation irreparably, and consequently her future prospects and that of her siblings, as well as potentially damaging a family's place in society forever.

The stakes were high, and it wasn't lost on Issy that they always seemed to be stacked against females - from the entail of property to sons, to the exclusion of women from the right to vote and have any real say in the major decisions affecting their lives, or even in those affecting their minor day-to-day activities. It was suffocating, but as much as Issy would have loved nothing more than to rally against it, she could not afford to draw attention to herself or to compromise her great grandmother's place in the world. So, she was dressed in a gown of midnight blue that emphasised her eyes beautifully, ready to attend the opera with Mr Walker - for whatever Lady Brampton had said to persuade Mama and Papa to accept the situation must have worked.

It was no secret that Mama could not tolerate Mr Walker one little bit, so it fell to Lady Brampton to escort Issy even though she was far from his biggest fan either, and as their chauffeur wound his way through the dark maze of city centre streets forming central London - streets that cut across all classes from absurdly wealthy to dismally poor - Issy wondered what kind of a night it was going to turn out to be.

'Was Mr Walker always this way?' she asked Lady Brampton, for it was hard to reconcile the man she had met with the man she knew he was to become.

Lady Brampton's mouth was solemn. 'No,' she said softly. 'To begin with he was as you find him - quite lovely. No-one is inherently bad in my opinion, but sometimes life changes us, and circumstance brings out something within us that may have always lingered just below the surface - for better or for worse.'

'I do not wish to marry him,' Issy said bluntly.

'No, I do not wish you to marry him either. But my boy, my dear boy...' She sniffed.

'It must be so hard for you seeing Mr Walker again after all these years.'

Lady Brampton nodded. 'What must be must be.'

But what if it doesn't need to be? Issy placed a sympathetic hand over Lady Brampton's and they rode the rest of the journey in silence.

There has to be another way, and somehow, I have to be the one to find it. As luck would have it, the solution - or so it seemed on the surface - practically presented itself.

'Isabelle, you look magnificent.'

Though the foyer was already crowded with ladies and gentlemen dressed in their finest evening dress, each intent on seeing and being seen by the upper echelons of society, Mr Walker was so tall and striking it was easy to spot him from afar.

'As do you, Lady Brampton.' He smiled winningly.

Issy thought he looked magnificent himself, with his sculpted features and tight, blonde curls contrasting with his formal black suit. She smiled up at him, and he offered them each an arm.

'Shall we?'

Against her better judgement, Issy enjoyed the feel of Mr Walker's firm, athletic build as they pressed against one another side to side to better negotiate the throng, the satin of her gown sliding between them, as close as they were permitted to be. She enjoyed the chivalry and attention as he held open doors for her, made sure she had enough to eat and drink, and ensured she and Lady Brampton were the first to be comfortably seated before he sat down himself. Though he had many faults, a lack of charm was certainly not one of them.

To date, Issy's experience of the theatre had extended only to annual Christmas pantomimes with her sisters at the local playhouse, and she had once seen Billy Elliot in the West End on a city break with her mum for her birthday. She could only imagine Mila's reaction if she told her she was going to the opera - something she struggled to associate with anyone below a certain age. But here she was, arm in arm with her dashing yet disgraceful suitor, dressed in the most luxurious fabrics and jewels that money could buy, to all intents and purposes putting her great grandmother's plan into action - or at least being seen to.

They perched (for Issy had learned the hard way that corsets didn't allow a lady to do anything more relaxing than perch) on red velvet seats paid for to provide the clearest view of the stage. Every single architectural and decorative feature of the auditorium had been carefully designed to exude grandeur, from the plush velvet curtains falling in folds to the floor, to the height of the domed ceiling and its ornately carved, gold-leafed cornicing.

'Lady Brampton, Miss Worthing.'

Issy looked up in surprise, as Lord Eltham and Miss Astbury negotiated their way through the throng in the row of seats in front of them. Miss Astbury sported the smuggest smile she could muster and clung onto her companion's arm that little bit tighter as she greeted Issy, but not so tight that Countess Astbury trailing behind them would notice anything amiss.

'And Mr Walker,' Lord Eltham added, almost as an afterthought, barely meeting either their eyes.

'Mr Walker, I believe we have yet to be introduced.' Countess Astbury extended her hand.

'Mr Walker is relatively *new* to society, mother,' said Miss Astbury.

'Better late than never, eh?' Mr Walker seemed unaffected by the slight, but Issy wondered what cumulative impact such barely disguised comments of prejudice and exclusion may be having on his ego, and whether this might contribute to the man he would become, or if the influencing factors were pre-determined long before his family's rise from poverty.

She didn't have time to ponder in too much depth, because the lights were soon dimmed and the curtain opened. The orchestra erupted into its opening stanza and Carmen herself stepped onto the stage, her voice almost ethereal in its depth and strength, and quite unlike anything Issy had ever heard before in her short lifetime. As the performance progressed, the music moved her and made her long for home - for her mum and sisters. As tears clouded her vision, she didn't notice Miss Astbury leave and barely blinked when soon after, Mr Walker absented himself to visit the men's room and get them another drink to beat the intermission queues.

'Issy dear, are you alright?' Lady Brampton whispered.

The tears were coursing now and Issy felt powerless to stop them. 'I'm fine.' She sniffed.

Carmen's voice rose and fell, her tone plaintive.

'Oh Issy.' Lady Brampton needn't say any more for she knew exactly how Issy felt.

'I'll be fine. I'll visit the ladies' room and pull myself together. Is that ok?'

Lady Brampton almost refused for it wasn't seemly for a young lady to be left alone. But Issy was from another time, it was almost the intermission, and she needed to wipe her nose and dry her eyes before Mr Walker saw her in such a state.

'Be quick. When the lights go up, you do not want to be seen to be absent at the same time as Mr Walker. These times are not your own, and you are doing so well we cannot afford to fail now. Everyone who has seen you here with Mr Walker tonight cannot doubt his intentions towards you.'

Issy nodded and slipped as inconspicuously as she was able into the darkness of the auditorium. Thankfully, the ladies' room was empty of company, so she didn't have to come up with a polite excuse to explain her flushed, wet face and red eyes. For once, she was relieved about the absence of mascara. She splashed her face with cold water, dabbed at it with a cloth, and finally satisfied that she would do, returned to the auditorium.

As the doors swung closed behind her, it took Issy's eyes a moment too long to adjust to the darkness and she almost careered into a young couple standing in shadow against the curtained wall. Issy saw the man's hand stroke gently up the woman's arm, but he pulled it back as though burned when he felt Issy bump against him, his back to her.

'I'm terribly sorry,' Issy whispered, her eyes low in embarrassment and keen to minimise the commotion lest they draw any unwanted attention to themselves.

She looked up and caught the pale face and panicked eyes of Miss Astbury, who shook her head slowly in a silent plea. The male turned and Issy gasped.

'Mr Walker!' she exclaimed; her voice strained. There was a great deal she would have liked to say - to both of them - but she couldn't risk making any more of a scene than they had already.

'Shhh!' The command came from somewhere towards the back of the stalls, but fortunately Issy doubted they'd be able to make out anything more detailed than their silhouettes.

She backed away, shaking her head in disgust before slipping past them into the darkness then resuming her seat beside Lady Brampton as though nothing untoward had happened. Moments later, Miss Astbury slipped into the seat in the row before her, soon followed by Mr Walker, who brazenly resumed his place beside Issy as though nothing actually *had* happened, and Issy breathed in his intoxicating scent of wine, tobacco and guilt.

A blissfully unaware Lady Brampton patted her hand in comfort, as Issy's head spun with the implications of everything she had just witnessed. A moment later the curtain opened, the lights came on, and the audience erupted into applause.

'I'm terribly sorry, Lady Brampton,' she said, 'but I've developed the most terrible headache. Do you mind if we go home?'

Mr Walker was all politeness of course, but when the pair made their hasty retreat Issy noticed he could no longer quite hold her gaze. As they exited through the crowd gathered in the foyer, Miss Astbury's anxious eyes trailed them all the way, until at last they found themselves alone and stung by an unforgiving wind, climbing gratefully into the Brampton's motor car to escape the elements.

'Anything you'd like to tell me, my dear?' Lady Brampton prompted.

Issy hesitated, unsure whether to divulge what she had seen. But Lady Brampton was an astute lady, and she doubted she could get much past her. 'I caught Miss Astbury and Mr Walker together.'

Lady Brampton gasped. 'Did anybody else see them?' Her voice was urgent.

'I don't believe so.'

'Then when next Mr Walker comes calling, as I'm sure he will - for men like him always do - you must forgive him.'

Issy's mouth was set. 'I will do no such thing.'

'Issy, please! You must.'

She was silent.

'You like him,' said Lady Brampton. It was a statement, not a question, and Issy knew she was right. 'In my experience, a young woman is often drawn to the wrong sort of man, but it is a *mature* woman indeed who outgrows this affliction.'

'And yet you would still have me marry him.'

Lady Brampton sighed. 'Remember Issy, it is I, not you, who must live with the consequences of that decision.'

'But you said yourself - you didn't live with it, you escaped it.'

'You speak out of turn.' Lady Brampton was affronted. 'I could see no alternative at that time, and I have chastised myself about it ever since. Perhaps this time I will make a different decision.'

Issy knew she was pushing things too far, but she couldn't help herself. 'You don't even know if you still can. Maybe that's why I'm here - because *you* left.'

It was obvious by Lady Brampton's silence and damp eyes that she was hurt. 'We'll never know. But this... this *spell* that binds us, whatever it is, we can assume it has been happening to the women of our family for centuries, and yet somehow everything has a way of working itself out in time. If you let it.'

'I desire only to protect you, grandmother.' Issy spoke softly. It was the first time she had addressed Lady Brampton as such. 'Can't you see? There are legal orders, rehabilitation programs, and prisons for men like Mr Walker in my time, no matter how rich and influential they might be - but in your time, you are entirely unprotected. There is no place of refuge.'

Lady Brampton touched her face. 'I *can* see. But the best way to protect me in my time is to protect my boy. That may be hard for you to understand at present, but one day when you have children of your own, you will see.'

Issy knew she was beaten. Even though the perfect escape route had presented itself, no matter which was she looked at the situation, she was still trapped.

*

The next morning an invitation arrived inviting Lady Brampton, Mama and Issy to tea with Countess and Miss Astbury and the young Misses Astbury. Miss Astbury greeted Issy as though they were as dear friends as the Countess, Lady Brampton and Mama were, and Issy had to marvel at her guile to pull that off. Perhaps she and Mr Walker were meant for one another, after all. But every time Countess Astbury dropped Lord Eltham's name, which she was sure to do liberally, Issy could see that Miss Astbury (and, for entirely different reasons, Mama) winced - but given she knew the sort of man Mr Walker truly was, she could take no pleasure in it.

'Lord Eltham has invited us to the hunt at Upton Hall in April, will you be going? I believe King Edward himself is likely to make an appearance - you know how much he enjoys a hunt.'

'We are otherwise committed,' said Mama swiftly, 'for my younger daughters will be joining us for the holidays.'

Countess Astbury knew as well as the others that the arrival of Issy's siblings would not be enough to prevent them from attending such a prestigious event had they genuinely received an invitation.

'You'll be giving your apologies then?' Countess Astbury persisted, as beside her Miss Astbury shifted uncomfortably in her seat. 'It would be a shame to miss the King himself.'

'There will be no need, for our commitments are common knowledge, and my Isabelle has already made quite an impression upon the King.'

'A fine day it is today, is it not?' Lady Brampton was keen to divert the conversation onto safer ground. 'And your gardens are magnificent, Countess.'

Countess Astbury didn't just have a townhouse, she had a townhouse *and* a large formal garden, something Issy didn't think there would be quite enough room left to wedge into this part of upper-class London. The full height window of the drawing room looked out upon a neatly paved terrace with steps leading down to a lawn dappled by blossom trees in becoming shades of pink and white, signifying that spring had finally sprung upon the capital.

'Perhaps we should take a turn?' Miss Astbury suggested, who seemed as keen to put an end to this awkward conversation as Lady Brampton was. 'It is rather clement for this time of year – we should make the best if it, should we not?'

'Splendid idea,' Lady Brampton agreed. 'I do admire the enthusiasm of youth.'

And as the three elder ladies strolled at a slower pace, each lost in the nostalgia of their shared memories, and the two youngest Misses Astbury ran on ahead of them at a pace that was a little more than seemly, it was only natural that before long, Issy and Miss Astbury should find themselves walking together, quite unheard.

11.

The blast was deafening, closely followed by the sound of falling rubble and windows shattering. They could no longer hear the hum of enemy aircraft, and Susan hoped the immediate threat had passed. She made to get up, her heart racing, but Will grabbed her arm and pulled her back down again.

'Not until you hear the all clear!' he said.

'But-.'

'No!' said Mr Rogers, his expression grave. 'Will is right, Miss Worthing. It isn't safe out there.'

Beside her the men tensed. They could hear the sound of an engine approaching, only it wasn't a jet or a fire engine – Susan felt she would recognise that sound anywhere.

'Elizabeth! Elizabeth!' a man's voice cried, closer now.

Her cheeks flamed. 'It's Father.'

'Come to rescue the little lady of the manor, has he?' said Will. 'Well, I can't say I blame him – I suppose I'd probably do the same in his position.'

Her shoulders stiffened. 'I'm not leaving.'

The all clear sounded and Susan dashed up the narrow steps of the cold, damp shelter and out into a night that felt entirely different from the one she had left behind only minutes before. Her father accosted her in the village hall, still dressed in his night clothes with a jacket pulled hastily about his shoulders. Around them wardens poured out of the shelter, through the village hall and out into the street, yet above the noise of the sirens and the shouting Susan could hear only Lord Worthing's panicked voice.

'Elizabeth! Oh, Elizabeth, thank goodness you're safe!' He tucked her under his arm and motioned her towards the car. 'I must get you home at once - your mother is beside herself with worry...'

THE DEBUTANTE

'I'm staying right here, Father,' said Susan, her stance defiant. 'I am a warden and there's been an explosion - I can't leave - I must assist. It is my duty, and it is what's right.'

He studied her for a moment, those Worthing-blue eyes intent upon her face. He looked as if he was about to admonish her, to argue his point, then conceded there was no use. Instead, he rolled up the sleeves of his jacket.

'If you stay, then I'll stay with you,' he said, and Susan knew there was no use arguing with him.

The street was a hive of activity as the residents of Worthington village exited their shelters to survey the damage. The munitions factory had been left remarkably unscathed, however there was smoke and tall flames coming from the direction of the last house in the row just beyond the clocktower.

'Mr Gardener!' Susan yelled.

She fled in the direction of the flames, and Lord Worthing had no option but to follow her.

Fortunately, the bomb had hit only the lean-to and had knocked flat Mr Gardener's shed and part of the property's surrounding wall. There was a steaming crater of earth at the point of impact, and each of his windows had shattered from the force of the blast. The firemen were doing their utmost to put out the fire before it claimed not just Mr Gardener's lean-to, but his home and the entire street. To his credit, Lord Worthing did not hesitate to tear off his jacket and lend a hand, doing anything he could to assist the men in stopping the spread of flames.

Susan felt sick with grief. She knew they shouldn't have left the old man alone - they should have insisted, if not dragged him to the shelter. But then emerging from the smoke amidst a backdrop of black sky was the shadow of Will, and gripping his arm as he coughed into a handkerchief was the unmistakable stooped figure of Mr Gardener.

'The boy's a hero!' declared Lord Worthing on their drive back to the manor as the sunrise splashed its lemon glow across the horizon. 'I shall see to it myself that old Joe Gardener gets the best pair of glasses money can buy – whatever it takes to get him using that shelter of his. I'm so relieved that Mrs Baker was able to accommodate him until the lads patch up his property.'

Susan was careful to wear a neutral expression upon her face, lest he have cause to suspect any hint of her true feelings towards the young William Manning. 'Mmm.'

'Your mother will have kittens when we get home.'

'Quite,' Susan agreed, the hint of a smile upon her lips as she surveyed her father's bright-eyed yet exhausted face, with what looked like grey ash smudged beneath his nostrils from a night of breathing in the smoky air. 'I suspect you are quite right about that.'

*

Miss Astbury grasped Issy's arm and she stiffened. 'Issy, I can explain,' she said.

'There's really no need,' said Issy, for whom nothing Miss Astbury could say could halt the inevitable - she would marry Mr Walker for her grandmother's sake whatever arguments stacked against it. 'Your blossom trees are quite lovely.'

As they strolled, a soft breeze showered petals upon the pathway, the blooms giving way to the buds of leaves beneath and creating a soft pink carpet underfoot.

'You must understand, there is nothing between Mr Walker and I.'

'I'm sure.'

'No, really - I don't know quite how it happened. He happened upon me as I exited the ladies. He talked to me, held the door open for me, complimented me if you like. Then... Well, perhaps he'd had a little too much to drink. I was flattered at first - Mr Walker is very charming, as you're well aware. But I gave him no encouragement, you must believe that. Lord Eltham will-'

It was obvious to Issy that whatever one might have to say against Miss Astbury, in this instance she was quite earnest. Whatever had passed between her and Mr Walker, Issy could see she was not at fault.

'Lord Eltham will be just as he was,' she said, 'for he need never know.'

Miss Astbury exhaled in a combination of surprise and relief. 'But... But I thought you had your sights set upon Lord Eltham for yourself. You have been presented with the perfect opportunity to win his affections from me and you are not taking it.'

'Then it is fortunate we do not all see the world as you see it, or it would be a very sorry world indeed,' said Issy. 'There are more good men in society than Lord Eltham, and *many* who are more agreeable. I wish you every happiness with him, for he will hear nothing from me.'

It was evident that Miss Astbury could scarcely believe her luck. There was a spring in her step that hadn't been there before, and a hopeful optimism to her expression, as though a great weight had been lifted from her shoulders. 'Do you really mean that, Issy?'

'I do.'

'Then you do me a great kindness, one that I do not deserve.'

'Kindness should not have to be earned, Alice.'

'If ever you need something, *anything*, from me in return, I would be glad to do it.'

Issy thought that never having to spend another moment in her company would be a nice way to return to the favour but didn't say so. 'Perhaps your mother could stop dropping Lord Eltham's name into the conversation every five minutes,' she said instead, then broke into spontaneous laughter. She couldn't help it, and neither could Miss Astbury.

'I may be capable of many things, but even *I* am not capable of that.'

'What are you two girls giggling about?' Lady Brampton asked.

'Nothing, Lady Brampton,' said Issy, and the girls broke into fits of the giggles all over again.

'But seriously,' said Issy, when at last she'd composed herself. 'I'm not without fault myself, Alice, and I have my own reasons for keeping your secret. Like you said, you did nothing wrong - the fault lies entirely with Mr Walker. All you did was to have the misfortune of being born female in the wrong century.'

Miss Astbury smiled, a blossoming affinity between the pair - or at the very least a truce. 'I'm sorry if this incident has caused you pain, Issy, especially if you have come to care for Mr Walker. I'm sure it will not be long before you meet a nice new gentleman - and one with far better manners.'

'No-one is without fault, Alice, I will see what Lord Walker has to say for himself then make my decision from there.'

Miss Astbury was aghast. 'Surely not! You cannot - you must not. How could you even-'

'I do not expect perfection in a husband.' Issy was abrupt. 'Only duty - and several thousand a year, of course.'

She tried to laugh it off, to make light of the situation, but this time her laugh sounded hollow even to her own ears. And though Miss Astbury said nothing, her thoughts on the matter were obvious - and absolutely right, of course.

*

It didn't take long for Mr Walker to come calling with a fresh bunch of hand-picked tulips entwined with baby's breath - daffodils had passed by now. Issy had wondered when he might have the gall to show his face, though she was still surprised he would show it at all. Mama made herself scarce, and Lady Brampton gave Issy a meaningful look before sitting as unobtrusively as she could manage at the farthest end of the drawing room to give the pair some space.

'Miss Worthing.'

'Mr Walker.'

Issy did not intend to make this easy for him. She said nothing and waited for him to speak. He proffered the flowers and when she did not reach out to take them, simply nodded at Delia who took them from him.

'They are beautiful, Mr Walker,' said Lady Brampton. 'Please excuse me while I help Delia find a suitable vase.'

Lady Brampton and Delia excused themselves, and Mr Walker paced to and fro before settling himself awkwardly into a seat opposite Issy. He looked at her with those penetrating eyes of his, and Issy's heartrate quickened.

'Are you well? You said you had a headache. I was concerned.'

'As you see, I am quite well.' Indeed, Issy looked more than well in her cerise gown trimmed with trails of delicate flowers.

'Ah.' Mr Walker nodded. 'Good. You look well - very well.' He looked directly at her and Issy could feel her cheeks redden.

'Perhaps not as well as Miss Astbury?' She arched her eyebrows.

'Isabelle, about last night. I'd had too much to drink - I was not myself. I do not usually behave in such a way, and I loathe myself for it. I had lost badly at cards only that afternoon....' He did have the grace to look somewhat tortured.

'That's a relief,' said Issy. 'Then we'll forget all about it.'

'I mean to say... Hang on, what?' He frowned.

'I said, we will forget all about it. We all have our faults, and they need not be permanent.'

'Issy, I promise - I guarantee - this particular fault of mine will not be permanent.'

He reached out a hand towards her, his eyes earnest, pleading even, and Issy tried her best to ignore it, though no small part of her longed for him to take her in his arms so that she could breathe in the scent of him and feel his strong frame against hers once more.

'Did you stop to think how Miss Astbury might feel about it?' she said instead. 'In one moment of entitlement you risked damaging her reputation irreparably, and a fine match with Lord Eltham in the process.'

'She did not seem too concerned about that last night.' Mr Walker was abrupt. 'And you do not seem to care much for Lord Eltham yourself – or Miss Astbury, come to that.'

'I have spoken to Miss Astbury, and I am satisfied that the fault in this matter is entirely yours. I am no-one's fool, Mr Walker, but against my better judgement I am happy to continue our *courtship*, or whatever this is, provided no such incidents of this nature occur again, and you pay attention to addressing these very real faults in your character.' If the real Isabelle had to have him, Issy could at least try to influence a better version of him.

'I... Isabelle Worthing, you surprise me. I will do my very best to become the man that you deserve.'

'Good. Then perhaps you can begin by demonstrating that at the charity auction this weekend. And by staying away from the brandy, the cards, the sports – whatever it is that causes you to act with such open impropriety.'

'Anything.'

'And by apologising to Miss Astbury.'

Mr Walker hesitated. 'If you insist.'

'Then that concludes our business here today, I believe.' Issy rose when the door opened and Lady Brampton re-entered the room, with Delia trailing in behind her with the tea trolley.

Mr Walker nodded. 'As you please, Miss Worthing. Until the auction.' And he exited as though he couldn't quite understand what had just passed between them.

Issy, who could feel her heart beating at much faster than its usual pace, dashed tears of vexation from her eyes. In her heart of hearts, she liked Mr Walker – she couldn't help herself – and even though she knew what she was dealing with, he had still managed to hurt her.

'It's done,' she said to Lady Brampton. 'He is forgiven.'

'Let's hope this time round he comes to deserve it.'

Issy doubted that very much. She excused herself and spent the rest of the afternoon in her room drafting letters to her real sisters, the ones she missed more and more every day, telling them all about this confusing new world she found herself in as a means of feeling more connected to them. Letters she would burn on the fire each night and hope that somehow their sentiments would wind their way up through the mysterious passing of time to reach them.

*

Issy sat before the mirror of her dressing table as Mary fussed with her hair. Her view on Mr Walker had changed. If she could not escape the match, she would do her utmost to make it a better one for her great grandmother. Perhaps she could use this time to learn more about what made him tick? She would find out at the charity auction.

'Are you ready?' Lady Brampton asked when she came down, dressed in a lilac beaded gown with matching gloves. There were two things Issy was sure she would miss if she ever found her way home - the fabulous dresses (the likes of which she would only ever get to wear at her prom or on her wedding day), and, it went without saying, her great grandmother.

The men were waiting for them, and whilst Lord Brampton - a naturally agreeable sort of man - proffered her a warm smile of approval as he always did, Papa appraised her sternly as she grasped her wrap and cloaked herself in it.

'Quite,' said Issy, and they followed the men out.

'Off to spend an evening with the riffraff,' said Mama, who was not sure she could ever forgive Issy for rejecting Lord Eltham's attentions, 'and hand over good money for it, all in one evening.'

'Now, now Edith, remember - money is money.'

But Mama gave Lady Brampton a look as if to say that in her eyes, two pound notes could never be equal. 'Unfortunately for my daughter, there are some things money cannot buy - respectability for one.'

'Perhaps not, but one attribute can complement the other, can it not?'

Mama merely sniffed. 'Well, now she's been seen out by all and sundry with Mr Walker, if he is indeed respectable then a proposal will soon follow, and he will become our son-in-law. '

'Perish the thought,' remarked Papa icily.

It didn't get any less awkward at the dinner table. The saving grace was the addition of Earl Henwick and his mother, and his elder sister and her husband, who were all quite delightful and in the presence of whom Mama and Papa could not reveal their true feelings against their daughter's chosen match - for to be one's true self in the presence of society, or even in the presence of one's own family, Issy had learned, was simply not how things were done one hundred years ago. Another thing to be thankful to her own time for, she realised.

Nor could they cast aspersions as to why Earl Henwick had chosen to attend a charity event in which the expectation was to part with large sums of money in exchange for auctioned goods, when it was common knowledge he was near-penniless thanks to debts inherited from his extravagant father that the family had successfully concealed until his elder sister's celebrated marriage to Viscount Westwood. It was no secret that Earl Henwick needed as strong a match as his sister to secure the old Henwick name that had gone untarnished for generations - and all the property that came with it - something Mama would ordinarily thoroughly enjoy discussing with all and sundry at length, just not in their presence. In the meantime, being seated with a Viscount and Viscountess was excitement enough to distract them from their views on Mr Walker, at least for one evening.

'The next item has been donated by Earl Henwick. It is an original Selìn, in excellent condition, one of few surviving paintings of his winter series. We'll start the bidding at one-hundred and eighty pounds.'

'Do you think Earl Henwick intends to keep the proceeds for himself?' Mr Walker whispered with that mischievous grin of his. 'Or do you think he truly intends to donate it all to the hospital?'

The funds were required to build the Hollins wing as an addition to a large city hospital, specialising in research and modern treatments for children with tuberculosis, with Doctor Lisle at the helm, who was leading the evening's proceedings.

'Mr Walker,' Issy admonished, 'you're incorrigible. The very fact that he would donate to such a good cause when he is clearly in need himself is a credit to his character.'

Mr Walker laughed then raised his hand to bid again, and Issy wondered if he would find a perverse pleasure in securing an item of Earl Henwick's property, a man of new money in a position to buy property from a man of greatly reduced fortune but a respectable family name. She also wondered how long 'new money' would take to become accepted by wider society, for Mr Walker's education was to all intents and purposes on par with most of the men in attendance that evening, and yet there were still some things money could not buy - acceptance for one. But that problem wasn't unique to the Edwardian era - exclusion was a problem for humanity itself - one that was wrestled with every day in the confines of Issy's very own schoolroom.

'Ah, Mr Walker again at the back,' said Doctor Lisle. 'Going once, going twice, SOLD! Congratulations, it is a fine piece.'

Earl Henwick had the good grace to congratulate him. Mama merely arched her eyebrows. From the next opposite, Miss Astbury gave Issy a small smile that she was now happy to return, though she noticed Lord Eltham did not make eye contact with either of them all evening.

'Well, now that business is settled, shall we dance?' Mr Walker grasped Issy's hand, and she had no option but to acquiesce, for the auction was over and the violinists were already in position as couples begun making their way to the ballroom. They took their place near Miss Astbury and Lord Eltham. Issy had asked Viscount and Viscountess Westwood if they would like to join them, but the blushing Viscountess had revealed their happy news, so she was sitting out for the evening, content to watch on from the sidelines.

Issy felt like her heart and body were traitors to her head, as she could feel herself reacting to Mr Walker's physical presence in a way that was entirely new to her. If only he could find it within himself to be a better man to the real Isabelle Worthing, the man she hoped he could be and the one that she deserved.

As they danced, she realised it was the only time she felt truly at ease in his company, for their bodies spoke to one another in a way that words could not. But then she got the sense of all eyes being on her, and not in a good way, and as she glanced around the ballroom, she wondered if it was just her, or were people staring?

She rejoined her family, noting that Lady Brampton was pale and solemn whereas Mama's face was aflame. 'It is time to go now, Isabelle. Get your things at once.'

'What?'

'You heard me.'

'Goodness, whatever's the matter?' asked a breathless Mr Walker as he gestured for a waiter to bring him a drink.

'Don't play the innocent with me, my boy!' Papa's rage was barely concealed - though conceal it he must, for it was not the done thing to show one's emotions in public, no matter how valid they were. 'For you have been seen at the theatre with Miss Astbury, and if you know what is good for you, you will never speak to Isabelle or so much as set foot in my house again.' Papa's neck flamed as red as his face.

As Issy was steered out of the venue by a furious Mama and Papa, shielding their eyes from the scrutiny of society and leaving a disgraced Mr Walker in their wake, Miss Astbury and Countess Astbury were not far behind them.

Issy looked back over her shoulder, and as her eyes met Miss Astbury's, her lovely features conveyed nothing but wrath as she mouthed one simple word, 'You!' Issy, horrified, shook her head, but it was obvious from Miss Astbury's venom that she would never believe she was not somehow behind all this.

12.

'Papa, I'm sorry,' said Issy when they arrived at the Brampton townhouse following what was perhaps the most awkward car journey of Issy's life.

'Do not speak of it, Isabelle,' said Papa. 'You have done enough damage for one evening. You should have taken Lord Eltham when you had the chance, and instead you would disgrace us in front of all polite society. And for what? A common man with common manners.'

'Your father is right. I cannot understand you,' said Mama, tearing off her cape and gloves. 'You have not been the same since that bump to your head.'

Issy hesitated. 'If society is as polite as you say,' she spoke tentatively to Papa, 'then they should understand. For I did nothing wrong, and neither did Miss Astbury.'

Papa was puce - he looked as though he might blow an eyeball.

'Come now, old chap,' Lord Brampton intervened. 'How about a brandy? What's done is done, and things are bound to look better in the morning - they always do.'

When the men were gone, Mama fixed Issy in her steely gaze. 'Go to your room, this instant,' she said. 'For I cannot stand to even look at you.'

Mama cast off her cloak then was gone, leaving Issy and Lady Brampton standing awkwardly in the vestibule. Lady Brampton was unusually quiet, and Issy turned to face her.

'I'm sorry, grandmother. Truly, I am.'

Lady Brampton sighed, and her breath carried the weight of the private pain she was not supposed to reveal, not even to her own family. 'Get some rest, Isabelle. As my husband has said, what's done is done. Tomorrow we will work out what to do about it.'

Issy shook her head. If even Lady Brampton was mad at her, there was no hope. Perhaps she should simply put on her debutante dress, climb into her trunk, and go back home to leave the real Isabelle Worthing to sort this mess out - for she was bound to know what to do, better than she ever could.

*

Issy did not get into the trunk, though she certainly considered it. She'd even had the dress on ready to climb in, but she couldn't leave her great grandmother in this mess - mess that even if she wasn't entirely responsible, she'd had a hand in creating.

She'd had a restless night sleep, and not even the morning birdsong nor the warmth from the fire in her grate could cheer her spirits. She knew she would not be welcome downstairs any time soon, so she smiled gratefully at Mary when she brought up her breakfast, and did the only thing available to her after the tiresome business of getting dressed - she wrote to her sisters, her *real* sisters.

It was an outpouring of everything that had happened, and everything she had felt. All of the thoughts and feelings she had been stifling since her arrival in the past - and not just because her travel back in time was a great secret, but because sharing any feelings of meaning was simply not how Edwardians did things - not even between family, and for the first time Issy understood the true meaning of a British stiff upper lip and how suffocating that could be.

...Now I have destroyed our great grandmother's future by writing her dear son out of it. How could she ever forgive me? I've failed her, and in doing so I've failed our entire family - for without her son, we too cease to exist... How can I ever make things right?

The door opened and Issy jumped. Roughly, she folded the paper and stuffed it into the pocket of her dress as Lady Brampton herself entered the room.

'Miss Astbury is here for you, Issy. If it were up to your Mama, she would not let you see her; but since only Miss Astbury, you and I know the truth about Mr Walker, and Mama has taken to her bed for the morning, you may. Trust no-one and tread carefully.'

The porridge Issy had eaten for breakfast knotted in her stomach at the thought of another drawing room encounter. Miss Astbury was almost the last person she wished to see, but see her she must, if only to clear her name from the whole sorry affair. It was with that in mind that she dragged herself to her feet and down the stairs, her heart and mind as heavy as the burden of responsibility she'd had to carry.

'I'll leave you two alone for a moment while I check on your mother,' said Lady Brampton with a pointed arch of her eyebrows.

Miss Astbury was already seated, her tea poured. She was dressed in taupe, the colour a lovely offset to her dark hair that was gathered in a loose side plait.

'Miss Astbury,' said Issy wearily, taking a seat opposite her after going through the motions of pouring herself a cup of tea she had little intention of drinking.

'Miss Worthing.'

Issy didn't know what to say. How could she begin to defend herself when she knew that from Miss Astbury's point of view, the evidence against her was so damning? It looked as though she had been the one to let slip the incident she'd witnessed between her and Mr Walker, when in reality she would never have dreamed of doing any such thing.

Miss Astbury's pallor betrayed that she'd probably had as little sleep as Issy had. 'I know now it wasn't you who did it, Isabelle, so you needn't look so glum. It is I, if anyone, who has cause to be glum today.'

Issy's eyes widened in surprise. 'Then who?'

Miss Astbury sighed. 'I'm not entirely sure - someone sitting towards the back of the stalls must have seen us together. Mr Walker had little regard for discretion as you know, and it is I who will pay for it, far greater than he, for how could any man of means be at fault? They will say that I enticed him, or that I was too receptive to his charms.'

'But that's ridiculous!' Issy exclaimed. She was downright offended by this societal injustice towards another member of her sex.

Miss Astbury shook her head at the hopelessness of her situation. 'Lord Eltham will surely have nothing to do with me now. It seems my prospects have narrowed considerably overnight, and my mother will not let me forget it - you know how she is.'

'I'm so sorry, Alice, I never meant for any of this to happen.'

There was a truce between them again, albeit an uneasy one. Too much had passed between the pair, and not enough of it good.

'Of course not. No doubt you will move on from Mr Walker now also, for society will expect that last night was the last time you two will be seen out in public together.'

Issy hesitated, and Miss Astbury's mouth parted in surprise. 'You cannot possibly still be harbouring any romantic notions towards Mr Walker, surely?'

'Of course not.' Issy rose and began pacing the room as she wondered what on earth to do next. She had promised herself to Mr Walker for her great grandmother, and now she couldn't have him. What was she to do? Her mind had been circulating these exact same thoughts over and over ever since the previous evening.

'Unless...' Miss Astbury frowned as though she was trying to work something out - to get all of the puzzle pieces to fit together into just the right places in her mind all at once. She appraised Issy from top to toe as she walked. 'Isabelle, are you... Are you *with child?*'

Issy stopped in her tracks. Of all the assumptions Miss Astbury might make, this was the last thing she would've expected - and it was a dangerous one. Even if it was nothing more than speculation, it could damage her reputation irreparably. 'Absolutely not.' Issy spoke without hesitation. 'How could you suggest such a thing?'

'Well, I didn't think so. But I know how... persuasive Mr Walker can be. And you seemed to have your mind set on him despite all the evidence to the contrary - perhaps even still, and I simply cannot understand it. In fact, come to think of it, you said yourself you had your own reasons for pursuing him.'

When considered in that context, Issy could see it was not such a difficult conclusion for Miss Astbury to have reached. Could things really get any worse? She knew she should have gotten back into the trunk when she'd had the chance.

'Miss Astbury, I can absolutely assure you I am not with child. In fact, my courses began only yesterday. If it were not wholly improper, I would be willing to prove that to you right now.'

Miss Astbury was justifiably horrified. 'Please don't.'

'What a mess this is, what a mess.'

Issy's hands agitated as she moved, and a folded piece of paper fell from her pocket and landed on the floor beside Miss Astbury's feet, who immediately reached down to pick it up.

'You dropped this,' she said.

Issy's expression conveyed such panic that it gave Miss Astbury cause to pause as she reached up to hand it back to her.

'What is it about this letter that would have you looking quite so... agitated, Isabelle?'

'Nothing,' she replied quickly. 'Nothing at all. Just some frivolous insights about the season to share with my younger sisters.'

'Oh, then I assume you have painted me out to be quite the villain.' Miss Astbury gave a wry smile. 'Especially after last night. Perhaps that is why you look so pale.' As she moved to unfold the letter, more with a view to observing Issy's reaction than with any genuine desire to read the contents, her interest was only more piqued.

'Alice, now that you know it was not I who spoke of Mr Walker to anyone, perhaps you might be ready to keep a promise you once made - to do something for me?'

Miss Astbury tipped her head to one side. Of course she remembered, but now she was assessing whether it was a promise worth keeping. 'You want me to promise not to read the letter?'

'Oh, you can read the letter.' Issy assumed her best poker face. 'But I would like you to promise not to breathe a word to anyone about your *suspicion* - for it is incorrect, and it could damage my reputation, and that of my family, irreparably.'

'Like mine, you mean?'

Issy wondered if Miss Astbury would be prepared to keep her word now that she had nothing to lose.

'I kept *my* word,' said Issy. 'But can you keep yours? A respectable woman would, and to me you are no less respectable now than you were when I first met you. And whilst I may not be able to win over Lord Eltham for you - and I'm not sure that is quite as great a loss as you might think it is at this moment - I'm prepared to do all that I can to help others see that too.'

There was silence between the pair as they assessed one another. Then Lady Brampton entered the room and greeted Miss Astbury as warmly as she would have upon any prior occasion.

'I believe I can, Isabelle,' said Miss Astbury, handing the letter over to her. 'I must go.'

And when she left, Issy clutched the letter to her breast, exhaling with relief.

'I suppose I needn't ask how that went,' said Lady Brampton, pouring herself a cup of tea which she sipped reverently as she looked out of the window upon a garden of lush green highlighted by a low morning sun.

'Well at least she knows that the news of Mr Walker didn't come from me. I suppose I should be grateful for that. Miss Astbury could prove a formidable adversary.'

'I heard - Lord Brampton told me after his trip into town on business this morning.'

'Good. Perhaps that will go some way to recovering my - our - reputation. Though Miss Astbury accused me of something outrageous that she suggested could be the only reason I was so intent on pursuing Mr Walker. I suppose from her point of view, it does seem rather odd, doesn't it?'

'Something outrageous?' Lady Brampton frowned.

'Yes... She accused me of...' Issy wondered how to put this delicately, for she knew such matters were positively unmentionable. But then Lady Brampton did know she was not of this time. 'Of being with child.'

The colour drained from Lady Brampton so quickly that she began to sway on the spot, and Issy thought she was going to pass out. 'Grandmother? Grandmother, are you alright?' Issy fetched her a glass of water from the jug and raised her feet on a stool.

'I'm well, child, stop fussing.'

'You don't look well to me.'

Lady Brampton's eyes were of palest violet and her skin had turned sallow.

'Lady Brampton?'

Issy looked into her face, but Lady Brampton couldn't quite meet her eye. It was then that realisation dawned.

'Hang on... When Mr Walker proposed, were you already with child?' As Issy looked into her pained face, she knew that she was right. 'But I don't understand. Why didn't you say so? Why would you push me to marry Mr Walker if it was not even his child you were carrying?'

Lady Brampton was quiet for the longest time. 'Oh Issy, I have never told a living soul. It is a great scandal, and you are barely out of the schoolroom so what would you know of such things?'

Issy could have laughed were the circumstances not so outrageous. She suspected that whilst she might lack in practical experience, she probably knew even more about such matters than her grandmother did thanks to TV, the internet, her modern education, and what she had picked up from her mum and from conjecture with her peers.

'I know all about such things, grandmother, for it is taught to us in schools nowadays. It's no big deal, it's only natural after all - I mean, without it we wouldn't be here. In my time, very few people are married before they... do the deed, and lots of them have children together. In fact, some couples choose never to marry at all. And if they don't want to have a baby, that's ok too - birth control is readily available. Even same-sex couples can have children.'

Lady Brampton lips pursed, and her eyebrows rose to her hairline. It was plain to see she was horrified to hear Issy talk so openly about such things. 'Well, I'm not sure I care much for your time at all, if that's the way of things.'

'Who was the father?' Issy asked her gently. 'You needn't be ashamed.'

'Lord Brampton, of course. Who else? And though I should be ashamed, I am not, for Lord Brampton and I have loved one another our entire adult lives. I didn't know the baby would carry through into my time - but like you said, whatever lies beneath the dress travels with us.'

Issy could tell that she meant it about Lord Brampton. 'Well, then I'm afraid we're in a bit of a pickle, aren't we? Because I can't travel back in time to find Lord Brampton for you, and yet I must marry... What was the point in you ever pushing the match with Mr Walker when Lord Eltham would have done just as well? Better in fact, for he seems to be as good a man as he is a disagreeable one.'

Lady Brampton shook her head. 'I don't know, Issy, I don't know. You being here has changed the course of things. I thought that by you promising yourself to Mr Walker, I could get our destinies back on track.'

Issy nodded, though what if her very presence in 1904 was not to follow the pre-determined course of things, but to do the very opposite? Both parties were jolted of their reverie by the door opening to reveal a radiant Mama, for whom you could now barely tell the events of the last twenty-four hours had even happened.

'Edith, I was not expecting to see you up today,' said Lady Brampton in surprise.

Mama smiled and confidently entered the room, pouring herself a cup of tea and suggesting Delia prepare them all a light lunch. She barely acknowledged Issy, but she didn't altogether dismiss her either.

'Nor was I, but I have good news. An invitation has just arrived - to the hunt at Lord Eltham's estate! I have no idea how you've managed this, Isabelle, but it goes without saying that you are fortunate indeed, and I am prepared to let go all that has passed with Mr Walker provided you realise you cannot afford to put a foot wrong from here onwards. Neither I, nor Papa, will stand for it. From now on it must be duty before all else, do you understand?'

Duty. It had never been anything else. 'As you wish, Mama,' said Issy, for what other option did she and her great grandmother have now? And Lady Brampton had no choice but to agree with her.

13.

Since Hugo Harding, frustrated by the lack of progress in his courtship with Susan, had gotten himself engaged to another young lady from the next town, Lady Worthing hadn't spoken to her for days and it was a relief for her to escape the tension of the manor to attend a dance at the village hall. She'd had to leave dressed in her ARP garb of course, claiming an early start lest her mother hit the roof. Inside her satchel she'd just been able to squeeze in a calf-length magenta skirt, a pair of sheer stockings, and a cream silk blouse. She hoped she would blend in with the local girls, and as she cycled into Worthington, her stomach fizzing with anticipation, she couldn't help but imagine Will's reaction when he saw her.

She changed in the cramped loo and assessed herself as best she could in the small oval mirror. Her short, dark-blonde hair had been curled back from her face in sections as per the current trend, and whilst her grandmother's features were quite different from her own, she still had the distinctive cornflower-blue eyes and pale, creamy skin that seemed to characterise the children of the Worthing line. Taking a deep breath, she nodded and smiled at a couple of familiar faces, said good evening to Mr Rogers, then helped herself to some punch.

'Blimey, look at you!' said one of the village girls in admiration. 'Are them real stockings? I have to stain my legs with tea to get them lookin' even half so good. And is that real silk?'

Lingering near the wall, feeling rather more conspicuous now, Susan watched as the groups of local girls chatted and giggled, vastly outnumbering the young men of the party, as the beat of the music gained pace and what few couples there were took to the dance floor.

These were the young women Will had grown up with, thought Susan. What would he ever see in her, a lady of a class that had previously been untouchable until the unique demands of war had begun decimating these great social divides?

123

'If it isn't the little Lady Worthing herself.'

Susan felt Will's breath upon the back if her neck before she saw him. He was dressed in what she imagined must be his best suit worn for any special occasion from Sunday church to dances, weddings, and perhaps even funerals. It had been darned several times about the elbows and knees, but it looked comfortable and lived-in – homely somehow, just like him.

'Will!'

'You came.'

'I said I would.'

'Yes, well, after Hitler dropped a bomb on Worthington, I didn't think your father would be too keen on you visiting us again any time soon.' His hazel eyes sparkled with merriment.

'Of course not, however he didn't try to stop me. He understands how I feel about my work. And my mother is... Well, let's just say I'm not exactly in her good books at the moment – it's better for everyone if I'm out of the house.'

'What did you do? Drop a stitch on your sewing? Mess up the chords on the pianoforte? Mix up your French tenses? Create a distasteful flower arrangement?'

'We can't all be gifted artists like you,' Susan laughed. 'Worse – the man she wished me to marry has proposed to somebody else - an unforgivable sin over at the manor, I'm afraid. And my mother is the only Lady Worthing for the time being - I'm just a regular miss.'

Will looked at her intently. 'There's nothing regular about you, Miss Worthing, nothing regular at all. If that chap of yours couldn't see it, then he wasn't worth your time.'

'Oh,' Susan flushed, 'you misunderstand me. He was never mine...' She looked at him and smiled.

'Shall we dance, or are you too good to dance with the likes of us?' Will extended a hand towards hers, and in answer to his question Susan didn't hesitate to take it.

It was as if there was no-one else in the room but Will as he led her through dance after dance and the band played on and on until her feet ached and she knew she'd still have to somehow find the energy to attend for duty that night, and yet she didn't want to stop. After the bombing they all knew that life was short, and any opportunity to make merry was eagerly embraced but never taken for granted. It was as if they were all searching for the opportunity to prolong the best of the moments that came to them, for the party continued long beyond dusk, with great care taken to block out every chink of light.

Eventually Will led her outside to cool down, and as day drew into night and the others began dispersing around them and Mr Rogers made it clear they would have to change and report to duty sooner or later, Will wrapped one arm about her shoulders then leant towards her and pressed his lips to hers. His lips were soft, and his kiss served only to warm Susan right back up again. She carried the feel of him upon her mouth long after their shift ended.

*

'So, where is your engagement ring, sister, for I should dearly like to see it?' demanded a breathless Lottie the moment she crossed the threshold of the Brampton's London townhouse, a miniature whirlwind of excitement and energy. 'Is it *terribly* big and *terribly* grand?'

As Lottie grasped her left hand, Issy smiled at the onslaught, which formed a welcome reprieve from the usual staid rhythm of her days.

'Come now, Lottie, there's no such ring,' Flora admonished her. 'You must understand these matters are sensitive and take time, as you will find out for yourself one day. Hello, Issy.'

Lottie pulled a face as if to say the very idea was unthinkable, and Flora pulled Issy into a warm hug, her eyes bright with happiness to see her dear sister again.

Lottie tutted. 'Well then, what on earth have you been doing all this time?'

Issy knew the girls wouldn't believe the half of it.

'Oh, how I have missed you,' said Flora warmly, as Delia took their outer things and Mama and Lady Brampton ushered them into the drawing room.

'And I you,' said Issy, meaning it. She'd always thought it would be a blessing to be an only child, but her experience so far had taught her that life was lonely without her sisters, and she appreciated the presence of her provisional ones more than ever.

'Is he really *that* horrid?' Lottie persisted, for she couldn't understand how a man could fail to secure the hand of the beautiful Isabelle. 'Is there *nobody* else in all of London?'

'Enough of that, Lottie,' said Mama.

Issy wouldn't have hesitated to agree with Lottie, were it not for the fact that Lord Eltham's invitation to his hunt had stabilised her place in society despite the scandal her name had been dragged into association with on account of Mr Walker's actions. It was a noble thing to do, made all the more surprising by the fact it was *him* doing it. She had written to him agreeing to attend on the proviso that he granted Miss Astbury the same privilege given she had done nothing wrong, then held her breath awaiting the wrath of Mama depending upon his response, for if he withdrew his invitation, she would be in hot water indeed - and not just with Mama, but with Lady Brampton too. Her hope was that if they all continued to live as though Mr Walker was the one at fault, which was the truth, then perhaps it wasn't too much to hope that the rest of society would follow suit.

'You may decide for yourself,' said Issy, as she linked Lottie's arm in hers, 'for we have an invitation... to a hunt at his manor! We leave tomorrow.'

'Oh!' said Lottie, her grey-blue eyes wide with excitement. 'Really? But we've only just arrived! And if I ever have to set foot inside a carriage again it will be too soon.'

Issy laughed - she remembered the feeling all too well. 'Well, I for one will be terribly pleased to have you there to relieve me of his dull company. And it isn't quite as far away as Worthington, thankfully - about a day I should think.'

'Oh, Issy,' Flora giggled, 'I'd forgotten how rotten you can be sometimes!'

'Honestly,' said an exasperated Mama, shaking her head, 'if this is the nature of the conversation between young ladies nowadays, there will be no further invitations for us Worthings to anything! Can we please just sit down to tea and be civilised for *one* moment.'

'Leave them be, Edith,' said Lady Brampton. 'For we were just like them, once.'

'There's a letter for you, Miss,' said Delia, presenting it to Issy on a silver tray.

Mama raised an eyebrow at Lady Brampton, as if to say whatever calamity could befall them next?

Issy took the letter and excused herself from the others to perch on the window seat and read, all the while relishing the new liveliness that Flora and Lottie's arrival had brought to Lady Brampton's sedate old drawing room, their chatter receding to the back of her awareness as she read.

Miss Worthing,

You will be pleased to hear I have taken the liberty of inviting Miss Astbury to the hunt. Given what has passed she can be under no illusion of entering into any arrangement with me, and I am sure that she, and by extension her family, would benefit from what this act represents given their current undesirable circumstances. It is a credit to your character that you would seek to support your dear friend at such a time. I look forward to seeing you and your family at the hunt.

Yours with esteem,
Thomas Eltham.

Issy exhaled with relief. It seemed Lord Eltham was more of a gentleman than she had given him credit for, and in terms of character he was about as far a cry from Mr Walker as one could imagine. It was, if not as exciting as her liaisons with Mr Walker had been, then at least a little intriguing... Perhaps more of his character would reveal itself at the hunt.

'What is it, Isabelle?' Mama asked, wearing the worried frown that had become her trademark of late.

'It is nothing, Mama, just Lord Eltham writing to tell me that he looks forward to welcoming us all to the hunt.'

Mama's frown dissolved into a wide smile. 'Did you hear that, Monica?'

'Indeed, I did, Edith, did I not tell you that everything would turn out well?'

'How ghastly,' said Lottie to Flora, and this time even Mama was simply too pleased to correct her. 'For I do not look forward to meeting *him* at all, especially given he has yet to declare his intentions towards our sister.'

'Another letter for you, Miss Worthing,' said Delia, and this time nobody batted so much as an eyelid when Issy excused herself from - a for once most enjoyable - afternoon tea to read.

Dear Issy,

Would you believe that Lord Eltham has invited us all to the hunt? Mama still thinks he means to marry me, and whilst I can scarcely hope for it myself, perhaps he is one of those men whose feelings run stronger and deeper than words can express?

Isabelle, I find myself once again in your debt. We look forward to seeing you at the hunt!

Your grateful friend,
Alice Astbury.

It was all Issy could do not to hold her head in her hands in dismay, but it was imperative that she did not draw any further attention to herself. Contrary to Miss Astbury's belief; in her experience, Lord Eltham was a man who did not pull any punches with his true feelings at all, and she realised that a match between him and Miss Astbury would have been most discordant.

'Is everything well?' asked Lady Brampton, who missed nothing.

'Everything is well,' said Issy, doing her best to appear as though she believed it. 'Miss Astbury will be joining us at the hunt too, I believe.'

'Miss Astbury?' Mama was aghast. 'What on earth for? She must realise that a man like Lord Eltham will never have her now.'

'No,' said Lady Brampton, 'but Lord Eltham does her a great kindness. This act alone should go some way to restoring her to good society even if he no longer intends to marry her, which I am certain he does not, given he has already extended an invitation to Issy. And his courtship with Miss Astbury – if it can even be considered such - was so brief it will soon be forgotten by all those who truly matter.'

Lady Brampton was right. If a man of wealth and status did not disapprove of Miss Astbury, then what cause could anyone with lesser wealth or status have to disapprove of her?

'I see,' said Mama, 'then he is a man of character indeed, for I doubt anyone else would trouble themselves to do the same. You are most fortunate, Isabelle.'

'Indeed,' said Issy, who in that moment could honestly say that she felt anything but. For if Lord Eltham *was* to declare his intentions towards her, she knew Miss Astbury well enough by now to realise she could become a most formidable adversary.

*

Worthington Manor was large, but Lord Eltham's estate was easily twice its size and at least twice its age. It was magnificent, with its four wings wrapping around a central courtyard, ample stables, a huge ornamental lake, and vast untamed lands stretching all the way to the peachy horizon beyond Upton Hall's formal gardens.

It also had the benefit of being less than a day's journey from London by carriage, and even less by motor car, much to Lottie's displeasure given the motor car was too small to transport their entire party and luggage all at once, and she had never travelled on one before. Lord Brampton's promises to take her could not come fast enough for her liking.

Mama, Papa, Issy and the girls had been relegated to the carriage as Lord and Lady Brampton travelled on ahead of them in relative comfort, just as their years necessitated, and Papa made no secret of the fact he was as displeased as Lottie was about it. It wasn't seemly to leave a group of women to travel alone if it was avoidable - though the days of highway robberies were long behind them, they could easily throw a wheel or come to some such misfortune. Unfortunately, carriage travel was far more dangerous than it was romantic, especially when crossing country terrain on unsealed roads.

'I've never been to a hunt,' said Lottie, her eyes wide with the promise of adventure. 'Will I get to shoot some deer, do you think?'

'Don't be silly, Lottie,' said Mama. 'You know as well as I do that women do not hunt. There will be other amusements for us ladies, or if you'd prefer, perhaps you could join Lord Eltham's sisters in the nursery?'

Lottie was aghast. 'But that's *boring*,' she moaned. 'I may just as well be at home painting and sewing all day long. What is the purpose of inviting ladies to a hunt, if we can't actually hunt?'

'The men will hunt, and we will... eat,' supplied Flora, who knew her place in the world and bore it well. 'Just as it has always been.'

'Just because we've always done something a certain way,' she persisted, 'who is to say it is the *right* way, or that it cannot or should not be changed?'

'Silence, Lottie, for you are making my head hurt.' Mama sighed. 'I can see that once again I have let you spend far too much time with Aunt Cassandra - she and I will have words when I return. You are only fortunate that Papa cannot hear you.'

Indeed, she was, for Papa was sleeping, and he snored so loudly that not even the roar of the carriage wheels upon the stones could dull the noise he was making, and the newspaper he'd been reading still was still spreadeagled across his chest. Aunt Cassandra - wealthy, widowed and with no children of her own, was a heroine in Lottie's eyes. She could do as she pleased whenever she pleased. She was accountable to no-one.

'Take heart, Lottie, dear,' Issy whispered, her heart hurting for this young girl who dreamed of a world far bigger than the one she'd been raised to inhabit. 'Times are changing, and faster than you could possibly imagine. It may not happen in your lifetime - but by the time you have granddaughters of your own, the world will be a very different place for them.'

'A fat lot of use that will be to me,' complained Lottie, who turned towards the window where endless fields rolled by, lost in her thoughts about the many injustices towards her sex.

'Trust me,' said Issy, thinking of Emmeline Pankhurst, whom she'd learned about at school, and about the First World War, which would compel women to participate in the workforce like never before. 'The wheels have already been set in motion.'

And whilst Issy felt for Lottie more than she could ever imagine, her own thoughts followed a different track. She found herself enjoying the beauty of a land unmarred by power cables and pylons. She liked seeing the men hard at work in the fields, working the earth with their own strength to reap nutritious produce unspoiled by the micro-plastics and chemicals of her era. As much as she appreciated the medical and technical advances that gave her a life of comparative ease to her Edwardian peers, and as powerless as she was to halt the industrial progress that was now steaming ahead at unprecedented speed; in her own time, the earth itself needed saving just as much as in this time the poor, the lowly, the sick and the marginalised did.

Perhaps, thought Issy, the countryside was not so bad after all. It was in this new spirit of awareness and appreciation that she greeted Lord Eltham, for she suspected, given his honourable actions towards both her and Miss Astbury, she had judged him unfairly.

'Miss Worthing.' Lord Eltham limbered over to the carriage to assist Mama, Issy and her sisters to alight with the closest thing to a genuine smile Issy had ever seen him produce - for her, at least. He was clearly more at ease in the country, and Mama simpered at him as though he was already earmarked as her son-in-law. Issy was once again struck by his attractiveness - those dark, sensual eyes that usually held such an intensity about them that was for once absent. It only served to increase his physical appeal, but she was still unsure quite how far his character might follow suit.

'My servants will assist you with your luggage. Please refresh yourselves, then you are welcome to join us for afternoon tea on the terrace when you are ready. The weather is surprisingly fine today, and we are still waiting on a few more guests. Lord and Lady Brampton have already arrived safely, you'll be pleased to hear.'

With a nod to his rather attractive valet (for the more attractive a superior servant, Issy had learned, the higher their status and the greater the wage they could command), the servants struck into action around them as they were ushered into the lavish interior of Upton Hall then straight back out the other side to the gardens, Lord Eltham linking his arm in Issy's the entire way, until even Mama's satisfied grin could not get any wider.

'I thought she said he was insufferable,' complained Lottie to Flora a little too loudly, as she gazed at their lavish surroundings in awe. When Mama shot her a look that could turn Medusa to stone, she was silent, but not for long - for the lawn games and the presence of Lord Eltham's younger sisters proved the perfect distraction, with whom she made sure she and Flora wasted no time in becoming acquainted.

Beneath a marquee sat Lord and Lady Brampton who rose to greet them. Papa was clearly relieved to have been reunited into Lord Brampton's company after a long afternoon with the ladies, for it didn't take them long to embark on an animated discussion on hunting strategy. There were also some familiar faces Issy had met during the course of the season - she recognised Earl Henwick and the Viscount and Viscountess Westwood from the hospital auction; Doctor Lisle, whom she could only assume was taking a well-earned break from the sanitorium; and then there was Countess and Miss Astbury, among several others.

Issy felt awkward standing arm in arm with Lord Eltham, and made to remove her arm before Miss Astbury could notice the gesture, but it was too late.

'Ah, there's your friend! Miss Astbury, here's Miss Worthing to see you!' And with a cheerful smile, Lord Eltham led Issy right to her.

Mama couldn't help but raise a smug brow at Lady Brampton when she witnessed the hopeful smile drop from Countess Astbury's face as she encountered the pair, especially after the Countess had gone to such great pains to rub her face in Lord Eltham and Miss Astbury's brief courtship, but Issy took no pleasure in it - she was acutely uncomfortable. She really did not want to be the cause of further hurt to Miss Astbury, for Mr Walker's actions had already harmed them both enough.

'Alice,' said Issy, warmly. 'It's so nice to see you again.'

'Issy,' said Miss Astbury.

Miss Astbury gave Issy a flat smile that, try as she might, could not meet her eyes, as Lord Eltham continued to engage them both in conversation, seemingly impervious to the undercurrent of tension running between them.

14.

Recalling his kiss, it was hard for Susan to make eye contact with Will in Mr Roger's presence when next she reported to duty. As they made their usual rounds to enforce the blackout, no longer needing to call upon Mr Gardener since he'd gotten his new glasses and had the no-nonsense assistance (or interference) of the widowed Mrs Baker, Will seemed unusually distant.

'I hear your brother is back, Will,' said Mr Rogers. 'How is he?'

'Wounded and no longer in service, Sir,' said Will. 'He lost part of his foot on the Western Front. He's been discharged.'

'How frightful!' said Susan, relieved that Will wouldn't reach the age of conscription until the following year, and with luck, so late into the war that it would be practically over, which she hoped would greatly increase his odds of survival.

Will looked at them both in turn. 'I may as well tell you that I've joined up. I leave at midday on Friday.'

Susan felt as though she'd been forcibly pulled down from the lofty heights her heart and thoughts had been resting in ever since their kiss. 'But you promised...' she said, her face pale, her voice a whisper.

Friday. So soon. And what then? Long unendurable days and nights without him, at home with her surrogate family, not even sure if she'd ever see her own family again let alone Will. Reporting to duty with only Mr Rogers for company, and not the cheeky livewire she had come to know - and even love.

'I promised I wouldn't leave my mother until at least one of her boys was safely home, and now that Dean's come home, I must go and do my bit.'

'But you're too young!'

'Huh, they didn't check that closely. Need men, don't they?'

Yes, thought Susan bitterly, they needed boys who were barely men to sacrifice themselves for King and country, and Will had no idea what he was walking into or if he'd ever walk out again – something his brother had unfortunately learned the hard way.

'Oh, don't look at me like that, Elizabeth,' he said later as they sat on watch together side by side, Mr Rogers dozing beside them. The night was balmy as summer reached its peak. 'It's the memory of your lovely face as it was before tonight that I want to carry into battle with me. You always knew I'd join up at some point, and now's as good a time as any – I can't expect my brothers and men like them – many younger than I am - to shoulder the load for me.'

He grasped her hand. 'And when I get back, we can get married – if you want to, if you think his lord and ladyship will permit it. For you must have realised by know that I quite like you, and I've suspected for some time now that you quite like me too. I can't say I blame you!'

Susan gasped. 'Married?'

Will grinned. 'Mmhmm, why not? Unless you still think you're too good for the likes of me - which you are by the way - so I won't be offended if you say no, that's the sensible thing to do. I think I'd be more surprised if you said yes. Actually, my mother and brothers might be the most surprised of us all!'

Susan suspected that accolade would go to her own parents. She didn't at all think she was too good for Will, but she knew her parents would never support it, not in this time nor in any other – for even her own mother from her own time had wanted her to do everything the proper way; the way it had always been done.

'What if we didn't wait?' said Susan, wanting to somehow snatch the moment – selfishly, to find a way to keep Will with her forever now that she knew she was at very grave risk of losing him.

'You mean, Gretna?'

Now that they'd said it aloud, it didn't seem like such a crazy idea. She had no idea how far away Gretna was or how they'd get there, but she knew they'd find a way. They had to.

THE DEBUTANTE

*

The vegetarian in Issy, the animal-lover, the nurturer - everything in her recoiled at the idea of hunting animals for sport, so it was hard to summon the requisite degree of enthusiasm that the rest of their party seemed to have in spades. Her grandmother had scoffed at the very idea of vegetarianism (for hunting was the sport of Kings, so what had the world come to?), especially in an age where most of the population had so little they were grateful of anything to assuage their gnawing hunger - they simply did not have the luxury of choice. Well, Issy supposed, it was just another area of her adventure in which she had learned to step far out of her comfort zone.

For the women, Issy had learned that a hunt was little more than an opportunity to while away half the day in bed; and the other half was divided between eating, taking turns about the grounds in a half-hearted effort to compensate for all they had eaten, gossip (given Issy and Miss Astbury were the source of gossip, she could only imagine how frustrating it must be for everyone to hold their tongue whenever they were present), and affirming the men's great sportsmanship when they returned - rugged and ravenous from their cross-country expeditions. The elders among them, Doctor Lisle, Papa and Lord Brampton included, preferred to fish, with enthusiastic reports that Lord Eltham's lake was positively teeming with catch.

Lord Eltham had shown Issy and her family every courtesy, a fact which had not escaped the Countess and Miss Astbury's notice - nor anyone else's for that matter. They had the best rooms in the best part of the house, and her every need was taken care of before she had even thought of it herself. Whilst he had not exactly afforded her a great deal of personal attention, something she found odd for a man who otherwise gave every appearance of desiring to court her, he had invited her to ride with him that afternoon, something Issy was positively dreading - for Lady Brampton's tutelage had not stretched that far, and she was certain she was going to break a leg. She was not confident in the Edwardian approach to medicine if she did.

'You will have to invent an ailment of some sort and ride pillion,' declared Lady Brampton.

'Women's troubles?' Issy suggested.

'Heavens, no! You must never allude to such things, and certainly not in the company of a male. Use your imagination - a simple headache, or perhaps a pulled muscle, would suffice. You must appear incapacitated, but not so incapacitated that you cannot accompany him and find out what he has to say for himself.'

'Ok,' Issy nodded. 'Got it.' Was nothing simple in 1904?

'What are you two talking about so fervently?' asked Mama, in surprisingly good cheer since Lord Eltham's favour had once again fell upon them, and the tension between her and Issy had eased somewhat.

'Didn't you hear? Lord Eltham has invited Isabelle to ride out later,' said Lady Brampton, 'to show her more of his estate. One can only imagine why. Perhaps he seeks her approval before he seeks her hand, as if anyone could disapprove of such a bounty.'

Mama's eyes widened with pleasure. 'Is that so? Well, then it is fortunate that my daughter is a competent rider, for Lord Eltham's grounds are vast. And it explains why you have changed into your riding habit.'

Issy paled. It seemed it was going to be a long afternoon, and she did not even have the pleasure of Lottie and Flora for company, for they spent every waking moment getting up to mischief with Lord Eltham's younger sisters. She had barely seen them since they'd arrived.

They were perched on picnic blankets at the far edge of the lawn closest to the stream, where the youngest amongst their party paddled and splashed, and the boys clamoured upon rocks with their fishing nets. Every now and then Lottie would wave at Issy and call her over, and, tempting as it was to join her surrogate sisters, Mama was having none of it. She was to be strictly on her best, most ladylike behaviour at all times.

There was a canopied area containing food and refreshments, and lawn games should anyone feel like a game of quoits or such like. As Issy stretched out beneath a high afternoon sun alleviated by a breeze, fronds of willow providing just enough shade to be comfortable in all the layers of fabric a lady was expected to wear whatever the season, she wondered what it would be like to be mistress of such a vast property - planning all of the meals and entertainment for her husband and guests, paying calls, and constantly keeping on the right side of good society, scrupulously avoiding any fall from grace. Having child after child and living a life of restricted luxury in which she would never be free to pursue any dreams of her own, only to support her husband and sons in achieving theirs, all the while trying to secure illustrious matches for their daughters. It was hard not to pine for the simpler world she had left behind.

A shadow fell across Issy, bringing an end to her reverie.

'May I?' asked Lord Eltham.

'You may.'

He pulled loose his cravat and sat down beside her to catch his breath, his legs spread wide and his elbows resting upon his knees as he looked out across the fields – his fields. All around them the other men were doing the exact same thing, rugged and exhausted, yet buoyed by the thrill of their hunt. Issy couldn't help but notice once again how handsome he was, as his clothing clung to every muscle and sinew of his lean form.

'So, how was it?' she Issy, keen to make their close proximity to one another a little less awkward. If only conversation could come easily between them like it had with Mr Walker, but there was something impenetrable about Lord Eltham.

'Excellent!' he said. 'The game has already been delivered to the kitchens. There will be feasting tonight.'

Issy's stomach knotted at the thought.

'How was *your* afternoon?' he asked, almost as an afterthought.

'Lovely,' she replied honestly. 'Your grounds are beautiful, and *my* sisters have been enjoying yours immensely, as you can see.'

She waved at Flora and Lottie, and Lord Eltham smiled to see the girls all at play with one another. Lottie waved back enthusiastically. It seemed she did nothing without a strong dose of enthusiasm.

'I'm glad my estate pleases you, Miss Worthing – and that my sisters please yours.'

The conversation between them quickly ran dry. 'I can see you are hot and parched,' said Issy. 'Shall I fetch you a lemonade?'

'Nonsense, allow me, and then we shall go for our ride, for there is much to see.'

'You have not ridden enough for one day?' she asked hopefully.

'Certainly not,' said Lord Eltham. 'I never tire of a good ride.'

Here we go, thought Issy, as Mama and Lady Brampton, and of course Miss Astbury and the Countess looked upon their every move.

Overhead, clouds that had been sparse to begin with now grouped together to form one single white canopy almost blotting out the sun, and a chill suddenly struck the air, not that anyone seemed to notice in their languorous state. The laughter from Flora and Lottie and the other children retreated into the distance as the pair walked together in uneasy silence, Issy linking Lord Eltham's stiff arm as Lady Brampton, their self-nominated chaperone, kept just enough distance to afford them some privacy. If Issy had to force her grandmother to marry this man, she determined, the least she could do was find out what made him tick, otherwise she couldn't bear the idea of tying her forever in matrimony to someone who was about as engaging as stone.

'Thank you for inviting Miss Astbury to the hunt, Lord Eltham,' she said. 'You have done her and her family a great service and I truly appreciate it.'

'A friend of yours is a friend of mine, Miss Worthing. It was the least I could do, given the circumstances.'

'Many in your position would not have done what you did.'

'Perhaps not, but I know what it is like to feel...,' he wrinkled his brow, 'somewhat on the edge of things. It is not a feeling I would wish upon an innocent young lady.'

'Yet you will not marry her,' said Issy flatly, 'though she is innocent as you yourself acknowledge.'

'Certainly not! We have spoken of duty before, Miss Worthing, and my first duty is to my family. It is unthinkable that I would marry Miss Astbury now that she has been tainted by Mr Walker, but at least by our society she is no longer rendered completely ineligible, and in that she is more fortunate than most.'

How could he be so dismissive of another person's entire future, Issy wondered? 'Oh well, that *is* something,' she said, unable to withhold the edge from her tone. She couldn't fathom how heartless these times could be.

'You disagree?'

'I just think these times are cruel.'

'Perhaps so, but it is as it has always been. There is much to be endured about the human condition, is there not?'

'Like marrying without affection?'

Lord Eltham sighed, as though keen to avoid retreading old ground with her. 'If I recall correctly, duty was once as important to you as it is to me, until your head was turned by a certain Mr Walker, and we both know - all of society knows - how that turned out. Mr

Walker was a deceitful cad, and not worthy of the affection you held for him. With me, you can take me as you find. I will continue to be unapologetically myself, and I would invite you to do the same - though I believe you require no invitation, Miss Worthing - it is one of the reasons I am drawn to you above other young ladies. I find it quite refreshing.'

'But you are a man of means. Doesn't that free you up to make a choice based on more than duty?'

'Not in my case, but then I am not a sentimental man. My duty began when my brother died and I became heir. I must consider my mother and sisters above all else. It is what my father and brother would have wanted, and my greatest wish has always been to please them.'

Issy was quiet for a moment. If nothing else, at least he knew his responsibilities and did not shirk them, and his family always came first. 'Lord Eltham, if you don't mind me asking... Is there somebody else?' She risked a sideways glance at him over her shoulder.

He pursed his lips, and for a moment Issy didn't think he was going to answer, which only piqued her curiosity even more. 'I intend to be honest with you, Miss Worthing,' he said eventually, 'so I will start as I mean to go on. There *was* someone, but let me reassure you it is finished. It's not something you need worry about for it will not impact our marriage. My first responsibility will always be to you as my wife, and to any children we might have together.'

Aha, thought Issy. Well that explained his complete lack of affection towards her. 'So, you *do* mean to marry me?'

'I should think that was obvious. The question is, do you mean to accept me?'

Issy sighed. Though her heart hurt for her great grandmother, for whom she dearly wished a love match, Lord Eltham was by far the best choice, and it was what Mama and Papa and even Lady Brampton herself wanted. No matter how difficult it was for her to understand, in these times, a match of duty was not at all unusual. Perhaps in some circumstances, love could still enter the equation somewhere down the track. 'I do,' she said at last.

'Then that settles it. Now,' said Lord Eltham, his dark eyes suddenly alight with mischief, 'what say we set aside all our quarrels for one afternoon, and try to enjoy this venture across the land that is to become as much your home as it is mine, if you so desire it?'

'So, we are betrothed?'

'Well, I had not intended to ask you quite like that, but since the subject came up, why not? You must know I was intending to ask you anyway. You will have my mother's engagement ring, of course. It is already set aside and will be adjusted to fit.'

'Ok.' Issy nodded, resigned that this was about as romantic as Lord Eltham could get - towards her, at least. 'You have yourself a deal.'

'A deal? What a turn of phrase. You do amuse me.'

'A... a truce!' said Issy quickly. She had forgotten herself for a moment.

'We will announce our engagement at dinner tonight, after I have spoken with your father. I'm sure your mother will look forward to getting involved in all your wedding plans.'

And just like that, Issy was engaged to be married. It was hard to get her head around. She would just have to make the best of it, or hope that if she didn't, the real Isabelle might.

'It was not the most romantic proposal, Lord Eltham. It will not make the best conversation piece when I am asked to recount it to all your guests.'

'Does this help?'

He dropped to his knee upon a tuft of tall grass speckled with daisies and dandelions and smiled up at her. It was as though that now the business of marriage was settled, he had recovered a sense of humour and lightness of manner Issy hadn't realised had been lurking in him. 'Isabelle Violet Worthing, will you do me the honour of becoming my wife?' He reached up towards her with an empty hand holding an imaginary ring.

Issy laughed in spite of herself and slipped her hand into his. 'If you continue in this vein, I will.'

'I am glad of it, for my knee has happened upon a damp patch.'

'Was that a *proposal* I just witnessed?' asked a breathless Lady Brampton as she finally caught up with them, walking stick in hand and her violet eyes bright. She didn't *have* to chaperone but she didn't like to miss a trick, and Mama had had to stay behind anyway to keep the younger girls out of mischief.

Lord Eltham hauled himself to his knees and brushed off the blades of damp grass from his trousers. 'Indeed it was, Lady Brampton.'

'Well, that's a relief, for now as a betrothed couple you two will have less need of a chaperone. I don't think these old hips of mine can carry me much further across all this land of yours, Lord Eltham! It is simply too vast – you should have to sell some of it off.' She grinned. 'Congratulations to the both of you. Your Mama will be so happy for you, Issy.'

'Thank you, Lady Brampton.'

'Well, now that's settled, Isabelle, I suppose we had better ride before the afternoon escapes us. Gosh, I'm going to have to get used to calling you that - and you must call me Thomas, of course.'

Issy blushed. 'Thomas,' she said, his Christian name feeling unusually intimate on her tongue. If Lord Eltham had been this gregarious all along, she might not have had so many reservations about him. Perhaps the real Isabelle could come to care for him after all - if he could ever get over the love he could not have, an intriguing subject upon which she hoped to one day learn more.

15.

Lady Worthing had a mother's sixth sense, and that mother's sixth sense was telling her to be watchful, even if she didn't fully understand exactly what it was telling her to be watchful for. There was something different about Elizabeth that evening, she just couldn't put her finger on what it was. When Cook told her some of her fresh batch of buns had gone amiss, and a pork pie, a couple of boiled eggs and a wedge of fruit cake, in this day of austerity where every last ingredient was rationed and accounted for regardless of class, she initially assumed it must be one of their more hard-up servants. But Elizabeth hadn't been quite herself lately, ever since she'd taken up that darned war work.

'There's something going on with that girl,' she remarked to Lord Worthing as they dressed for bed that evening, 'you mark my words. Can you think of anything?'

Lord Worthing frowned then shook his head. 'No' He thought the recent changes he'd seen in his daughter – her increased sense of responsibility, independence, and awareness of the souls beyond the manor's boundaries were a good thing. Or he would have done, if one of the village lads was not at that moment about to overstep that very boundary.

Susan peered out of her bedroom window across lawns damp with morning dew and said a quiet goodbye to her childhood home of both times. Dawn was vast approaching, and she'd barely slept a wink. Her suitcase was packed, she had a basketful of snacks for the journey, and a couple of pieces of jewellery to sell as a last resort if her parents didn't welcome her return to Worthington as a married woman. All she had to do now was get out of the manor before anyone awoke.

But what if he didn't come? Then she glimpsed movement on the horizon and her heart sang. Any misgivings she had dissipated at the sight of him. Soon, she would be his.

The safest way out was through the front door – if she went through the kitchens, she'd be more likely to bump into Cook or any other member of their threadbare staff. The problem was that she couldn't find the key – she wasn't entirely sure where it was kept, and she hadn't factored this into her plan. She sighed. She had no option but to go through the kitchens.

To her great relief it was still too early for Cook – rationing meant the family's elaborate breakfasts were a thing of the past and too early a start was no longer required. Upstairs however, Lady Worthing couldn't sleep. She'd tossed and turned all night, the uncertain future of her eldest daughter coming of age during wartime of all times, having been at the forefront of her mind. Cook wouldn't be up yet, and what she needed was to nurse a pot of tea as she watched the sunrise from her window. What was it the villagers said? Make Do. Well, for once she would make do and do it herself.

'Will!' said Susan, throwing herself into his firm embrace as she opened the back door to find him there waiting for her just as they'd agreed, a grin splitting his face when he saw her. He showered her in tiny kisses and buried his head into her neck to breathe in her scent.

'Elizabeth.' Lady Worthing's voice was frosty as she absorbed the scene before her and its significance. Her daughter with her luggage about her feet, and a village boy in her arms. 'What do you think you are doing?'

*

Lord Eltham linked arms with the two women, and, setting a slower pace for Lady Brampton's benefit, he led them across the cobbled courtyard to the stables, where it was cool and dark apart from the thin shafts of sunlight that streamed into its farthest crevices. The groom had already brought out a grey and white mare for Issy, as well as Lord Eltham's own striking stallion who was now rested and replete and gazing at his master with adoration.

'Gosh, she's adorable,' said Issy, forgetting for a moment that she couldn't ride. She couldn't help but be drawn to the mare, and she patted and fussed over her as if she were a dear friend, pressing cheek to cheek and stroking her velvet fur. The mare relaxed, and Issy felt herself relax too after all the unexpected turns of the afternoon.

'It seems the feeling is mutual,' said Lord Eltham, bestowing Issy a rare smile as he fondly patted his own horse. The infrequency of his smiles put her in mind of Papa.

'That's Darcy, and this is Dart. Consider yourself formally introduced. She is to be yours – unless you wish to bring your own horse here, of course. I'll leave that up to you.'

Issy smiled, the ice between them broken by the unconditional regard of these two steadfast creatures. From the bench opposite, Lady Brampton gave her one of her looks, and Issy knew she had to quickly come up with an excuse as to why she simply couldn't ride out today, as hard as it might be to part herself from Darcy.

She needn't have worried, for just as the groom prepared to help her mount her horse, there was a peal of thunder followed by a torrent of rain that lashed in almost sideways through the unglazed windows and doorway. The downpour was so loud they could barely hear themselves speak, and suddenly it became imperative to calm the horses before they were spooked, something Lord Eltham and his groom were able to get quickly and skilfully in hand.

'We must gather all of the guests back to the hall at once,' announced Lady Brampton, her face pale with concern as droplets of water splashed onto her sleeves through the open window. 'Anyone could catch their death in a downpour like this. Oh! And my William is out in it, fishing of all things. If only I'd insisted he join us at the picnic! He is no longer as young as he thinks he is, not that he will hear it from me. Stubborn to a fault...'

The level of concern Lady Brampton had voiced made Issy uneasy. Rain was not something she'd ever had cause to fear in her lifetime, but she hadn't fully appreciated how quickly it might become disastrous in this one without the privilege of medicines she had always taken for granted.

'Please,' implored Issy, 'make for the Hall. Lord Eltham... Thomas and I will ride out and do what we can to assist the others.'

Lady Brampton was askance. 'But you will be soaked through!'

'I insist!' Issy was grateful for the vaccines she had received growing up. 'I'll be fine. Go and warm yourself by the fire and wait – perhaps you can organise some blankets and hot drinks for the others when they return. Lord Brampton and Papa will be fine – no doubt they will be riding back as we speak. And Doctor Lisle is there too, remember, should anything go awry.'

She knew that if Lady Brampton was kept occupied, she would worry less about her husband. Issy looked at her in such a way that brooked no argument, and, almost as if she were deferring to the soon-to-be Lady Eltham, Lady Brampton rose, grabbed her walking stick, and did as she was bid. Issy exhaled with relief.

Once she had seen Lady Brampton safely inside, Issy sought the assistance of the housemaid to fetch as many umbrellas and parasols as her arms could carry, then fled through the rain back to the stables, barely aware of the cold water penetrating her riding habit. It seemed she and Lord Eltham would ride out together today, after all.

The groom assisted Issy to mount side-saddle behind him, and she clung to Lord Eltham for dear life as the thunder pealed and lightning cracked over the fields ahead beneath a bulging grey sky.

'Thomas, this will not do!' she screamed, her voice lost amidst the wind and the sound of Dart's galloping hooves. 'I will fall!'

'Whoa!' he yelled, drawing Dart to a reluctant stop. 'What is it, Isabelle?'

'I cannot ride like this. I feel as though I might be thrown off! I need to sit astride. I know it's not quite proper, but given the circumstances perhaps an exception can be made? We are betrothed, after all.'

'Quickly then, we must make haste!'

Without even alighting, Lord Eltham assisted her to manoeuvre her sodden skirts so that she was sitting astride Dart, the bunch of parasols and umbrellas piled on top of one another between her chest and his back. Rainwater teemed down their faces, and Issy wiped it from her lips. Dart made no complaints as his master rode him hard downhill towards the stream – despite having already been ridden out once that day, the horse seemed to imbibe a sense of the urgency of the situation. Issy clung to Lord Eltham, her body moving in unison with his to compensate for the rise and falls of the land. If he were in any way interested in her, it could almost have been considered romantic.

When they arrived at the picnic site it was to find a number of servants frantically rolling up picnic blankets and crockery, whilst those of the guests who hadn't yet made for the hall took cover beneath the canopy that was now bulging in the centre from the accumulation of rain. Lord Eltham sprang from his horse just as a gust of wind tugged at the canopy. One half tore free from its restraints causing the material to fold in on itself, releasing a gush of water upon all those seeking shelter below. There were gasps and cries as the chill hit them and they were soaked. Somebody was screaming, and it took Issy a few moments to work out that it was Mama.

She was pointing towards the stream, where right up until that moment the children had been playing, enjoying the novelty of the water and the rain together despite the commands of the adults around them to get out and take cover. One of the children had slipped whilst scrambling over the wet rocks to get to the other side, but Issy couldn't make out who for the others crowded around the child where she lay sprawled upon the rocks, clinging to her ankle and crying out in pain as water teemed over her skirts. The children parted to make way for Lord Eltham, who strode knee-deep into the stream in his riding boots. It was Lottie.

'Lottie!' Issy cried.

She could feel her heart racing in concern for this child who had become almost as dear to her as one of her own sisters. She ran towards the stream, followed by a panicked Mama.

'Stay back, both of you!' Lord Eltham dipped to his knees in order to get a firmer hold of Lottie, his hands sinking into the water to release her skirts where they had become caught between the rocks.

He picked up Lottie as if she weighed little more than a kitten, and she posed a sorry figure indeed with her vibrant red hair hanging in wet ropes about her face, her dress dripping wet and her feet worryingly bare. 'Don't worry, I've got her. Quick! Assist the others and I will ride her back to the hall before returning to collect the less ambulant guests.'

As Lottie groaned in pain, the pair were trailed by a pale-faced Flora and the other children, Lord Brampton's sisters among them, as they clamoured out of the stream one-by-one with a lot less reluctance than they had demonstrated before the accident.

'I told you to get out of the water, you silly girl!' Mama admonished Lottie, panicked. 'Why didn't you get out when I asked you to? Look what happens when a child does not listen to their Mama.' It was evident that Mama was as angry as she was worried. 'Lord Eltham, will she be alright?'

'It's her ankle,' he said. 'I suspect it may be broken. I will get her back to the hall and make her comfortable so that Doctor Lisle can take a look upon his return. Try not to worry.'

Mama nodded, her brow knitted into a frown.

Lord Eltham's groom appeared and assisted him to mount Lottie onto Dart as quickly and as comfortably as possible, then he gave his command and made abruptly for the hall. When he left, his groom took one look at Mama's anxious face then instinctively went to help her mount his horse with the intention of riding her directly behind Lord Eltham to be with Lottie.

'No!' cried Issy, holding out an arm to prevent Mama from alighting. 'You must take the Viscountess first, for she is in a delicate condition.'

Red-faced by this obvious reference to her pregnancy, the groom nodded, and Viscountess Westwood stepped gratefully forward from the crowd who clung together shivering, almost immobilised beneath what was left of the broken canopy as the unforgiving rain continued to lash upon them.

'Thank you, Issy,' said Viscountess Westwood with evident relief, as Issy wrapped a reassuring arm around Mama's shoulder before handing her an umbrella and leading her to wait with the others.

Issy sprang into action. She and Flora handed out umbrellas and parasols and instructed those who could run back to the hall to do so as fast as they could, with the barefoot, chastened children leading the way. Countess and Miss Astbury barely acknowledged Issy as she pressed an umbrella into Miss Astbury's hand for them to share and instructed them to hurry and make for shelter. Issy was too focussed on assisting everyone else to give much heed to what they thought about her.

She was so caught up with the adrenaline of the moment that she no longer felt the cold or the wet. All she wanted was to get everyone safely inside so she could finally exhale. It was hard to believe that only an hour ago they had all been lying on picnic blankets beneath the sun. It was even harder to believe that but half an hour ago she had gotten betrothed to Lord Eltham, when now the weather unleashed its worst across her fiancé's land, potentially compromising the health and wellbeing of his most vulnerable guests in the process. She only hoped that Papa, the doctor, and Lord

Brampton had made it back to safety, and that Lottie's ankle was not too badly injured and would heal well, the poor child.

Issy stayed until the very last guest was gone, assisting the servants to clear up and reassuring them all in the meantime that Lord Eltham and his men would soon return to bring them to the warmth and comfort that was awaiting them at Upton Hall. All the while the rain did not relent, and the thunder got louder as it drew ever closer, until Issy could barely count the seconds between each flash and thunderclap. She watched in awe as she stood alone as forks of lightning struck the moors, waiting for Lord Eltham to collect her. This was the closest she had ever gotten to a storm, and as awesome as it was in its strength and power it was also an unsettling reminder that humanity was not in control, as if her and her ancestor's travels through time were not evidence enough of that.

Soon enough she could hear hoofbeats. 'Thomas!' she cried, as he appeared over the crest of the hill and rode downwards towards the gushing stream, its depth increasing along with the rainfall until it began spilling over its banks. On the fields opposite, cows and sheep huddled together as though in as much need of warmth and protection as their human counterparts, and birds shrieked as they sought shelter amongst the trees.

Lord Eltham leapt from his horse and assisted Issy to mount as inelegantly as her heavy, saturated skirts would allow.

'Is everyone back safely?' she cried, brushing her wet fringe from her eyes. 'Papa and the doctor? Lord Brampton? Is Lottie ok?'

'Everyone is accounted for,' said Lord Eltham. 'All is well. You need not worry, Isabelle. Doctor Lisle is with Lottie now – she has been asking for you.'

'Thank you,' Issy pushed her hair back from her face as she looked earnestly at him, 'for all you have done.'

'Thank *you*,' said Lord Eltham. 'You have placed others before yourself all afternoon, I only hope you do not come to pay a price for it. Look at you – you are soaked. We must get you warm and dry at once.'

He pushed his horse into a gallop, and Issy leaned forward gratefully, pressing herself against Lord Eltham's back. She wrapped her arms about his waist and held on tight, the adrenaline leaving her almost as fast as it had arrived until she felt cold, thoroughly exhausted, and grateful for the amber glow of the hall emerging from the mist that signalled they were almost home. For the briefest of moments, Lord Eltham removed one of his hands from the reins to squeeze hers in his, and to her surprise, Issy did not recoil but squeezed back.

16.

Lady Worthing had taken measures to ensure it was impossible for Susan to leave the manor's grounds unseen, but by Friday morning she simply didn't care – nothing was going to stop her from saying goodbye to Will. She tore past her mother and Cook, who were fortunately engrossed in discussions regarding the lunchtime menu, then she mounted her bike and rode as hard as she could towards the village, ignoring her mother's belated cries to stop.

The train was already at the station, and there were men, women and children milling about on the platform. Most of the men were in uniform, either joining up or returning from leave – Susan could tell from their war-weary or anticipant expressions which camp they fell into. Worthington was only a village, so the train was just passing through, but entire families had turned out to see their loved ones on their way. She knew she didn't have long – it was two minutes to twelve. She desperately needed to see him, to feel him, to hold him in her arms one last time.

'Will!' she yelled as she pushed through the crowd, scanning all the while to make sure she didn't miss him. 'Will!'

'Elizabeth? Elizabeth!'

He was already on the train, and it was jampacked with soldiers. He pointed towards the nearest door and they both jostled through their respective crowds towards it. He burst off the train and onto the platform and pulled her into his embrace, kissing her firmly on the lips as she trailed her fingers up his back. Though he wore the uniform of a man, his chestnut hair was so floppy, his eyes so bright – even his freckles had become more pronounced in the sun during his laborious working days that he just looked like a boy playing pretend, and Susan's heart ached for him.

'You came,' he said, smiling down at her.

'Of course, I came! Please don't do this,' she begged.

'It's too late now, my love, but I'll be back before you know it, and then we will be married and we can start out lives together at last, with or without your parents' approval. Though I'd far rather it was with – perhaps once I've served King and country they might soften towards me?'

Susan imagined it would take far more than that to soften Lady Worthing towards him, but she didn't say so.

'In the meantime,' he unfolded the piece of paper he was carrying in his breast pocket – his sketch of her, 'I'll carry you here with me, close to my heart, and I'll write to you as often as I can, and you must promise me you'll do the same.'

'I promise,' Susan cried. Hot tears streamed down her cheeks and Will kissed each one of them away.

The departure whistle sounded and wordlessly he took his leave, still smiling at her as he boarded the train where he watched her through the window, his eyes on hers the entire time as she followed him along the platform until the train gathered speed and was gone, leaving her empty, broken and alone.

She exited the station, and her father was there waiting for her in his motor car. He gestured for her to get in, and Susan did as she was bid.

'The young chap was it, that night of the bombing? The one who rescued old Joe Gardener?'

Susan nodded. She didn't trust herself to speak.

'Ah...' he sighed, then he tenderly patted her on the knee before driving them back to the manor.

*

As soon as Issy dismounted, she fled up the few steps into Upton Hall then up the grand staircase. A well-intentioned servant had tried pressing a warm blanket into her hand, but she'd ran straight past her unseeing, desperate to get to Lottie to see her condition for herself.

'Oh, Doctor Lisle! How is she? Is she alright?' Issy asked anxiously when she encountered him on her less than ladylike dash up the staircase – not that she cared for such trifles in that moment.

'Heavens, Miss Worthing!' said Doctor Lisle as he took in her bedraggled hair and sodden riding habit that had left a damp trail all the way down the stairs to the front door. 'You must get yourself warm and dry at once! The youngest Miss Worthing is safe and well. Her ankle is swollen and there'll be some bruising, but that is all. And whilst I cannot claim to have X-ray eyes, these old eyes of mine have served me well the past forty years and I'm confident I haven't missed a break yet. Can't trust those darned newfangled contraptions anyway, they'll be putting us all out of the job soon,' he muttered. 'Imagine, a world run by machines!'

In that moment the irony was lost on Issy as she gripped the stair-rail tightly.

'Now, I really do insist you take off those wet things. Your sister is quite well enough to wait the few minutes that might take you – your mother and sister are in with her now and we don't need an extra casualty. I'll see that you all get hot drinks brought up, then it is my professional opinion that you should try to get some rest after your adventures this afternoon.'

'Thank you, Doctor Lisle,' said Issy, without the least intention of heeding either of his recommendations, no matter how well intentioned.

Lottie did not at all make the sorry sight Issy had expected, though her mother and sister did, as their earlier distress had yet to fully dissipate. She was sat up brightly in bed, her fiery hair like a mane about her face, quite enjoying all the fuss now she'd been reassured her injuries were nothing serious. Her leg was propped up on a few cushions, and the fire had been lit opposite her bed enabling everyone to slowly begin drying out.

'Look at your face, Issy!' said Lottie. 'As you can see, I'm quite alright, did nobody tell you?'

'Oh, Lottie,' said Issy, crossing the room to take her small hand in hers. 'You gave us all such a fright! It's so good to see you are unharmed, though that ankle does look nasty and will take some time to heal. How is your pain?'

'Fine,' was Lottie's nonchalant reply. 'Doctor Lisle gave me a little something. It won't stop me joining the others in the nursery though, Mama, will it? For I would dearly like to tell everyone all about it.'

Flora and their Mother looked at one another and shook their heads.

'I will tell them for you, sister,' said Flora, 'for you shall be going nowhere today. You must give your leg rest if it is to have the best chance of healing. You heard what Doctor Lisle said.'

'Oh, but you won't tell it the same!' Lottie complained. 'And we're playing Ludo against the boys tonight with Suzanna and Harriet - I don't want to miss it! That wouldn't be *fair*. Why should I miss just because I have a sore ankle? It isn't broken. I don't need my ankle for Ludo anyway, and the rest of me works just fine.'

There was a petulant set to her mouth that Issy couldn't help but find endearing. She laughed.

'Don't be ridiculous, child,' said an exasperated Mama. 'Don't you think you have done enough injury to yourself for one day? The least you can do is do as you're told for just *one* afternoon. Especially when you've already discovered what can happen if you do the opposite.'

But it was an empty threat, for they all knew just as well as Lottie did that she would end up getting her own way.

'How's it going with the ghastly Lord Eltham, Issy?' Lottie was keen to divert Mama's attention from herself. 'You never said.'

'Well,' said Issy, unsure how much to divulge, 'that is because you and Flora have been so busy spending time with Thomas's not-so-ghastly younger sisters.'

'Thomas? When, exactly, did Lord Eltham become Thomas to you?' Mama asked, raising her brow.

'Right after he proposed to me this afternoon, Mama, and I accepted. Provided you and Papa approve, of course. I believe he is seeking Papa's blessing as we speak.'

Issy figured there was no point in withholding the one piece of information that would bring her family great joy, especially on a day like today, and she was right. Mama beamed at Issy. Her entire countenance softened, as though ever since Issy's debut, her concerns about the uncertainty of her daughter's future marriage prospects had settled insidiously into her very frame.

'Oh, Isabelle, your Papa will be thrilled! And I am too.' She kissed Issy's cheek in a rare gesture of affection.

'Issy, that's wonderful!' said Flora, who did not hesitate to press her into a warm hug. 'Congratulations! I'm so happy for you.'

'But was there *truly* nobody else?' Lottie persisted. 'Somebody a little less... stiff?'

Lottie was less than thrilled at the prospect of her beloved sister throwing herself away on a man who didn't seem to inspire a great deal of passion in anyone, let alone Issy, even if it did mean gaining Harriet and Suzanna as sisters-in-law. Issy didn't get a chance to answer, because Lord Eltham himself was at that very moment shown into the room.

'And how is our little invalid?' he asked.

'I'm not little, I'm ten now,' said Lottie with an unmistakable edge to her tone, 'and almost as tall as Flora.'

'So you are,' said Lord Eltham, with the hint of a smile about his mouth that made Issy feel warm inside, despite her dripping wet corset (her riding habit was starting to dry out a bit). What was happening to her – was she beginning to develop *feelings* for him?

Mama, however, was horrified by her youngest daughter's poor manners. 'Charlotte Elizabeth Worthing, did you hit your head as well as your ankle when you fell? Lord Eltham is merely enquiring as to your health - if it were not for him, you might still be in the stream. If you keep going, he might carry you back there and he would have my blessing to do so.'

'He is to be my brother soon, is he not?' It was clear Lottie felt this excused everything.

Mama's cheeks flamed.

'Oh, Thomas, I do apologise,' said Issy.

'No need to apologise,' said Lord Eltham with a dismissive wave of the hand. 'What is a little squabbling between a soon-to-be brother and sister-in-law? I imagine your family were in need of some good news today – and it *is* good news, for your father has given us his blessing.'

Mama looked as if she would have hugged him on the spot, were it not for the fact he was even more dripping wet than Issy was, a fact Issy regarded with some approval for it was clear his first thought was for the wellbeing of his guests and her own family as opposed to himself.

Mama and Flora congratulated them, and Lottie reluctantly joined in.

Lord Eltham nodded. 'We can share the good news at dinner tonight.'

Issy smiled. 'How is Dart?' she asked him. 'For I fear he may have fared worse out of all of us, given Lottie is quite well now.'

Lord Eltham smiled at her, and it was a smile that Issy was heartened to see reached his eyes. She sensed something of a thaw emerging between them, a developing sense of – if not the passion Mr Walker had conjured within her – a mutual respect. He was particularly handsome when he smiled, and she wondered whether to tell him he ought to try it more often.

'He is being taken care of by my groom as we speak and enjoying an extra feed in the warm and dry. No doubt he will sleep well tonight - I think we all will.'

Issy smiled back at him, unusually coy.

Lord Eltham cleared his throat. 'Well, now that we've established all is well with the youngest Miss Worthing, perhaps it is time for us all to get out of our wet things and join the rest of our party, for we only have one day left together before we return to London to complete the season.'

'I would like to check on your guests first,' said Issy, 'if you don't mind. Just to make sure everyone is well and then I will change, if not to at least appease Doctor Lisle.'

'My thoughts exactly,' said Lord Eltham, who had received similar advice from the old doctor himself. He offered her his arm and Issy took it. 'Very well, I'll take you down.'

As they left, Mama watched the exchange between the pair with obvious approval.

'Your sister is as a vivacious young thing,' said Lord Eltham when they were out of earshot.

Issy felt acutely aware of her arm in his, of his damp lean body by her side as they moved, a teasing glimpse of his shirt clinging to his torso beneath his sodden riding jacket.

'Oh, I'm sorry-'

'No need to apologise, my dear, it seems it is a family trait.' He looked at her pointedly with those fathomless dark eyes and Issy blushed. 'Actually, she reminds me of a distant cousin of mine, a certain Mrs Pankhurst.'

Issy's eyes widened in awe – they had covered the Suffragette movement in school. '*Emmeline* Pankhurst?'

Lord Eltham could not hide his surprise. 'Yes, do you know of her? I suppose it should not surprise me if you did. Our connection is a poorly kept family secret. She's considered as something of a troublemaker, you see, women's lib. and all of that. But I have to say, I for one have always admired her passion and her commitment to the cause, provided she does not take matters too far, of course.'

Issy wished this was a society in which there was no need for women to have to take things *too far* to be treated fairly, something she would always be grateful to her own time for – as well as for the women of this time who had suffered to pave the way for freedoms that were now accepted as a right.

'Would you ever introduce the two of them?' she asked, for she was unsure as to whether Lord Eltham would appreciate her thoughts on the matter of women's suffrage, though she was certain that Lottie would find the hope for change she so yearned for in this one formidable woman.

'Lottie and my cousin? I'm afraid that may do your sister more harm than good, for the movement is rapidly gaining in strength and support. I've heard about some of the things she has planned to attract attention to the cause, and I strongly suspect your parents would not approve.'

'Well,' Issy was undeterred, 'that *is* true. But what if Mrs Pankhurst happened to visit us one day, whilst Lottie comes to stay? No one could have anything to say about that – she's family, after all.'

'It is good to hear you are thinking so far ahead into our married life together. Perhaps you do regard me as something of a match for Mr Walker, after all.'

And as Lord Eltham grinned, Issy couldn't help but grin back. Perhaps she did. 'If we agree on little else, I think we can both agree you are twice the man that Mr Walker is, my lord.'

*

'A rainbow,' declared Lord Brampton affably, when Issy and Lord Eltham entered the sitting room. Just like the rest of them he had a woollen blanket about his shoulders, but unlike the rest of them his cheeks were made rosy by the second or third glass of port he now held in his hand.

'Indeed, who would ever have imagined all that happened here but an hour ago?' remarked Papa as he peered out of the mullioned windows where a murky grey sky gave way to brightest sunlight as though one sort of weather were in competition with the other. 'I must say I'm pleased we have all lived to tell the tale of our adventures, my youngest included, the silly girl.'

Papa was in unusually good spirits, and Issy attributed this to the excitement of the afternoon's events and the bottle of port that he, Lord Brampton and Doctor Lisle were wasting no time in working their way through together – that, and the fact she knew Lord Eltham had wasted no time in asking his permission for her hand.

Now that the afternoon's excitement had past, a strange sort of lethargy hung in the air. Everyone was warm and comfortable at last, many had changed out of their wet things, those who hadn't were wrapped in blankets and positioned closets to the fire, and each were simply grateful for the lavish comfort to be found within Upton Hall and out of the elements. Everyone was accounted for, and all was well. It was because everyone was well (and not a little due to the drinks they were consuming) that they could now regard the afternoon's events as something of an adventure.

'Oh yes, and how is dear Charlotte now?' asked Mrs Eshott, a genteel older guest with whom Issy had yet to become properly acquainted.

'She is well,' Doctor Lisle replied. 'No broken bones, fortunately. It was just a bad twist of the ankle. Nothing a little time and rest won't heal – if she can find it within herself to stay still, that is - these youngsters never do like to stay in one spot for long.'

'She will have lost no time in regaling all her new friends in the nursery of her antics, I am sure,' said Mama, who had just come down to join them.

'What a weekend you have thrown us, Lord Eltham!' said Lord Brampton. 'One that will provide us with conversation fodder for dinner parties for quite some time to come, though perhaps not as much as your own and Miss Worthing's exploits will have afforded you, I'm sure.'

As Issy took a seat beside a warm and rosy-faced Lady Brampton, her cheeks burned, and she was fairly sure it wasn't just the blankets, the fire, or the wine she had been given. She couldn't bring herself to look in Miss Astbury and her mother's direction, whose keen eyes she had felt on her for almost the entirety of their visit. She glanced at Lord Eltham instead, to see if he would make their announcement now when the opportunity had almost presented itself or wait until dinner as they'd discussed.

'I agree - you make quite the striking hero and heroine,' said Viscountess Westwood approvingly.

'Yes, I believe I must thank you, Miss Worthing, for taking care of my wife,' said the Viscount.

'Yes,' said Earl Henwick, her brother. 'Thank you, Miss Worthing.'

'Anyone in my position would have done the same,' said Issy.

'Actually...' said Lord Eltham, poised to speak further.

Issy held her breath.

'Well, I for one am not sure how wise it is for a lady to ride like a man in the middle of a thunderstorm, brazenly exposing herself to the elements in the process,' interrupted Countess Astbury as she peered down her aquiline nose at Issy. 'You're lucky you haven't caught your death! I would never have allowed Alice to do such a thing – it's not proper for a young lady to behave so. I'm sure most of you would agree.'

'Mother,' whispered Miss Astbury through gritted teeth.

Issy couldn't help but feel for her. Whatever had passed between them, her destiny – or her grandmother's at least - was secure, whereas Miss Astbury's still was not. It was not an enviable position for any young lady, not least a young lady in the marriage market who had brushed with disgrace.

'As I recall,' said Mama, 'if it were not for my daughter, you and Miss Astbury may not have been so fortunate as to make it to the hall with barely a drop of water upon you. I'm at a loss as to understand quite how you both managed to stay so dry when the awning collapsed. Anyway, you were saying, Lord Eltham?'

'Well,' said Lord Eltham with a small smile, 'what's a little improper behaviour between a betrothed couple?'

'I'm glad he said it,' Lady Brampton whispered, 'or else I would've been tempted to do so myself.'

Issy was relieved she had not. She did not think Lord Eltham would have appreciated the announcement of his own news being made by somebody else, a female no less, for the second time that day. There was good-hearted laughter all round, and many a pat on the back for Lord Eltham and complements and good wishes for Issy.

'Magnificent!' declared Lord Brampton. 'What *magnificent* news! My sincere congratulations to the both of you. You have already proven yourselves quite the team - if you can just keep that up for another forty years, then you might be as happy as Monica and I.' He topped up his glass and the glasses of those nearest to him then took his wife's arm. 'It is fortunate we already have drinks to hand. A toast,' he declared, 'to Lord Eltham and Miss Worthing's engagement!'

Everyone was happy for the pair. Everyone except the Countess and Miss Astbury. And as glasses were refilled and the happy news lent an air of optimism and excitement to the gathering following the events of the day, only one of their party was dreaming up ways to sully it.

17.

All of Lady Worthing's worst fears had come true. There were no eligible men in the vicinity for Elizabeth, who had fallen in love with a village boy of all people, and now the manor's ballroom had been turned into a makeshift hospital for wounded soldiers and there was simply no escape from their pain, for their cries haunted her dreams every night. The Worthings had only been permitted to remain in their home if they assisted with the running of the hospital in some capacity, and since she knew the countryside was the safest place for her family, and she could not imagine what would become of the manor without her there to oversee everything, she'd had no choice but to acquiesce.

Upstairs, Susan's heart leapt. Will had been writing to her, and fortunately Lord Worthing had not prevented his letters from reaching their intended destination despite his wife's best efforts. She unfolded the letter as though she was handling a precious artefact and read:

My dearest Miss Worthing,

Golly, how presumptuous that sounds, even to my own ears! To think that a man like me could ever dream of calling a woman like you mine. It's a privilege I will be thankful for until the day I die.

I've come to see that you were right – I should never have left you. I carry your portrait everywhere, for it brings me great comfort in these difficult times. War is not at all what I imagined as a boy, and looking upon your face is the only thing that takes me far away from here.

I recently shared some of my drawings with my commanding officer who thinks he may be able to get me a commission as a war artist. It would mean something of a change of scenery for me – and I can only hope that turns out to be a good thing. It gives me hope that I might have a skill I can one day use to keep you in the manner to which you have become accustomed.

I will make our parting up to you, my dear Elizabeth, when we meet again - then I can truly call you mine.

All my love,
Will.

Oh Will, thought Susan, clutching the letter to her breast, careful not to dampen it with her tears. I am yours. I have always been yours.

*

Issy was disoriented when she awoke. She'd slept so well, she'd almost expected to find herself back in her family's little three-bedroom semi with her mum and sisters, her best friend Mila only a text message away. Those days seemed so far away, so unreachable, it was as if they'd been little more than a dream. But now she'd let the thoughts and memories creep in, they swamped her, and her heart filled with longing for nothing more than a hug from her mum. For movie nights and popcorn on the couch with her sisters, fighting over what film they'd watch until their mum put her foot down and chose for them. She even missed Jasmine and Ella's constant demands for her to play – demands she usually ignored in fear of appearing childish, though on the occasion she did indulge, she secretly quite enjoyed the games she was expected to have outgrown.

Now she was a betrothed woman of the twentieth century, and she had no idea how her fiancé felt about her, yet the expectation was that she would share her life - her entire future - with him, and of course divorce was nothing short of a scandal if it didn't work out. She didn't even know how Lord Eltham took his tea, let alone much else! She determined to find out – not just how he took his tea - but how he felt about her. The least she could do was embark her grandmother upon a married life with someone who, if they weren't quite there yet, could at least see themselves one day growing in affection towards her. But first, breakfast.

As usual, Issy didn't need to lift a finger. Her fire had already been lit, its heat and crackle something she'd miss if she ever found her way back home. There were jugs of hot and cold water waiting for her on her washstand, and a maid on standby to help her dress – a task that in this era was quite impossible to do oneself. She was ashamed to say she'd gotten so used to being waited on that she no longer woke up when the servants took it upon themselves to enter her room and get everything prepared. She'd quickly learned that even if it didn't sit right with her, to do anything more than simply accept it would give her away.

Breakfast was no different - there was a spread laid out that would have done old Mrs Lamb proud, and Issy slotted in at the table next to Mama and her younger siblings, who, to Lottie's excitement, had been permitted to join the adult guests for their final breakfast together before their departure back to London. Lottie was holding court with the entire table, telling them all about her brush with danger – a slightly embellished version - and exhibiting her injuries to the polite interest of most, and the great embarrassment of their mother.

'Issy, you're finally up!' said Lottie. 'Look,' she raised her skirts above her ankle and thrust her leg towards her, 'the bruising is coming out! It's all red and purple, and Suzanna thinks this part looks like the Americas.' Proudly, she pointed out the offending area, and it did look somewhat look like the United States. It put Issy in mind of the cloud game her sisters used to play.

'That's most impressive, Lottie,' Issy grinned, 'and I'm pleased you have been taking your geography studies seriously, but please try not to add any more continents to the mix if you can help it.'

'Heavens!' remarked Countess Astbury, affecting a laugh. 'When I was growing up, ankles were never a feature of the breakfast table. Perhaps I have slipped behind the times.'

Issy noted that nobody laughed with her – for they were all aware Lottie was set to become the sister-in-law of their host, and Miss Astbury looked most uncomfortable. Lady Brampton seemed about ready to lamp the Countess, were it not deemed impolite, so Issy quickly stepped in.

'And was your sore ankle a barrier to beating the boys at Ludo last night?'

'It was not!' said Lottie. 'We beat them three games out of five, despite their cheating.'

'We didn't need to cheat,' said the young Mr Eshott. 'We were going easy on you because you're girls.'

'Yes,' said the second Mr Eshott, 'because you're girls!'

Lottie pursed her lips. 'Girls or not, we beat you fair and square.'

'Such competitive spirit,' said Countess Astbury. 'Don't worry, Lady Worthing, I'm sure she'll grow out of it before she comes out.'

'And yet you still demonstrate it in spades.' Lady Brampton threw her a sweet smile, and the Countess was sensible enough to venture no further, for everyone knew Lady Brampton was not someone to trifle with.

'Well,' she said instead, 'I think I had better make a start on our packing before we get too wrapped up in the festivities Lord Eltham has planned for us. Excuse me.'

Even Miss Astbury looked relieved when she left. 'I will join you when I have eaten, Mother.'

Miss Astbury was unusually subdued for the remainder of their meal, and as she leaned over to fetch the marmalade that was placed out of reach near the centre of the large oval table, just as Issy went to pass it over, Earl Henwick covered the distance and handed it straight to her.

'Thank you, Earl Henwick,' she said politely.

'You're very welcome, Miss Astbury,' said Earl Henwick, maintaining eye contact with her for just a fraction too long, until Miss Astbury blushed in such a manner that only made her appear even more becoming than she already was.

Issy watched the exchange with interest, as she topped her plate with fresh fruit and pastries, omelette and hot buttered crumpets and tucked in, eagerly making up for the previous day when she'd been too worn out by the afternoon's events to have much of an appetite for dinner. Beside her, Lottie began to cough.

'My,' said Flora concerned, 'did something go down the wrong way, Lottie, dear?'

'It's nothing,' Lottie dismissed. 'Just a frog in my throat. It certainly won't prevent me from joining in the fete today.'

But she kept on coughing, and Issy didn't like the sound of it one little bit.

'I say,' said Doctor Lisle, who until then had been absorbed in conversation with Papa and Lord Brampton. 'I have just the tonic for that nasty cough. I will prepare it for you, then you must take it easy. That's doctor's orders, for we do not want to add illness to injury.'

'I'll see that she rests, Doctor Lisle,' said Mama, though Issy suspected it would be a futile task.

*

Issy didn't see her fiancé until the fete, for he had spent most of the morning coordinating it in his mother's absence. Lady Eltham had been called away to assist an elderly relative, but she was due back that afternoon. Issy was as curious to see what she would make of her son's choice of wife as she was to discover what Lady Brampton would make of Issy's choice of mother-in-law.

Lord Eltham led her across the lawn, where there was a coconut shy and a hired merry-go-round for the children; croquet, quoits and boules for the adults, rowboat rides on the lake, and a large marquee to provide the guests with shade, lunch, and refreshments. Later there would be dancing and party games, and Issy was intrigued to see what those would entail for she suspected that pass-the-parcel and musical chairs would not be among them.

A band was set up in the bandstand playing lively music, and there was a general air of merriment as the sun shone high above them and the children's laughter punctuated the air – Lottie's included, for though she was on makeshift crutches, there was no way she was going to be persuaded to miss out. As was customary they were all dressed in shades of cream, white, and beige, and the whole thing put Issy in mind of a Pinterest-inspired summer wedding at a stately home – all that was missing were the hay-bales, hog-roast and donut wall. And the wedding, of course.

'This is just gorgeous,' said Issy. 'I'm sure you'll have done your mother proud.'

'I'm glad to hear it, Isabelle, for trust me – she would not have it any other way, and she had already set much of this in motion herself before she was called away.'

'I am anxious to meet her.'

'You need not be anxious, dear. She will be relieved I have made my choice at last, for it is something she has been most determined upon for some time.'

'I know the feeling,' said Issy, with a glance towards her parents, and they laughed.

She had to admit that Lord Eltham looked fine in his relaxed attire - from his boater hat to his light linen suit and white shirt that formed the perfect contrast to his dark hair and molten eyes. Issy had decided upon a latte-coloured dress trimmed with lace and swept her tresses into a loose chignon at the nape of her neck. Unfortunately, her corset was as restrictive as ever, but she barely noticed it now – it was amazing what a human being could adapt to, for she was convinced that if she could adapt to a corset, she could adapt to anything.

Issy looked to her fiancé for signs of affection, even desire. Disappointingly, whilst he did smile back it was clear he felt uncomfortable beneath her scrutiny, and Issy wondered why it felt like for every step forward, they seemed to take a step back. Perhaps it was this mysterious ex-love of his holding him back. Could she find a way to help him move on?

'What a pretty parasol,' she remarked, in efforts to steer their conversation onto more comfortable ground. It was of cream lace and would accessorise her outfit nicely. The catch was that in order to obtain it, one first had to win it.

'If the lady likes it, then she shall have it,' said Lord Eltham chivalrously.

He took off his jacket and rolled up his sleeves, revealing muscular forearms lightly darkened with hair.

'Stand behind the line, sir,' said the stallholder, handing him five wooden balls and directing him to take a couple of steps back. 'Knock down three coconuts to choose any prize. Good luck.'

Lord Eltham drew quite a crowd as he muttered expletives beneath his breath when his first ball missed and his second brushed against a coconut but not hard enough to dislodge it from its stand. He only had three balls left, and Issy thought it best to let the idea of ever becoming the owner of such a parasol go. But her fiancé was nothing if not determined, and the next two balls made strong enough contact with a pair of coconuts to knock them clean over, the latter glancing off one with such force that at first it only wobbled from side to side before suddenly taking them all by surprise and toppling over too.

'I say, old chap,' said Earl Henwick good naturedly, 'I reckon you've done this before.'

There was a round of applause, and Mama observed the events with obvious pride as Lord Eltham allowed Issy to choose her prize and put up her new parasol to afford her immediate relief from the sun.

'I think I should like a go myself,' said Earl Henwick. 'Perhaps Miss Astbury would be so kind as to help me choose the prize.'

Miss Astbury blushed, and Issy smiled. It would be a great relief should Miss Astbury develop genuine feelings for Earl Henwick. Though his financial situation was questionable, his family name was an old one that still commanded great respect. And the Astbury family were not without money themselves – no doubt a handsome dowry would soon follow any proposal the young lord might happen to make. She suspected this development would not be lost on the rest of their party, ever poised to latch onto the next piece of gossip.

Next there were egg and spoon races for the children, in which Lottie was awarded first prize sheerly for the effort she had gone to to participate – and not least because she made quite the spectacle trying to compete with a crutch in one hand and an egg and spoon in the other. This was followed by what Issy considered a truly bizarre game in which the men were to take part in a bicycle race, in the middle of which they were to hop off their bikes and decorate a straw hat as best as they could using all manner of accessories provided by the ladies, then wear their design as they raced back to the starting line. There would be two prizes – one for the fastest rider, and one for the best hat. Issy could not imagine how much port must have been consumed when this game was invented, for it seemed such an odd combination of elements that not even her own youngest sister could dream up, but she supposed it might be fun to watch.

'Where is your fiancé?' asked the affable Lord Brampton. 'For it's just about time for the race, and I'm keen to get the whole escapade over with so we can make a start on the buffet.'

'And the port, no doubt,' said Lady Brampton, with all the certainty of one who has been married for forty years. 'I'm pretty sure I saw him walking towards the hall. Perhaps he had something to attend to.'

'I will go and find him,' said Issy. 'His mother may have arrived; in which case I should probably be available to meet her.'

Lady Brampton nodded her assent.

The hall stood proud in the sunlight amidst a backdrop of lush greenery and cobalt-blue skies that put Issy more in mind of the Mediterranean than southern England, and as she negotiated her way across the lawn towards it, she thought she saw a glimpse of beige disappearing through one of the side doors. Thomas? She was surprised he hadn't taken the main entrance, for the other door was usually utilised by service staff. Nevertheless, she followed him in there. There was no unfamiliar carriage out the front, so no doubt Lady Eltham had yet to make her entrance, and most of the servants were busy assisting with the fete.

'Thomas?' she ventured, but there was no response.

Once she'd passed through a small wooden porch, the door opened into what could best be described as a boot room. Ah, thought Issy, perhaps he was getting changed into something more suitable for the race. She wasn't sure why, but she instinctively felt she should tread more lightly and speak more softly. When she pushed open the door between the porch and boot-room, nothing could have prepared her for what she found there – it felt like she'd found the missing piece to a jigsaw. There was Lord Eltham. And his valet. Only his valet wasn't helping him dress - quite the opposite, in fact. And, if she were still in any doubt, they were kissing.

Thankfully the door had not yet made so much as a creak, so she left it ajar and fled to the fete before she could be missed. She had no idea what to do with her discovery, but she hoped her grandmother's constitution was strong enough to handle it, given she'd lived most of her life in the Victorian era. What Issy didn't notice, however - what nobody caught up in the merriments noticed - was that she and Lord Eltham were not the only missing guests.

18.

An impatient Lord Brampton was the first to accost Issy. 'Did you find him?' he asked.

'I must've just missed him,' she replied, trying her best to appear normal, even though she felt it was written all over her face that something was most definitely amiss.

'Damn and blast! We're almost ready to go but we can't set off without him! That buffet has been calling my name all afternoon - especially the trifle - I do love a good trifle.'

'You love a good anything if you can eat it, Kenneth,' said Lady Brampton, 'you always have. Oh look, it's the man himself! I'll be sure to have a glass of port waiting for you at the finish line. Now remember, peacock feathers for the win – I do love a hat with peacock feathers.'

'Peacock feathers, got it.' He greeted the surly Lord Eltham. 'I say, old chap, we were wondering where you had gotten to! Has your mother arrived yet?'

'She has not,' Lord Eltham clipped. 'You may proceed without me, for I have matters I must attend to. Isabelle, I would like to speak with you before my mother arrives.'

A prickle of uncertainty ran down Issy's neck. What on earth had gotten into him?

'Start? Without our host?' Lord Brampton exclaimed. 'Certainly not! You must join us, man. You said yourself that your mother has yet to arrive, and how could she fail to be enchanted by the lovely fiancée you have chosen? Whatever you have to say to prepare Miss Worthing to meet her mother-in-law can wait a few moments, surely?'

Lord Eltham pursed his lips. 'If you insist, Lord Brampton.'

'I do!' He grinned. 'Come lad, that's the spirit. Best make that *two* glasses, Monica.'

But Lord Eltham had spoken through gritted teeth, and as the pair departed, he threw Issy an icy look that sent chills through her. Perhaps, when she'd happened upon him in the boot room earlier, she had not been as discrete as she'd thought?

'Is everything well between the two of you?' Lady Brampton asked as she regarded Issy with those penetrating violet eyes. It was clear she was as worried as Issy was that something was amiss.

'I can think of no reason why it would not be,' said Issy, for in truth even if Lord Eltham had seen her, she could think of no reason to justify his sudden change in demeanour towards her. Perhaps if she'd caught the eye of a certain member of the Astbury party surreptitiously re-joining the merriments as if she'd never been away, she may have thought differently.

The gentlemen took their places on their bicycles at the starting line, and they were the most smartly dressed cyclists Issy had ever seen. For all there was much to dislike about the Edwardian approach to class, sex, and status, she could not help but admire their dress sense - corsets aside - for the men looked so fine in their suits, and the women were so elegant in their dresses, their arms adorned with silk gloves and their intricate hair styles topped with elaborate hats.

Lord Brampton, who had decided against riding at the last moment due to a tickly cough, sounded the whistle, and the men rode as fast as they could the four-hundred metres or so to the hat stop, where they leapt from their bicycles and had five minutes to create the most appealing straw hat from the natural embellishments that had been gathered for them by the ladies – from pebbles, flowers and foliage to grasses, feathers and straw – whatever they'd been able to find about the estate grounds.

There was a great deal of competition amongst the men to acquire the best of the adornments available, and to stuff them into the most accommodating gaps of their straw hats as fast as they possibly could. The spectators were helpless with laughter by the time the men had jumped back on their bicycles balancing their creations on their heads, before racing back to the finish line for the final part of the competition - the judging.

Lord Eltham was fast - he seemed to have been spurred on by whatever it was that was on his mind, tailed by Earl Henwick, whom Miss Astbury seemed to be watching rather intently. It was Lord Eltham for the win, until his front wheel hit a rut and his hat flew off his head and landed in a muddy puddle. There was an outburst of laughter as the ladies urged him to put his hat back on and finish the ride – in third place, as it happened.

'And who will be judging this spectacle?' Lord Eltham asked, as he set his bike aside and wiped his handkerchief over a spot of mud spattered onto his forehead.

'Oh, come now,' said Lord Brampton, in as good spirits as ever – especially now he was only minutes away from the buffet's opening, 'your fiancée, of course. Who else?'

The men were lined up hopefully, and if Lord Eltham was in better spirits Issy would have enjoyed her role immensely. She was secretly quite impressed with what several members of the party had been able to achieve with only a few strips of grass and some feathers, though her fiancé's effort was now something of a write-off. She could hardly award Lord Eltham the winning prize in fear of being perceived as biased, so as she scanned the line and wrote-off even Dr Lisle's impressive peacock-feather creation (which was undoubtedly best) in favour of Earl Henwick's less striking effort. It was Issy's offering of an olive branch to Miss Astbury, but whilst Earl Henwick smiled at her gratefully, Miss Astbury still did not meet her eyes.

The buffet was opened, and the bottles of port too – thereby putting Lord Brampton out of his misery at last – but no sooner had the hungry crowd dispersed than Lord Eltham took Issy by the arm and steered her back towards Upton Hall.

'So, how long have you known?' he spat, once they were safely ensconced inside the library and out of the earshot of guests and servants alike.

'But half an hour,' said a bemused Issy who was unsure exactly why, given the circumstances, she felt like the one being attacked, on a day that had had all the makings of having been such a wonderful day, no less.

'Huh! I find that hard to believe.'

'It was not obvious at first,' said Issy, 'but now I cannot be mistaken.' It certainly explained Lord Eltham's apparent lack of attraction towards her, and she recalled Mr Walker's implication that he was disinterested in the female sex. He must have known.

'I see. And now you are not mistaken, what do you intend to do about it?'

'I'm not sure.' The day had been so busy, she'd had too little time to consider.

'I'm a tolerant man, Miss Worthing, but even I will not tolerate raising another man's bastard as my own, least of all Mr Walker's. You have played me for a fool, in my own home, no less, and I will not stand for it. And now my mother will be here at any minute, to meet my *fiancée*... This is inexcusable.' *Fiancée* was spoken with obvious disgust.

Issy was gobsmacked. 'Lord Eltham, I...' she shook her head, as she tried to wrap her head around this surprising turn of events. It didn't take her long to reach a conclusion – that a certain Miss Astbury was no doubt behind this. Despite the promise she had made never to mention her suspicions to another living soul, the green-eyed monster had obviously gotten the better of her during the short period in which they'd been forced to live in such close quarters. Issy now regretted awarding first prize to Earl Henwick.

'Is that all you have to say for yourself?'

Issy breathed deeply. 'Lord Eltham, you are mistaken. I am not with child, and I would never set out to entrap any man. This is what comes of getting engaged to someone you barely know, let alone care for - it sets the conditions to allow for such grave misunderstandings to occur.' She could not prevent bitterness from creeping into her tone.

Lord Eltham exhaled. He threw himself into a leather armchair and rubbed his knotted forehead as though his very thoughts hurt. 'I do not know what to believe.'

'No doubt the Astbury's were behind this?'

He nodded, and Issy sighed. She took a seat opposite him, but he would not meet her gaze.

'Nothing improper ever occurred between Mr Walker and I,' she said. 'I'm not saying the thought never crossed my mind, and I cannot deny that I would not have been tempted had the opportunity presented itself as our courtship progressed - for we both know I was attracted to him initially, before I learned of his true nature.

Once you told me you admired my honesty, so I am asking you to please believe that I am speaking the truth right now. As we are both aware, the Astbury's have cause to dislike me – in fact, they have made little attempt to hide their feelings towards me during our stay here. Even I did not think Miss Astbury would stoop to this level, however.'

Lord Eltham sighed, holding his head in his hands. Eventually, he raised his molten eyes to hers, and Issy looked earnestly into his face before reaching out a hand towards him. He did not take it.

'What did you think I was talking about?' he asked.

'What do you mean?'

'Before, when this conversation began, what did you think I was referring to?'

Issy wondered whether she should tell him the truth. Hadn't they just spoken about honesty? She supposed should start as she meant to go on.

'I saw you two together,' said Issy.

'Countess Astbury and I?'

Issy's lips parted. 'Was it *Countess* Astbury, not *Miss* Astbury, who spoke with you?'

'Of course it was Countess Astbury! *Miss* Astbury has barely spoken two words to me this entire time.'

'That makes two of us. Though I'm sure the countess made up for it, for she seems to have a good deal to say on any topic that concerns my family and I.'

'If it was not Countess Astbury,' Lord Eltham cleared his throat, 'then to whom are you referring?'

Issy hesitated. 'To your valet,' she said.

Lord Eltham coloured. 'I don't know what you mean - my valet was assisting me to get dressed for the race.'

'We both know it was a little more than that, Lord Eltham. It's ok, you can speak of it.' Issy now felt as uncomfortable as he did at the prospect of using his Christian name. 'There will be no judgement from me.'

Lord Eltham exhaled, and Issy wondered what torment he must have gone through in his lifetime in order to keep his true self hidden in a century in which he was not permitted by society, nor even by law, to be who he was or to feel what he felt. 'What a sorry state of affairs.'

'It's ok. We can't help who we're attracted to, whatever form that might take. Look at me and Mr Walker! Truly, I hold no ill feeling towards you, and I will speak of it to no-one without your explicit consent. Is your valet the 'someone else' you were referring to?'

Lord Eltham sighed. 'Yes. But you must believe I did not intend to continue our... arrangement. I intended to be a good husband to you, just as my father was to my mother – and as I know my brother would have been had he gone on to marry. Temptation and opportunity got the better of me today, and now not only am I a disappointment to you, but I have disappointed my father and brother's memory as well.'

'It cannot be helped,' Issy was sincere. 'I'm sure that if your father and brother were here to see the man you have become – a man who only has good and honourable intentions towards others, who prioritises his family as much as you do yours – they could only have been proud of you.' As she spoke, Issy wondered how he could ever have hoped to achieve the charade of a typical marriage with her, for she could no sooner force an attraction towards a female than he could. 'The question is, how will this affect our betrothal?'

Slowly, Lord Eltham reached a hand towards her face, and Issy could see that his eyes, clouded with unshed tears, had softened towards her. But just then the door opened, and Lady Eltham was shown in.

'Mother,' said Lord Eltham, rising to his feet.

'Tommy,' said Lady Eltham, crossing the room to kiss his cheek.

Issy rose to her feet to dip into a curtsy, affording her a moment to compose herself. 'Good afternoon, Lady Eltham, it is a pleasure to meet you.'

When she looked up, it was to meet eyes of the same molten brown as Lord Eltham's, and she noticed they shared the same creamy complexion, though her son's height must have been all his father's, for Lady Eltham was as petite and delicate as he was tall and lean. She was also young – to Issy, the mothers of this era all seemed so young to have such grown up children. She looked as if she had only just passed forty, and she had a nurturing quality that, were circumstances as she'd hoped them to be, would have instantly set her at ease. Issy couldn't help but wonder what Lord Eltham's father and brother must have been like, for Lord Eltham had none of his mother's easy warmth - but then she supposed his life had been one of hidden adversity.

'The pleasure is all mine, Miss Worthing,' said Lady Eltham, 'for I have waited so long to see my son betrothed and here we are at last. I was starting to worry I may not see this day at all, for he has kept us all waiting! But it was worth the wait to meet the lovely bride he has chosen.'

The irony in Lady Eltham's words was not lost on the pair as they regarded one another awkwardly.

'Thank you, Lady Eltham,' said Issy. 'Won't you join the festivities? Your son has done you proud in arranging it all in your absence.' She was convinced things would feel far less awkward between them amidst company.

'I do not doubt it,' said Lady Eltham. 'I will refresh myself, and then perhaps you and I could have a bite to eat and get to know one another better.'

'I'd love to,' said Issy, though she had a feeling it was going to be a very long afternoon.

19.

To escape her constant thoughts of Will, Susan threw herself into caring for the wounded men in the hospital. She was no nurse, but she could offer them a kind word, a listening ear, a glass of water and a hand to hold. They made it clear they appreciated any small kindness or comfort that was offered to them as they lay afraid and in pain, often with life-altering injuries and far from home – far from those who loved them and who cared. She could only hope that if anything ever happened to Will, someone would take the time to do the same for him.

His letters had dried up, and Susan couldn't escape the gnawing fear that something terrible must have happened. As she held the hand of one particular soldier, most of his head bandaged from some terrible injury and his eyes swollen and face bruised beyond recognition, she thought of Will on the battlefield, taking his chances against weapons and machinery designed with the sole purpose of killing and maiming men, and wondered how in the world he or others like him could ever stand a chance.

'This one will not survive,' said the nurse, her expression grave. 'We have done all we can. Can you stay with him?'

Susan knew what she was asking, for she had now done this countless times. She would comfort the stranger until he took his last breath. She wondered, as she always did, who his family were, and knew they would give anything to exchange places with her, to be there sharing their final moments with their son or brother.

The man became agitated, and Susan moistened his lips with water. He was mumbling something incomprehensible, and she rose and placed her ear close to his lips. 'Pocket,' he was saying. 'My pocket.'

She patted his jacket and sure enough she felt something in his breast pocket. It was a folded piece of paper. 'This?' she asked.

He prised open an eye and nodded, wincing with the pain the effort had caused him. Carefully, Susan unfolded the paper and gasped. It was a sketch. Will's sketch of her.

It couldn't be. Not Will. She gripped his hand and her tears fell so fiercely she could barely see.

'Will?' she asked. Perhaps it wasn't him. Perhaps a comrade had kept the sketch in safe keeping for him. But when she looked more closely at his face, she could just see the smattering of freckles she knew as well as the stars above Worthing.

'Will, it's me - Elizabeth,' she whispered. 'Do not be afraid, for you have come home and I am with you. I will always be with you, Will, I am yours. I have always been yours.'

He squeezed her hand, and Susan realised that despite his injuries and his pain, he knew that she was with him in the moment he needed her. She would always be grateful for that.

'Thank you for loving me,' she said. 'I love you.' She leaned her head on his chest as he took his last breath, his heart stilled, and he left her for the very last time.

From the far side of the room Lady Worthing, who had happened to observe what had passed, burned with pain for Elizabeth. Lord Worthing had seen it too, and he crossed the room to stand with his wife, taking her arm in his as they both shared in their daughter's sorrow. Lady Worthing, her eyes misting disconcertingly, grasped his hand.

*

The imposing backdrop of Upton Hall was softened by bright sun and a cloudless powder-blue sky that lent the lush lawns a more vibrant hue. The band played on, and as the port and champagne went down, the laughter and jollity became steadily more raucous and the volume increased. Issy wished the awkwardness between her and Lord Eltham would dissipate so she could better enjoy the afternoon, for what an afternoon it was. The food was sublime, and the sun felt warm on her skin, but not so warm that she cooked beneath the many layers of gown, corset and undergarments she was wearing. She enjoyed Lady Eltham's company immensely, and fortunately so did Mama and Lady Brampton.

No-one was more surprised than Issy when Miss Astbury approached and asked her to join her for a turn about the lake. Even her own mother looked surprised, and Issy was certain she glimpsed Earl Henwick staring at Miss Astbury longingly as he watched the pair retreat.

'How are you enjoying the fete?' Issy asked.

'I believe I have yet to congratulate you on your engagement to Lord Eltham in person,' said Miss Astbury at the exact same time.

'Oh,' Issy smiled, 'thank you. Though please believe I am terribly sorry if our engagement hurts you in any way. I wasn't expecting an engagement to be the outcome of our visit.'

'Then that makes both of us,' Miss Astbury returned Issy's smile, 'for Earl Henwick intends to seek my hand in marriage before the season is out. He has declared a formal courtship.'

'That's wonderful,' said Issy. 'How do you feel?'

Issy was relieved, but she would be much happier for Miss Astbury if the affection Earl Henwick clearly felt for her was returned, though Miss Astbury would never know she did not find herself in such a promising position with Lord Eltham.

'I feel good about it,' said Miss Astbury, who was unusually coy. 'Very good, in fact. Though I'm not sure my mother feels quite the same way.'

'I'm sorry to hear that.'

'I'm not concerned, for what Earl Henwick lacks in fortune he makes up for in family name, and it is quite possible that my own dowry, used wisely, could be enough to secure the future of his estate once again. My mother will come around, though I am aware I owe you an apology on her behalf. Please believe I said nothing – she made her own assumptions.'

'Speak nothing of it,' said Issy, waving a dismissive hand but hoping all the while that no-one else amongst their party had leapt to similar conclusions, though she doubted the others held the same level of spite towards her that had empowered the Countess' creative imagination. 'Your mother's actions are not your responsibility, and I am certain it comes from a good place – she only wants the best for you as her daughter, just as my mother does for me.'

'Perhaps,' Miss Astbury acknowledged, 'though I'm not sure I could be quite as gracious in your position, Issy.'

'I suspect we will both be just as bad when we become mothers ourselves.'

The two young women laughed, and Miss Astbury linked Issy's arm. Issy squeezed her hand, and it felt as though once and for all, a truce had been reached between them. As they walked, Issy couldn't help but wish she could have secured a little of Miss Astbury's happiness in her match with Earl Henwick for her own dear great-grandmother.

They re-joined the gathering in good spirits, and Issy ignored the questioning looks from her own party who were clearly as surprised by this turn of events with Miss Astbury as she was. Someone suggested a spot of dancing, and as Lord Eltham drew her into his disinterested embrace, Issy wished they did not have to feign the affinity that it was obvious came naturally to Miss Astbury and Earl Henwick.

As Mama, Lady Brampton and Lady Eltham looked on with obvious approval, Issy wondered what to do. She should talk to her great-grandmother, but now that she and Lord Eltham were publicly betrothed, she doubted there was any recourse for them – especially not after all that fuss with Mr Walker. It was, indeed, a sorry state of affairs.

When the children began joining them on their makeshift dancefloor by the lake, Issy couldn't help but notice that Lottie was a little more flushed in the face than the others. Perhaps it was due to the effort involved in getting about on her sore ankle all day, but nonetheless she made note to encourage their Mama to urge her back into the hall to get some rest, just as Doctor Lisle had ordered. She had just parted from Lord Eltham to speak to her Mother about it when Lady Brampton took her to one side.

'Issy, is everything alright?'

'Is it really that obvious?' Issy was concerned the rest of the gathering could begin to suspect something was amiss.

'It is to me, but then I am highly invested in your relationship with Lord Eltham.'

'We have hit upon a snag, Lord Eltham and I, and I'm not sure it's something that can be overcome.'

'After the scandal with Mr Walker, any difficulties with Lord Eltham *must* be overcome if you are to retain your place in society, there's no question about it.' Lady Brampton's expression was determined, her mouth set.

Issy sighed. She'd thought as much. She wondered how to put this delicately for the benefit of her great-grandmother's sensibilities. She did not feel that now was the best time, but she knew Lady Brampton well enough to know she would not let the matter drop any time soon.

'Is there someone else?' Lady Brampton persisted.

Issy grimaced. 'Yes.'

'Not Miss Astbury?'

'No - nothing like that.'

'Then who? Someone here?'

'Well... Yes, someone here, though not amongst the guests.'

'What are you implying? That it is someone among the... *servants?*'

Issy nodded, thinking this whole thing would be so much easier if Lady Brampton could reach the truth herself.

'A housemaid, I assume? For he would not be the first gentleman to fall foul of the great social divide.'

'No, grandmother. His valet.'

'His *valet*? You mean, Bentley? But, he's a... He's a *man*!'

Issy was unsure what was worse to Lady Brampton – that Lord Eltham was gay, or that he was having intimate relations with a member of the lower class. Lady Brampton took a couple of steps back as though to make extra certain they could not be overheard. Issy watched as a myriad of thoughts crossed her face in quick succession, from shock and disbelief to anger and frustration, eventually settling, to her credit, somewhere towards compassion and grace.

'I promised not to tell anyone without Lord Eltham's express consent.'

'And who would we tell? He could be imprisoned if word got out, and Bentley may find himself shipped over to Australia for hard labour. With the way servants talk, I'm surprised they have been able to keep their secret for so long.'

'What are we to do?' Issy was certain they had now exhausted all their options.

'*Do*? For once I admit I have no idea. We will return to London tomorrow and think it over, and in the meantime, everything must remain just as it was – we can give no cause for anyone to suspect there is something amiss between you, for I think it is highly likely there is nothing to be done except go ahead with the marriage as planned.'

'That's as I feared, grandmother.' Issy fixed Lady Brampton in her anguished gaze. 'If you only knew how I long for so much better for you.'

'You need not worry about me, child, for I have lived my life, and it has been a fulfilling one of love and security with Lord Brampton. Together we will work out what to do next and all will be well. Look - Lady Eltham is trying to attract your attention, so put your best foot forward.'

Issy wished she could agree with her grandmother, but given the complexity of their circumstances she could not see how the situation between her and Lord Eltham could possibly be resolved. She was still turning the matter over in her head as they made their way back to their group when a commotion on the dancefloor drew her attention, and everybody else's too. There was a gasp and the crowd stepped backwards around a figure slumped on the floor, echoing the scene at the picnic the previous day.

Somehow, Issy knew instinctively that it was Lottie, even without even catching sight of her fiery red hair and assumed she must've stumbled and fallen over given she shouldn't be dancing on an injured ankle anyway. But it was worse than she feared.

Mama cried out, one hand flying to her mouth. She and Doctor Lisle were with Lottie in a matter of moments, and the old doctor crouched down on the floor beside her.

'Miss Worthing? Charlotte, can you hear me?' He placed a hand to Lottie's flushed face, and though she blinked several times and murmured, it was as though she was not truly present. He shook his head. 'The child is burning up. We must get her inside.'

Without a word, Lord Eltham strode over to Lottie and gently lifted her over his shoulder as though she weighed little more than a baby, then walked her all the way back to Upton Hall and up the winding staircase to her room, as Flora and Issy and their distraught Mama followed behind him.

'I knew I should not have allowed her to join the fete,' said Mama as they walked, 'I should have *insisted* she stay in bed. But would she have listened? Of course not. Stubborn, headstrong girl.'

'She'll be alright, Mama. Doctor Lisle will take good care of her,' Flora reassured her.

But Issy was not convinced, for what medical treatment was available to Lottie in 1904? She recoiled inwardly as images of leeches and bloodletting passed through her mind, and she wondered what rudimentary, ineffectual treatments Doctor Lisle might suggest on behalf of the poor girl and felt entirely powerless to stop him. Unless...

With great care and a solemn expression marring his handsome face, Lord Eltham eased Lottie from his grasp and onto her bed. She barely stirred, her eyes were closed, and when she did speak her mutterings made little sense. Doctor Lisle rushed to retrieve his medical kit, and after taking Lottie's temperature and listening to her chest his expression was grave.

'She is delirious. Her temperature is thirty-nine degrees, and we cannot afford for it to get any higher. Her lungs are crackly. We must prepare ourselves for the worst, but hope for the best. She has youth on her side - it could go either way.'

Mama threw herself into the armchair by Lottie's bed, grasping her hand and kissing it. 'You must help her, Doctor Lisle, for I cannot bear to lose another child.'

Silently, Lady Brampton entered the room, and she embraced Mama as she cried. Flora and Issy glanced at one another, helpless. They did what they could to make Lottie comfortable – they pressed cool, damp cloths upon her head, covered her in only a sheet and a nightdress to help lower her body temperature, and raised her bruised and swollen leg. Flora read pages of her favourite adventure stories to her – the sort Mama would usually frown upon but permitted given the circumstances.

For hours they sat vigil by Lottie's bedside as the sun retreated beyond the horizon, bathing the little room in a rosy hue that belied the sense of hopelessness they all shared but were too scared to express aloud. Meanwhile, well-meaning guests would knock and ask after their young patient in hushed voices, offering to prolong their stay and do whatever was necessary to support the family. But the Worthings were all in agreement that what they needed most was privacy to enable them to find the courage to face whatever may come next, so it was agreed that all guests aside from Doctor Lisle would leave the next day as planned.

To Issy's horror there was talk of bloodletting, which no-one among their party foresaw a problem with, and she knew she needed to get Lady Brampton alone somehow and come up with a plan – a plan that had already begun formulating in her mind to save this little girl who had become so dear to her, just as she would do whatever was in her power to save one of her *own* sisters. She had to act, and quickly, before Doctor Lisle, despite his good intentions, made matters gravely worse for Lottie.

It was getting late, and the room grew dark and cool. It was still too early in the season for the day's heat to permeate the hall with its massive, single-glazed windows, and for once Issy was glad of it, because what Lottie needed most was to be kept as cool as possible.

She cleared her throat. 'Mama, Flora, you are exhausted. Why don't you take a hot drink and something to eat? Lottie is safe for the time being - I can stay here awhile, then you are welcome to take over if you'd like. If anything changes I'll alert you at once, but some rest will give you the strength you need to be there for her.'

Mama did look tired. Her face was drawn, her back stiff, her hair was coming loose from its tightly contoured style, and her dress was uncharacteristically crumpled. The fine lines around her eyes looked deeper, and her skin was washed out from tears.

'Thomas, will you take them down?' Issy asked. 'Perhaps you can arrange a light supper and let your mother know we will need to stay on a bit longer.'

'Of course, anything you need.'

Lord Eltham appeared surprised to hear his Christian name spoken from her lips once more, but he recognised it as the peace offering that it was – a mark of Issy's continued commitment to him. Mama said nothing, she merely allowed herself to be led by Lord Eltham, who nodded at Issy as he left, an emotional Flora trailing along with them.

Lady Brampton sniffed. It was, after all, her very own sister who lay in that bed, and Issy wondered what early childhood memories were playing through her mind of the life she had exchanged for a life with Lord Brampton.

Issy sighed. 'Grandmother,' she said gently. 'I must go back. In my time there are medicines that can save Lottie, and I must get them quickly and bring them back here for her before... Well, before it's too late.'

'Nonsense, Doctor Lisle has decades of experience. It is just a chill from her fall in the stream yesterday and all that rain - perhaps a chest infection at worst – and he will prepare her a tincture and help reduce her fever then she'll get better. She must.'

Issy shook her head. 'I fear not, grandmother. Trust me, please. Medicine has advanced greatly in my time – faster than ever in history. Doctor Lisle *thinks* he can help her, but I *know* I can help her. I must, while there's still time.'

'But what about Lord Eltham? What if you can't get back to us? How do you know your plan will work?'

Issy looked towards Lottie, her face almost as fiery red as her hair that was spread out across the pillow like a halo. She slept fitfully. It was a sorry sight, especially when they both knew the spirit of the girl trapped within the fever. Lady Brampton followed her gaze as though reading her thoughts, and her violet eyes misted with tears.

'What if we are not supposed to interrupt the course of history?'

Issy grasped her hand. 'Lady Brampton, I think it's a little too late for that, don't you? Imagine if something similar happened to your son and there was a chance that someone could save him, wouldn't you want them to take that chance?'

Lady Brampton nodded.

'You would what, Lady Brampton?' Lord Eltham asked. The pair had been so intent on their conversation, and he had entered the room so quietly, that neither one of them had heard him enter.

'It's nothing,' said Lady Brampton.

'No,' said Issy, looking to Lady Brampton as though first seeking her approval, before fixing her earnest cornflower gaze upon Lord Eltham. 'It *is* something. Today I discovered something about you, Lord Eltham, but I'm afraid there's also something about *me* that you ought to know.'

She gestured for him to sit down and hoped that despite the breach of time between them and all that had changed in society within it, he would be as understanding towards her as she had endeavoured to be towards him.

20.

Elizabeth Worthing had gone on to marry a doctor with the blessing of both her parents, for her mother had witnessed firsthand the significance of the contribution medics had made to the war effort, and she'd approved, even if he was only middle class (it's not as if there'd been a plethora of other options).

When Susan returned to her own time, estranged from her mother and estranged from herself, she'd married the first man who'd asked her, the first man who'd promised to take her far away from her memories and from the life she'd always known. Her children's father had been a good man, but she'd measured him by a standard to which he could never hope to compare, a standard set by the late William Manning. She had kept the portrait he'd drawn of her, had brought it back with her under the dress and framed it, but she'd left it behind at the manor, for she knew she should not allow Will to encroach upon the new life she was intent on making for herself. But it had been no use, of course, because he'd encroached anyway. Her love for him had filled every fibre of her being for many years, and in that respect both their futures had been snatched from them.

She looked at the portrait now and remembered the young man she had lost to the futility of war, futile for despite the lessons that nations had learned from it, humanity had taken no heed of its own warning, had not tempered its greed, and conflict continued to occur at one point or another in every corner of the earth.

There was a knock on the door.

'It's time,' said Mrs Lamb gently, a kindly smile upon her face, looking at her with those warm, maternal eyes that had offered her comfort since she'd been a small child. She was dressed smartly in sombre black, and it was strange for Susan to see her out of the uniform she had always insisted on wearing long after formality required it.

Susan nodded. Her mother's funeral. How she wished things could have been different - that she hadn't allowed the past to get in the way of her own future or prevent her from rebuilding her relationship with her mother. All that wasted time. Life was short - if Will had taught her anything, it was that. Even Lucinda Worthing had learned it, and from the feedback Susan had received from those who'd known her, she'd changed considerably over the years. Susan resolved that if Issy ever came home, she would not make the same mistakes.

*

'Do you trust me?' Issy asked.

She had taken extra care to ensure she was dressed just as she had been that fateful afternoon in the attic of Worthington Manor, an afternoon which felt so long ago now she could scarcely believe that if her plan worked, she could end up back there in a matter of moments. She studied herself in the gilded mirror and wondered at how quickly she had adjusted to her new life in Edwardian England since she had first put on this dress. She no longer needed her grandmother to tell her to stand up straight and keep her shoulders back and her head up – the posture came naturally now, even without a corset.

'Do I have a choice?' Lord Eltham asked, wryly. 'Though how you dressing-up as a debutante could possibly assist your sister, I cannot imagine.'

'We have to hurry - we don't have much time.' Issy was unperturbed. 'We are about to go to a place where you can be free to be whoever you choose. And if you like it - you may just choose to stay there.'

Lord Eltham raised his eyebrows as though to indicate that he hardly thought so. 'I've been to places like that before, and I can assure you they were not located at the bottom of a young lady's trunk.'

A little frantically, and with not less than a little difficulty, Issy flung open the great trunk and stepped inside, gathering her train about her legs then gesturing to Lord Eltham to join her.

'Isabelle, this is ridiculous, truly. I must implore you to focus on the matter at hand.'

'Just trust me. Please.' Something about the urgency in her voice caused him to set aside his doubts for the moment, and a little gingerly, step into the bottom of the trunk by her feet.

'Now, it's going to be uncomfortable – but the discomfort should only be momentary. I need you to somehow arrange yourself beneath the layers of my dress then I'll pull the lid down over us.'

'Isabelle, if your plan is to entice me into heterosexuality by permitting me to admire your feminine wares, I can assure you it will not work, no matter how attractive the subject. It is not the first time I have encountered the female form, and yet my predisposition has not changed. And once again, I fail to understand how any of this can help your sister. Surely we are simply wasting valuable time?'

'If we continue to talk about it, we are. Please, Thomas!'

'What on earth are those things you are wearing, anyway? Long johns? If my memory serves me correctly, I would have thought the standard was petticoats – dreadful things to manoeuvre under – like some sort of frilled chastity belt!'

He was referring to her carefully preserved black leggings, but Issy simply ignored him. And though Lord Eltham sighed, and though it was indeed ridiculously uncomfortable for him to contort his tall, lean frame to fit inside the trunk alongside Issy and to arrange himself beneath her layers of tulle and train, he did as he was bid. Then she pulled the lid closed and everything went black.

'This is ridiculous,' he repeated a moment or two later, his voice muffled by layers of fabric.

Issy bit her lip as tears filled her eyes. It hadn't worked. Poor Lottie.

With a heavy sigh she lifted her skirts to enable Lord Eltham to take in a great lungful of stale air, then pushed back the lid of the trunk. It was dark, and at first they couldn't see a thing. But when Issy's eyes eventually adjusted, she could just make out the old eaves of the attic's rooftop above, and Lord Eltham's astonished face as he clamoured out of the trunk and smoothed down his trousers. Worthington Manor. The first part of her plan had worked.

'What in the world just happened?'

'Welcome to 2024,' said Issy, her relief evident. 'I'm a descendant of the Isabelle Worthing to whom you are betrothed. I'm named after her, in fact. It's a little complicated, but the *real* Isabelle Worthing is actually Lady Brampton - only she went back in time just as I did, but to Victorian England where she married Lord Brampton. They fell in love, and she decided not to come back here to reassume true self. Here, they call me Issy.'

Lord Eltham swiped a hand over his brow. 'It can't be!'

'That's what I thought too, at first. But it can. There's a lot more to explain, but too little time. I have some acting to do if I'm to get Lottie the medicine she needs to get well, and in the meantime, you should go into town and ask for Georgie Stevens. Tell him I sent you and ask him to show you around. You will find that in this century, being who you are is not only legal, but greatly encouraged. I thought that perhaps by sharing my truth with the man I am betrothed to marry, you could also decide for yourself if that is what you still want.'

Lord Eltham looked at her. He was so handsome, with his dark, impenetrable eyes and brooding mouth. If only things were different. But they were not.

'You are free, Thomas! If you want to, you can choose to put all those the years of responsibility, duty and deception behind you for good.'

It was obvious that Lord Eltham could scarcely believe what was happening, but he looked as though a great load had just been lifted from his shoulders, for as she spoke, his chest puffed outward and his stance grew taller and somehow stronger. His shining dark eyes conveyed his mixed emotions. 'Thank you, Issy. I wish you and your family all the very best – especially Lottie.'

'Follow me,' she instructed, as she carefully slipped off the dress then picked her way around all the old furniture, covered in white sheets like ghostly spectres, to grapple for the attic door, 'you can sneak out through the servant passage. There's an old bicycle in the boot room – keep riding for about two miles towards Worthington. You'll see it just over the hill.'

'I can't believe I'm doing this.'

'Me neither, but then lately I've grown accustomed to doing things I can't believe. I should require several hours – a full day at most - to get what I need from here. If you decide to come back with me, you'll need to make your way back to the attic by sundown to meet me.'

He nodded. They crept down the narrow staircase, pushed aside the threadbare velvet curtain and found themselves enveloped in the draughty embrace of the servant's passage. Just beyond the horizon, the sun was coming up, and it shone into the hallway bathing them both in its soft, buttermilk glow. If Issy was quick, she could creep into bed as though she'd never been gone. What a surprise that would be to her mother and sisters, whom she assumed must have been searching tirelessly for her these past few weeks!

Waving Lord Eltham on his way, she slipped off her shoes and crept as quietly as possible along creaky old floorboards towards the staircase and down to her bedroom, which she found just as she had left it. Even her mobile phone, which previously she could not have stood to go an hour without, was plugged in to recharge at her bedside. Overcome with relief and from the exhaustion of pretending to be someone who was not for so long, Issy pulled the bed covers up to her chin and waited.

It had been so long since she hadn't awoken to the disturbance of servants that she slept through until past eleven, then cursed herself for wasting precious time. She was just stretching out and considering her next move when in burst her sister, Jasmine, unannounced, her impish features pinched with curiosity and concern.

The moment Issy caught sight of her beloved sister, her eyes clouded with tears of joy. 'I'm back!' she declared. 'Oh, Jasmine, I've missed you so much.' She threw back the covers and drew her sister into her embrace, just as Flora had once done to her.

'Back? What are you talking about? You haven't been anywhere but bed, and that's not exactly unusual.' Jasmine's eyes narrowed. 'Mum's been asking why you haven't come down for breakfast - I think Mrs Lamb has put something aside for you because she needs to clear up.'

'Jasmine, don't you remember the game of hide and seek? The attic?'

She wrinkled her nose. 'Course I remember, but that was weeks ago, before grandma's funeral. You were grounded for a week when we eventually found you. Why are you bringing it up now? Are you sick or something? 'Cause you're acting really strangely. *Again.*'

Issy slumped against the pillows. It was almost as if to Jasmine, she hadn't been gone at all. But how could that be? Jasmine had said herself that quite some time had passed here in 2024, just as it had in 1904.

'Actually,' said Issy, one hand on her brow, 'I do feel unwell. I think I might need a doctor.'

'Is *that* why you didn't come down to eat? I'll go tell mum.'

'Thanks.'

Jasmine peered at Issy strangely, and Issy realised it was because her sisters weren't really accustomed to her thanking them for anything. She recalled that when she'd first gone back in time, she'd thanked one of the servants and it had caused her to stand out straight away. Now here she was making the same mistake again.

The moment Jasmine had left, Issy tugged her mobile phone from its charger and checked the date. Whilst at least eight weeks had passed of the London season, she tallied that here in her own time she'd been gone for only four. She determined that life in Edwardian England must run at double the pace – Lady Brampton had warned her that time wouldn't pass the same. The unfortunate thing about it was that it not only halved the amount of time she had to do what she needed to do and get back to Lottie, but it was also just shy of being enough time to get her through this tedious period of study and revision and out onto the other side of her A Levels.

It seemed odd to Issy that given how long she'd been gone, she'd received no messages or notifications, until she went inside her phone and realised that not only had there been dozens of messages – from Mila mainly, and the odd one from Chad Connor, whom she'd practically forgotten all about in all honesty - but what caught her attention was that there were replies. Sent by *her*. Had her mum or sisters been through her phone? Nothing made sense.

'Issy!'

Susan entered the room, and for a moment Issy couldn't quite decide whether she preferred every visitor to be formally announced by a housemaid so that she had time to prepare herself, or for them to simply announce themselves.

'Are you ok? Jasmine said you're sick?'

Issy regarded her mother – she looked older somehow, more tired and wan. The fine lines about her eyes had deepened, and Issy suddenly felt overwhelmed by how much she had missed her, and from something more – a combination of guilt and regret for the once close relationship they'd shared, that as she'd grown older had somehow been cast adrift. She promptly burst into tears, and Susan rushed to her side, maternal concern etched on her face.

'Mum,' she sniffed, pulling Susan down towards her so that she could once again find herself enveloped in the most comforting of arms after what felt like the longest time. She couldn't imagine Mama ever allowing her to do something like that.

'Shh,' Susan soothed, stroking her hair as she had always done. 'Hush. It's ok.'

Issy's slender frame shook.

'Issy,' said Susan after a few moments. 'I *know*.'

Issy sniffed and looked up into her mother's pale blue eyes. She definitely knew. 'But... how?'

'I was young once too, my girl.'

'What happened?'

Susan sat on the edge of her bed beside her. 'I went back as your great-grandmother, Elizabeth Worthing, and I fell in love... with a stable groom. We were going to elope, but at the last moment we were discovered. He had already enlisted into the army without telling me, after I'd begged him not to go because I knew what was likely to happen to him if he did, and I was right. He was sent to the front line during the Second World War in 1944, and he never came home again.'

'Oh, Mum.' Issy didn't know what else to say. She could only imagine her pain.

'Did anything bad happen to you while you were gone?'

'No, not at all! I went back to the Edwardian era, and once I got used to it, I found that I quite liked it. Apart from the corsets.'

Susan arched her eyebrows. 'I was terrified of you finding the key to the attic in case you had your heart broken just as I did – or worse - in case you decided never to come back... Especially after how things have been between us lately. Issy, I could not have borne it if you never came back.' Susan's shoulders shook with the emotion she had been holding in for so long. 'I begged my mother never to give you the key, but she did it anyway. I found it and I hid it, but Mrs Lamb must have put it back there under strict instructions from your grandma, to whom she has been loyal her entire life.'

'Did grandma go back in time too?' Issy asked.

'She did. She secured an illustrious match that prevented our family from losing just about everything, thanks to a previous Lord Worthing who'd had a penchant for women and gambling. She just couldn't see the problem with the time travel thing – was disappointed I hadn't done as good a job of it as she had for the benefit of our family – and that, and I suppose the grief I blamed her for, drove a wedge in our relationship.

'When I fell in love with your father, she felt I was once again turning my back on the family name and all the expectations that came with it, but I just wanted to escape the pain... I wanted an ordinary life with an ordinary man like Will. When your father and I divorced, she as good as said *I told you so*. She was quite the snob in her younger years, though from what I gathered at her funeral, she changed a lot in her later years. I wish I had not been so stubborn and had made more of an effort with her. Now I've lost that opportunity forever, and I will always regret it.

'Issy, I hope that nothing ever comes between us – in the grand scheme of things, there is nothing more significant, more meaningful, than relationship with those you love.'

'It won't, Mum,' said Issy, meaning it. 'I love you and I'm sorry.'

Issy wished she could have made it back in time for her grandma's funeral. Later, when they had the time, she would ask her mother everything and find out as much as she could about her. Perhaps one day if she had a daughter of her own, they would travel back in time and meet her for themselves.

'I'm sorry too,' said Susan. 'We'll never get everything right as parents – we all make mistakes - but we try our best. Just know that anything we do, is done from love.'

'Mum?'

'Mm?'

'If you knew I'd gone back to the past, then who's been sending messages from my phone?'

Susan simply raised an eyebrow and smiled through her tears. 'Your replacement, of course. Mya, from 2068.'

21.

From the moment Issy had offered to babysit the girls for her so she could attend to matters at the manner, she'd known someone else was occupying her daughter's skin – Mya, a mixed-race girl of the Worthing line from over forty years in the future. It had been quite an experience to have her own great, great granddaughter living in her home with her and a special affinity had blossomed between them. Susan and Mrs Lamb couldn't get enough of her tales of life in the twenty-sixties and all that had changed between now and then.

Mya didn't really seem to need them, but Issy she suspected, needed her. Perhaps that was why she had come? So, as she'd observed the blossoming friendship that emerged between Mya and Georgie Stevens, she'd known better than to interfere.

'The solicitor is here for you.' Mrs Lamb interrupted Susan's reverie. 'Mr Manning, the solicitor.'

She grinned, and Susan rolled her eyes. Mrs Lamb needn't get ahead of herself. What in the world could he want? she wondered.

'I'll watch the girls for you,' Mya offered, and Susan could see how happy that made them.

Mr Manning was as polite and efficient as he was handsome; with his chestnut hair, hazel eyes, and a smattering of freckles across his nose that put her in mind of a bygone time. As he shuffled the huge pile of papers he had brought for her to sign, she couldn't help but notice the telltale splatters of paint at the edges of his fingernails, the parts where it was hardest to clean. She remarked upon it, and he smiled.

'I am a solicitor by day, Ms Worthing, but an artist by... well not by night, exactly – the light's too poor. I'm the latest in a long line of artists, and we are fortunate enough to live in a landscape that constantly inspires. Unfortunately, I'm afraid I can't say the same about my day job – but I seem to have fared better than my ancestors in that respect.'

His eyes crinkled at the corners when he laughed. Susan glanced through the window beyond him and surveyed the beautiful colours of the Worthington landscape that she supposed had barely changed in centuries. 'You're right,' she said. 'Inspiring.' She hadn't appreciated it quite like that before.

'And you're really going to leave it all behind?'

Susan had been so certain, she'd already met with an estate agent that dealt with the sale of properties like hers, but now found she was unsure. 'Actually, I think I'll hold onto those papers a little while longer.'

'Very well.' Mr Manning handed her his card. 'When you're ready, I can come back to collect them. Otherwise, if you happen to be passing through the village, feel free to drop them at my studio and I'll give you the grand tour – which will take approximately three minutes of your time. Art is a darned sight more interesting to me than facts and figures, but unfortunately it doesn't pay the bills.'

Susan understood the problem, for if they stayed on at the manor, how could she possibly pay their enormous bills? She would have to monetise the property – and fortunately, Mya had given her some ideas in that regard if she had the confidence to pull them off.

She rose, and as Mr Manning shook her hand, a jolt of electricity shot through her palm at his touch, taking her entirely by surprise. 'I think I'd like that,' she said, and he smiled.

*

As curious as Issy was to find out more about Mya and how she measured up as her replacement, and as wonderful as it was to be enveloped back into her true family fold once again, and to see old Mr and Mrs Lamb, and not have to wear a corset or stand on ceremony all of the time, and to be able to wear whatever she wanted and lounge about the house comfortably and eat familiar foods, and be a vegetarian and not have her every move dictated by somebody else or be observed by servants; Issy found she still missed the

Edwardian world she had come to know. It was going to be a lot harder than she'd thought to leave it all behind, but hardest of all would be saying goodbye to her dear grandmother and surrogate sisters – even Mama and Papa.

Given her mum already knew the truth, Issy hadn't had to affect an illness, which made things a whole lot easier, and with Mrs Lamb's help they'd been able to locate a single pack of unfinished antibiotics in her grandma's medicine cabinet.

'Amoxycillin,' said Mrs Lamb with a wink, brushing her floured hands on her apron before plucking them out of the Tupperware box. 'Only a couple are missing. The doctor used to say these were the best at fighting chest infections and the like, but your grandma couldn't tolerate them - they made her too sickly. Best take some paracetamol with you as well, in fact, why not take the whole kit? There's antiseptic, steri-strips, plasters and bandages - all sorts of things they're sure to find useful back in 1904. Didn't you say the poor girl had hurt her ankle too?'

'I'll take whatever will fit under the dress,' said Issy, 'and whatever won't draw me too much unwanted attention or arouse the suspicion of Doctor Lisle.' It was going to be hard enough to get past him and Mama as it was.

'What are you ladies plannin'?' teased Mr Lamb, as he trundled in from the garden and sliced himself a hunk of freshly baked bread, smearing it liberally with salted butter. 'Up to no good again, are ya?'

'Never you mind,' said Mrs Lamb. 'What you don't know, I usually know for you. And what have I said about coming inside with those boots on? I've just swept and here you come traipsing mud and breadcrumbs all over the place.'

'I'm not immune to all the strange goings on in this place, let me tell you!' Mr Lamb was used to his wife's complaints. 'If these walls in here, and those old trees out there, could talk...'

'What strange goings on, Mr Lamb?' asked a breathless and rosy-cheeked Ella, who had come skipping in behind him before draping her skipping rope about her shoulders.

Susan narrowed her eyes.

'Oh,' he said mysteriously, 'all sorts of strange happenings. But yer mum wouldn't want me tellin' yer,' his voice dropped to a stage whisper, 'so I'll tell yer when we get outside to harvest those veggies and collect the eggs. Startin' with that unusual young gent' who stole a bicycle from 'ere this mornin' and took one of me biggest carrots for 'is breakfast.'

Ella grinned and eagerly followed Mr Lamb's retreating back out into the kitchen garden, leaving a trail of muddy dust from his boots behind him, and Mrs Lamb rolled her eyes. Issy's cheeks flushed. Thomas.

'Oh yes, I'd forgotten about Lord Eltham,' said Susan. 'What do you think he'll decide to do?'

'I really don't know,' said Issy, who whenever she thought she had worked Lord Eltham out, had swiftly been proven wrong. 'I wonder what Georgie Stevens will make of him – he'll stand out like a sore thumb dressed as he was and behaving as he does. I'll have a lot of explaining to do when I next see Georgie at school.'

'I don't think Georgie will mind,' said Susan. 'I think he may have guessed there was something a little unusual about Mya too – they struck up quite a friendship, what between his shifts here with Mr Lamb and your revision down at the school.'

'Oh.' Issy recalled Georgie's grass-green eyes and his look of disdain. She wasn't sure how she felt about that. And what about Chad Connor? That exciting moment with Chad in class seemed so long ago now, it was hard to believe it had even happened at all. She'd have to look through Mya's phone messages with him and Mila properly to see where she'd left things between them. 'Revision?' she asked.

'Yes, revision. Mya understood the benefit of an education as much as I imagine you do by now, after learning how little options there were for women without it not too long ago.'

'Yes,' said Issy. 'I just wish I knew what to do with it.'

Come to think of it, her mind did feel full of fresh snippets of information she was sure hadn't been there before – things she recognised her teachers had covered over the course of the past year, and some of it that could only have come from her schoolbooks. And had her heartbeat just accelerated slightly at the mention of Georgie's name? Mya had certainly kept herself busy during her visit - Issy only wished she had limited it to her schoolwork and left the romantic side of things to her. But then hadn't Lady Brampton wished the same?

'You'll work it out. You're a bright girl, Issy, you always have been. And you don't really have to know it all now – some people get to my age and still don't know what they want to do. In fact, I'm not even sure *I* know what I want to do if we move on from here. Often you find that the journey is just as important – perhaps even more so - than the destination, and who you spend it with.'

'She's not bright, she's stupid,' said Jasmine, who had followed the scent of freshly baked bread into the kitchen where she helped herself to a wedge and spread it liberally with butter and berry jam. She stuck her tongue out at Issy. 'She'll have to be an influencer – that's what all the kids in my class who don't do their homework want to be - only Issy's hardly got any followers.'

Susan bit her lip, anticipating a flare-up between the two sisters, but Issy simply grinned. If only she had the sense of direction her friends all seemed to have for what to do next once her schooling drew to a close.

*

At the top of the main staircase at Worthington Manor was an intricate tapestry of the Worthing family tree, and Issy paused before it. She must've walked past it a hundred times, but she'd never taken the time to study it before – she'd simply regarded it as part of the furniture, like everything else, but now it dawned on her that it was a tapestry of riches, for the tree portrayed the very people whose interweaving lives had created the foundation of her own identity.

It hadn't been added to since her mother's birth because they'd run out of space. There was her mother, Susan Worthing born in 1978, her grandmother, Lucinda Worthing born in 1952, her great-grandmother, Elizabeth Worthing, born in 1927 – but most interesting of all was her great, great grandfather, Ruben Walker-Worthing, the only child, a son, born in 1905 to Isabella and Otto Walker-Worthing. Walker-Worthing? That stood out, because Issy knew that a woman of the era always assumed her husband's surname upon marriage, when double-barrelled names were less commonly used. Before that was her great, great, great grandmother, Isabelle herself, born in November 1885; and before that, Mama and Papa - Monica and Kenneth Worthing - and so it went on and on...

The tapestry contained two poignant pieces of information that were of utmost importance to Issy's return to 1904 – that Charlotte Elizabeth Worthing died on the twenty-seventh of April 1904 aged only 10 years, and that Ruben Walker-Worthing married a woman named Mary Day in 1925. It was the twenty-fifth of April now. Lottie could not wait, therefore neither could Issy.

Casting her eye out of one of the picture windows placed either side of the tapestry, Issy gazed across her family's land for any sign of Thomas. She half expected him to come galloping towards the manor on Dart, and for a moment she had to remind herself which century she was in. It was getting late, with only the last mauve streaks of daylight splashed across the horizon. Perhaps he'd decided he couldn't go back to living a lie – perhaps he had decided to stay. Issy wasn't sure which decision would surprise her more.

'Couldn't you stay with us for just one more night?' Susan asked, hopefully. 'To give him a bit more time to decide what he wants to do?' As much as she'd enjoyed getting to know Mya, she was scared to let her real daughter go again.

'I can't,' said Issy, thinking of the tapestry. 'I'm not sure what's wrong with Lottie, but I do know that she can't afford to wait. We're running out of time.'

Susan nodded and her eyes brimmed with tears. 'Just don't forget to come back home to us.'

'I won't!' Issy smiled.

Mrs Lamb kept the children occupied downstairs whilst Issy and Susan snuck upstairs unseen, all the way to the attic. Issy had brought all manner of things with her that she thought might come in useful to leave behind in 1904, including several pairs of hard-wearing yet comfortable shoes for the servants - though she wasn't quite sure how she was going to fit them all under her dress, with or without Thomas. Quickly, she slipped off her t-shirt and stepped into the folds of the debutante dress, a task which was far easier with her mum's help. She left the black leggings on too, just in case.

'Issy!' Susan gasped. 'Look at you – you're stunning.'

They stood before the full length-mirror as Susan pulled the straps of the dress in tight at the back until the bodice cinched in, accentuating her slender hips whilst magically creating a bosom at the same time.

'Do you know what?' she said. 'I have an idea.'

'What?' Issy asked.

'I'll tell you when you get back!' But already her head was swimming with plans. She had to get everything just right.

'Mum? It's not so bad here at Worthington. Do we really have to sell the manor?'

'That depends,' said Susan, 'on you and your sisters - and don't forget about Mila and Chad and all your friends.'

'Well... We'll all be going our separate ways soon anyway.'

It was true. Mila had been accepted into a university in York, and whilst Issy had no idea what it was she wanted to do and seemed to have missed the boat on applying for university, she knew in her heart that she didn't want to go home because somehow, Worthington Manor now felt like the place she truly belonged. She was certain her sisters wouldn't mind – they loved it here already, and they'd soon make friends down at the village school. Lots of other places like the manor had been converted into wedding venues, country retreats and hotels – and with breakfasts like Mrs Lamb's, they could easily run their own B&B.

'I'll think it over,' said Susan. 'There's a lot of work and expense involved in keeping a place like this going, so we'd need to have a plan.'

'Isn't there just,' said a deep male voice. In their haste, Susan and Issy had forgotten to close the attic door behind them.

'Thomas!'

He stepped out from the shadows into the glow of the attic's single light bulb, and despite the seriousness of the task upon which she was about to embark, Issy couldn't help but crack up laughing at the sight of him. In the few hours he'd been gone, his moustache and thick sideburns had been shaved off, his hair had been cut into a fade, and wax applied until his thick strands of dark hair poked up at jaunty angles. Most entertaining of all however, was his outfit. It was so unlike anything Issy could ever have imagined him wearing that she could hardly contain herself.

'Is that... a tracksuit?'

Lord Eltham nodded. 'Your friend Mr Stevens thought I might be more comfortable riding your bike back to the manor in this get-up rather than in my fete suit. I wasn't sure, but I think he was right. My own things are in this backpack.'

He looked so stiff and spoke so formally that the overall effect was comical, and the addition of the backpack set Issy into an uncontrollable fit of the giggles.

'Look!' she pointed at the mirror. 'Have a look!'

Lord Eltham did so, and even he couldn't help but smile. 'As much as I have appreciated this most unusual experience, Isabelle, I'm not sure this century is for me.'

'That's a shame, because your new look suits you.' Not so much the tracksuit which seemed totally out of place, but the shave had taken years off him and emphasised the lovely structure of his face.

'That said, I would still very much like to come back with you.'

'You're sure?'

'I'm sure. I have a duty to my mother and sisters. Pursuing my own desires here would mean abandoning them to an uncertain future. Whilst that burden might feel overwhelming at times, especially given it was always intended to be my brother's burden and not mine, I am now their sole provider and protector, and since his passing I have taken that role very seriously. I care for my family, and I care for Bentley too. I... I do not wish to be without him – not without *any* of them.'

'That is very noble of you, Thomas,' said Susan in approval.

'I'm sure you were about to introduce us?' he said to Issy.

'Oh, that's my mum - Susan.'

'Lady Worthing.' He took her hand in his. 'If I was wearing a hat, I would remove it – though I could not quite bring myself to wear the cap your friend gave me. It is a pleasure to meet you.'

'Lord Eltham,' Susan grinned. 'Charmed!'

'Did you get what you came for, Isabelle?' he asked.

'Absolutely. Though how I'm going to fit you and everything else under this dress, I have no idea.'

'I can help. Come on!'

Between Susan and Lord Eltham, they were able to assist Issy into the trunk and lay out the pile of belongings in there with her beneath the dress.

'You may as well quickly change now,' said Issy, 'because that backpack will never fit in here.'

'Oh, Mr Stevens was most generous and said I could keep the new clobber. This outfit will make a fine nightdress, I think.'

The two women stifled a giggle. Lord Eltham climbed into the trunk then took a deep breath before disappearing beneath Issy's skirts, as Susan spread the fabric down over him and lowered the lid until once again, everything went black.

22.

This time was different. When Issy closed her eyes, dozens of images stole across her vision, grainy and fleeting at first, like a hundred barely recollected memories, before gradually increasing in duration and detail. The most consistent thing about each image was that they all contained the figure of a man Issy recognised but couldn't quite place. There was something familiar about him, and yet he was a stranger to her.

There were horses, one after another, getting faster and faster. There was shouting and cheering, and she found herself jostled by a raucous crowd. It was so bright that Issy could hardly see, and she lifted her hand up towards her face to shade her eyes from the piercing sun. In her hand was a cream lace fan, and she was wearing long gloves. The crowd were so intently focused on the race, and Issy so disoriented, that she didn't see where she was going until she heard a bellow of disappointment then felt an elbow jolt into her side. Momentarily, the pain beneath her ribs took her breath away.

'Dash it all, Rubicon! Oh, I beg your pardon, I'm dreadfully sorry, Miss,' said the man – a gentleman judging by the quality of his dress, though it was definitely not the same style of dress Issy had seen the men wearing in 1904.

She looked down. Crinoline. She was wearing a crinoline. It was cumbersome to move in. 'I'm afraid I am the one who was at fault,' said Issy, with a rising sense of panic. What was happening to her? She must have travelled too far back in time, but nonetheless, events continued to unfold, and she was powerless to stop them.

'Did you bet on Rubicon too? For you look as downcast as I feel.' The gentleman was sympathetic.

Issy could feel her mouth turning up into a self-conscious smile. 'I did not,' she admitted, 'however, I'm not sure horse-racing is entirely my cup of tea, anyway.'

'Nor mine after this,' said the stranger, clearly defeated but taking it in his stride. He was attractive. He wasn't a tall man – but he was sturdy and strong. Solid. Most appealing of all was the warmth he exuded – it was contagious. 'I'll tell you what *is* my cup of tea though – a glass of port to drown my sorrows. Would you, and whoever is accompanying you here today, care to join me?'

'Yes,' said Issy, without hesitation. She knew she shouldn't, but there was something about this man, a certain magnetism that made it impossible for her to pass him by.

'And to whom do I owe the pleasure?' he asked.

'Arabella Worthing,' said Issy. Arabella? She did not have time to question it, all she could do was allow the scene to unfold, like a spectator at the races, and relinquish herself to it.

'Excellent, Miss Worthing. My name is Kenneth Brampton.'

Brampton. Lord Brampton. When he took her by the arm, Issy led him to her party for the necessary introductions. She wasn't sure how she recognised them, but she did. They were all dressed in crinolines, just like her - only the older of her party wore high frilled necklines and stern expressions upon their faces. Issy felt static from the warm pressure of Lord Brampton's hand upon her milky, soft skin, and she knew in that moment that she didn't ever want him to let her go.

What followed were a series of images, and Lord Brampton was present in every single one of them. Stolen conversations at picnics and parties, Issy's beady-eyed chaperone monitoring their every move, the pair of them pressed together as they danced in ballrooms, their hearts racing and eyes interlocked, gloved hands entwined. All the while there was an unspoken yearning between them - and later, much later, she felt the delicious and heady sensation of him pressing his full weight against her beneath a cloudless sky as he showered her in kisses and tender caresses before completing her in a way she hadn't known she'd needed completing.

'Isabelle! What are you doing? I can't breathe under here.'

Issy awoke with a jolt to Lord Eltham clutching at her calf. She opened her eyes and blinked, but above her there was nothing but darkness. She was completely disorientated.

'The lid, please, Issy – the lid! Hurry!'

'Oh!'

She raised her arms and pushed forwards as hard as she could, then felt movement beneath her skirts as Lord Eltham flung them back from his face and gasped great lungfuls of air.

'Are you alright?' he asked.

'Quite,' said Issy.

Her plan had worked, and they were back at Upton Hall, but something was different. Issy felt nauseous. Her breasts ached, and she knew instinctively that she was carrying Lord Brampton's child.

'Oh, you're both back, thank goodness!' Lady Brampton came rushing to their aid.

She looked tired. Her violet eyes were tearful, her face lined even deeper. She appeared older somehow, and though she was a sturdy woman there was a new frailty to her stature that hadn't been there before. Issy realised that something was very wrong, and now was definitely not the time to broach with her this new complication of her pregnancy.

'Grandmother?'

The tears began to fall, slowly at first, then uncontrollably until Lady Brampton's whole body shook as she sobbed. Concerned for the worst, Lord Eltham assisted her to a nearby chair and Issy clutched both her hands in hers.

'Is it Lottie? Am I too late?'

'No,' said Lady Brampton between sobs. 'No. You've come at just the right time for Lottie, for I fear she is getting worse. But Ken, my Kenneth...'

'Lord Brampton?' Issy was confused.

'He's gone, Issy. He's gone.'

Issy shook her head. She looked to Lord Eltham, but his mouth was set – he knew only too well the pain of unexpected loss.

'He can't be,' said Issy. 'He just can't...' She thought of Lord Brampton – always affable, good-humoured, and kind, and with his rare enthusiasm and zest for life. He was big in stature, big in heart, and big in spirit. He couldn't be gone – to have lived so long only to have been felled so suddenly and so fast – it didn't make sense.

'It was his heart,' said Lady Brampton, as though answering her unspoken question. 'He had a weak heart, but still he drank like a fish and ate too much and did all of the things he knew he shouldn't. Then he caught a high fever, just like Lottie did after that ghastly afternoon out in the storm, but it was too much for him. His heart did not recover, and it was all over very quickly. I can scarcely believe it. Nearly fifty years have passed us by, just like that, and now he's gone. But who am I without him? I... I cannot be without him...'

Issy was torn. She needed to get to Lottie as soon as possible, but her great-grandmother needed her even more right now. The rest of Lady Brampton's sentence was inaudible, as Issy engulfed her in her arms and held her tightly, soothing her as she cried for what felt like a very long time. Silently, Lord Eltham slipped away to allow them the space to grieve and find comfort in one another, leaving only an embroidered handkerchief behind him – one that Issy later assumed he must have been carrying with him in his tracksuit pocket all along, a small detail she would have found amusing in other circumstances.

*

Issy gasped. It was true that Lottie was even worse than she'd feared. Her pale skin was damp and flushed, with strands of fiery hair stuck to her forehead, and her temperature was sitting at just over forty degrees (Issy had snuck a digital thermometer into the first aid kit she'd brought with her). Lottie's slender form was dwarfed by the large bed, and her breathing was laboured. Issy could hear a ghastly wheeze with every breath she took.

'Please say he didn't bleed her?'

'No,' said Lady Brampton. 'I have kept Doctor Lisle at bay for as long as I can, and I believe he has only entertained me due to my grief-stricken state, but I fear that unless he sees signs of an improvement soon, he will surely bleed her tomorrow. And what is so terrible about it if he does? It might just save her life.'

'Trust me, grandmother, it will not. But this might.' Issy did not think it was a coincidence that Lottie would pass away on the same day as Doctor Lisle intervened. Determined to prevent the inevitable, she filled a glass with water, and took out two paracetamol and an antibiotic. It was eight o'clock in the evening. 'What date is it tomorrow?' she asked.

'The twenty-seventh of April.' As she had guessed, time passed twice as quickly in 1904.

'And how long do you think we have before Mama or Flora return?'

'Minutes, I should think. They've barely left her side while you've been gone – it was difficult enough to convince them to take a break at all.'

'Then I must act fast.'

Immediately, Issy set about piling a couple of cushions beneath Lottie to help prop her up so that she could breathe more easily. She pulled back the blankets and dampened a towel at the washstand, using it to cool her face before handing it to Lady Brampton so that she could take over. Lottie was startled by the unpleasant sensation, and she clutched at the blanket in efforts to pull it back up over herself to keep warm, her eyelids flickering open from the chill. Issy wondered why it was that a fevered person rarely felt as hot as they were.

'Hello, darling girl,' she whispered. 'You may have a sheet over you, but no blankets, for you are burning up so we must cool you down. I have some medicine for you from the doctor. Here, I will help you take it. I promise it will make you feel better very soon.' Issy fervently hoped this was true.

With Lady Brampton's help, they were able to get Lottie upright enough to swallow the medication with a little water.

'We must keep her cool and hydrated until she gets through this,' Issy instructed, 'and give her these medications at regular intervals. I will persuade Mama and Flora to rest tonight so that I can stay with Lottie and keep on top of it all without them having cause for suspicion. With luck, she should show enough sign of improvement by morning to deter Doctor Lisle from pursuing any drastic treatment.'

Lord Brampton's passing had been enough to distract Mama and Flora from Issy's absence, as they'd assumed that given her particularly close relationship with Lady Brampton she'd been comforting her, and Lady Brampton had not disillusioned them of the notion. The pair were so exhausted they required less prompting than Issy had thought to take the opportunity to get some rest while she watched over Lottie. They knew that if they got some sleep, they'd be better placed to support Lottie first thing the next morning.

Issy made herself as comfortable as she could in the armchair by Lottie's bed, pulling a woollen blanket about her shoulders and not taking her eyes off Lottie, resting one hand on top of hers the entire time, until her eyelids grew so heavy with the onset of the night that she could keep them open no longer. Later, she awoke with a start. The room was in darkness, the fire was embers, and outside she could hear that a breeze had picked up. Otherwise, the great house was silent, and Lottie did not stir.

Issy checked her temperature. It hadn't gone up, but to her distress she found that it hadn't come down either. She fought a rising sense of panic, and decided to wake Lottie in order to give her one more dose of paracetamol - she would give her another antibiotic too, first thing in the morning. The main priority at that moment was to keep her fever at bay, and in turn keep Doctor Lisle at bay too. Lottie mumbled something, but her speech was indecipherable – she was most likely delirious, and her breathing was laboured. Issy had been so hopeful that her plan would work, but this was the first time she feared that it might not.

She begged for Lottie's life, both silently and by quietly speaking the words aloud. Asking whatever higher power that had sent her back to 1904 to keep Lottie safe and allow her to live her life. She told Lottie how things were going to change for girls like her, and how she might grow up to become one of the women responsible for leading that change. That she was living in a time of great advances for women. That there were so many things she was capable of and so many things she could do and be and achieve with her life. Then she read to her chapters from books she thought she might like by the light of a single flickering candle, and, eventually, despite her best efforts to fight it, sleep overtook Issy once more.

She awoke to first light streaming in through a gap in the drapes, and every part of her body was aching. As she stretched, she guessed it must be around five in the morning and she knew the servants would arrive soon to stoke the fire. She was scared to look at Lottie for she was afraid of what she might find, but she looked at her now and her face had lost some of its fierce glow. She appeared to be sleeping peacefully rather than fitfully like before. She re-checked her temperature - thirty-seven point nine. Much better, and Issy was overwhelmed with relief.

'Wake up, sleepy head,' she said, shaking Lottie gently by the shoulder.

Lottie's eyes flickered open, and instead of the dazed, void appearance of before, this time she looked truly present.

'Issy.' Lottie smiled.

'Take this.' Issy pressed another antibiotic into her hand, a wide grin splitting her face. 'Perhaps you might even manage a little breakfast this morning.'

Lottie did as she was asked without question, and though her chest was still rattly and her breathing difficult, Issy had a strong feeling that the worst had passed and she was going to be ok.

23.

Issy held her breath as Doctor Lisle examined Lottie, umming and ahing to himself every now and then at his findings, yet all the while maintaining the poker face that obviously had not changed within the medical profession in the last hundred years. Contrary to expectations, Lottie was sitting upright in bed, had taken dry toast, a little porridge, and some water, and in that inexplicable way of children, she had made a remarkably swift improvement overnight. She was not out of the woods by any means, but she was no longer ensconced so deeply into them that they'd have cause to question whether she'd even make it through the day.

'Remarkable,' Doctor Lisle exclaimed as he snapped his briefcase shut. 'We will continue with the bed rest and fluids and hold off on any further treatment for the time being, unless she deteriorates. If the fever returns, you must fetch me at once - I have arranged with my subordinate at the sanitorium to stay on here for as long as I'm needed. Fortunately for Miss Worthing, she has youth on her side – sometimes that is enough. In the meantime, I will indulge in a spot of fishing with your father, and whilst Lottie is stable, I suggest we all partake in a little breakfast and give our patient time to rest. That's Doctor's Orders.'

Issy exhaled with relief once Doctor Lisle's unsightly jar of leeches were safely ensconced back into his briefcase. Lottie was already dozing. Her breathing was a little easier, and her cheeks were cool and rosy rather than clammy and flushed like before. Issy knew she would have to keep on top of her fever, that even now she couldn't afford to miss a beat. She would stay with her until her last dose of antibiotics was administered, and then she would go back to her own time, where access to lifesaving medical treatment was a given, not a dream.

Issy brushed her hand across her still flat stomach and fought a wave of nausea. Breakfast. She needed breakfast. But she also needed to speak to her grandmother and Lord Eltham, because she knew that she wouldn't know peace in her own time until she could make certain that the real Isabelle Worthing knew peace in this one, and if Lord Eltham had cause to suspect she had been carrying an illegitimate child all along, then they were facing the terrifying possibility of everything she had achieved this season having been in vain.

'I know I have not said this to you enough, Isabelle,' Mama whispered, allowing the others to go on ahead then taking Issy to one side as they softly closed the door to Lottie's room behind them, 'but I am proud of you - we both are - for what you have achieved during our time here. How you have taken care of your sister and everyone else, how you have recovered from your disappointment with Mr Walker, and the fine match you have made with Lord Eltham – even the grace you have extended to Miss Astbury... You are a credit to us.'

Though her back was still ramrod straight and stiff, there was a rare softening to Mama's expression that Issy hadn't seen before. Perhaps the vulnerability she'd experienced due to her fear for Lottie's health had allowed her the necessary freedom for emotional expression that was so rare in 1904, and yet found abundantly in Issy's own time.

Issy grasped her hand. 'Thank you, Mama. That means so much to me. I hope you know I love you both very much.'

Mama bristled a little at that, and Issy wondered if she had gone too far, but Mama simply nodded. 'I love you too,' she said with a small smile. 'We both do.'

And Issy knew the real Isabelle Worthing would just have to take her word for it, for she was certain that no matter what the inner workings were of Papa's mind, he would never be heard to say such a namby-pamby thing in his lifetime.

*

To grant the Bramptons and Worthings their privacy, Lord Eltham's guests had departed for London and the awaiting season, aside from Doctor Lisle who insisted on remaining close at hand until Lottie was better. Breakfast that morning was a subdued affair, and though they all shared the relief of the improvement in Lottie's condition, there was still an underlying concern she may yet be taken from them, just as Lord Brampton had been taken so abruptly. Only Issy was confident the worst would likely no longer happen, and it was frustrating to have to hide the reason why from them all. Then there was the sad business of organising Lord Brampton's funeral, which Lady Brampton insisted must take place at their own estate. It was safe to say that the conversation was not an especially pleasant one.

Lord Eltham was late in coming down and his absence was notable. Issy hoped his mother would not suspect that anything was amiss between them. When he did make his appearance, he was slightly dishevelled, and after giving a polite nod to the rest of their party he gestured for Issy to join him for a moment, muttering something to do with Lottie that he stressed wasn't urgent.

'I must speak with you,' said Lord Eltham once they were out of earshot, and he spoke with a sense of urgency that made Issy's heart flutter, and not in a good way.

'Is there something wrong?'

He nodded.

'Can it wait until after breakfast?' Issy pleaded. She knew that if she didn't eat right away, she would throw up, and then where would they be? For the suspicion it would draw would no doubt make matters worse between them, and far sooner than she'd intended.

'I'm afraid not.'

Between Lord Eltham leaving Lottie and getting dressed for breakfast, Issy could not account for what could have happened to result in his dishevelled and obviously distressed appearance. He led her to the library, where he knew they would not be disturbed.

'What is it, Thomas?' she asked. Could he have guessed about her pregnancy? Surely not. She hadn't breathed a word of it to anyone.

'It's... It's Bentley,' he said, colouring slightly.

'Bentley, your valet?' Issy was momentarily distracted from her nausea by the direction their conversation had taken.

'He's gone.'

Issy gasped. 'Gone? Do you mean he is sick too, like Lottie and Lord Brampton?' She didn't think he had been called to brave the elements that afternoon, but then she didn't really understand the full extent of a valet's duties. Perhaps their sickness was contagious?

'No,' said Lord Eltham, 'I have made enquiries locally, and it looks as though someone threatened to expose us, so Bentley promptly left Upton Hall to protect us from the authorities and save my reputation. He is London bound apparently, but how am I ever to find him there? And what will he do, without references to speak of? If I hadn't gone with you to your time, Isabelle - if I hadn't been so selfish, I could have resolved matters before they went this far.'

Issy could see the pain in his eyes, and she suddenly understood why he did not appear to be as neatly turned out as usual, without his valet there to assist him with his dressing. She doubted Lord Eltham had ever had cause to dress himself in his whole life. 'Oh Thomas, I'm so sorry. Please believe I have said nothing about the two of you to anyone-'

He raised a hand before she could say anything further. 'I know you have said nothing – it would have been that blasted Countess Astbury. First, she tells me you're with child, and now this.'

Issy grimaced, recalling some of the comments Mr Walker had once made to her about her fiancé – he must have known too. But surely he would not have cause to stoop so low this late in the game?

Countess Astbury however, she could understand. 'Actually, there is something I need to tell *you* too,' she said.

There was a knock at the door, and when no servant appeared to open it, Issy did so instead.

'You are both missed at the breakfast table,' said Lady Brampton, peering from one to the other, 'particularly by your mothers. What message shall I give them?'

'Perhaps you can tell them I was checking on Lottie, grandmother,' said Issy.

'I tried that.'

'Then perhaps you ought to stay awhile and we can come up with some sort of excuse together, for there is something I must say and you should both be here to hear it.'

'Oh?'

Lady Brampton gripped her walking stick, and with one hand supporting her lower back she sat down in the nearest armchair.

'I am with child,' said Issy, and Lord Eltham paled, shaking his head in disbelief as though he couldn't imagine his day getting any worse. 'It is Ruben,' she continued softly to Lady Brampton, unable, despite the circumstances, to prevent the smile it brought to her lips to witness the softening in her grandmother's expression.

'Ruben? *My* Ruben? You're certain?'

Issy nodded. 'It is. Do you remember, Thomas, when we returned here to your time, there was a delay in me opening the trunk? It was because I was dreaming that I was with Lord Brampton, only it felt so real that it could not have been just a dream.'

'It can't be...'

'That's what I thought too,' said Issy, 'but just as I thought I couldn't travel back in time and I did, I am also carrying Lord Brampton's child, just as the real Isabelle Worthing once had when she married Mr Walker. Ask me something, grandmother – ask me

226

something that only you and Lord Brampton could know about the day you two met- a detail of some sort that I couldn't possibly know.'

Lady Brampton hesitated for only a few moments. 'What was the name of the horse that lost him the stakes?'

'Rubicon,' said Issy. 'His name was Rubicon.'

Lady Brampton's eyes were wide. 'That's right! That is why we called him Ruben – were it not for Rubicon, our paths most likely would never have crossed.'

'I don't understand,' said Lord Eltham, rubbing his forehead as though the very weight of his thoughts were giving him a headache. 'Do you mean to tell me, Isabelle, that you did not disgrace yourself before marriage, but your grandmother did?'

Lady Brampton was about to speak, but Issy was immediately defensive. 'What right have you to judge her?' she asked. 'You are hurting right now because you love Bentley, are you not? And you took risks with Bentley because of that love? Risks that led to me finding you both together that afternoon? I have been nothing but honest with you, Thomas, and whilst what happened between Lord and Lady Brampton may have been cause for exclusion from society in your time, surely you have learned enough about what exclusion feels like from your own experiences to understand the harm it causes? They were just a couple in love, doing what comes naturally, and Lord Brampton only ever had the most honourable of intentions towards her – eventually, they were able to marry.'

'Yes, after she had conned Mr Walker into accepting her child, no doubt.'

'We all know enough of Mr Walker's character not to be too concerned about his wellbeing in all of this – he is quite capable of taking care of his own needs. Heavens – Mr Walker is just as likely to have been the one who sent Bentley away from here as Countess Astbury, for it appears he already knew about you!' Issy was furious. Her corset strained across her bust and stomach and she felt hot, irritable and nauseous. 'I can't believe I am having to justify all of this to you. Relationships are complicated – you know this yourself! Not once in our acquaintance have I treated you with the lack of consideration and grace you have just demonstrated towards my grandmother and I.'

'It is most disappointing,' said Lady Brampton dryly, 'but to Lord Eltham's credit, it *is* a lot to take in, Issy, especially when he already carries his concern regarding Bentley's sudden departure, not to mention that his fiancé will of course be expected to produce a *legitimate* heir upon marriage...'

Issy shook her head. She had had enough. 'If Bentley means that much to you, Thomas, why don't you go after him? He can't have gone far without his own transportation and without having had access to the last of his wages. My grandmother and I will be just fine without you.'

'Don't be ridiculous,' said Lord Eltham.

'There is nothing ridiculous about it. You love him, do you not? Lady Brampton has just lost the only man she has ever loved, and she had no choice in the matter, but you – you have a choice.'

Issy knew it was hopeless, for Lord Eltham would never marry her now. She would return to her own time knowing she had ruined her grandmother's future prospects forever, and those of her sisters in turn. Her entire family would no longer be accepted into society... And the child... Who knew what would happen to the child. From the very start, all odds had been stacked against her match with Lord Eltham, yet despite all that, there was one relationship that was still salvageable in all of this.

'Get Dart,' she instructed Lord Eltham, who's molten eyes burned intently as he searched her face. Issy ignored him. 'Grandmother, you may tell our parents that Lord Eltham and I are going out for a ride.'

THE DEBUTANTE

*

They were able to cut directly across Lord Eltham's land to the departure point of the post-chaise a lot faster than a car would have taken them, given the roads were not developing at the pace of the rise in ownership of the motor car. Issy felt rather than heard above the pounding of the hooves, Lord Eltham's intake of breath at the sight of a solitary male figure waiting expectantly. Over his shoulder he carried a single bag of possessions, his head tilted in the direction in which the post-chaise would arrive.

Issy squeezed Lord Eltham's hand, but this time he didn't squeeze it back. When they dismounted, she wished him luck and told him she would walk back to the hall alone and see to Lottie before facing their families, for it was fine out and she was sure there would be no more incidents of torrential rain to scupper her plans. She no longer felt nauseous, she had simply surrendered to the whole host of competing emotions that propelled her forwards, so that she continued to put one foot in front of the other even if in the grand scheme of things, she didn't really know where she was headed.

She knew Lord Eltham and Bentley needed time alone, but just as she crested the hill that would take her out of the pair's sight, she glanced back to see Bentley's shoulders shaking within Lord Eltham's embrace, and just down the track ahead she could make out the approaching carriage that, depending upon what they decided, could become the first step of Bentley's journey towards London without him.

24.

Though Issy had begun making for Upton Hall some time before Lord Eltham, on horseback it looked as though he had beaten her to it, for she watched him dismount and walk Dart back into the stables, alone. She assumed Bentley must be London-bound after all, and her heart went out to them both. Still, she hoped she'd have just enough time to get into the hall and avoid an encounter, but Lord Eltham emerged just before she could enact her plan – the crunching of the gravel having given her away. He was flushed in the face from his ride on what already had the makings of a warm spring day, and dare she say it, he appeared far happier and more animated than any of his encounters with her had ever made him.

'Lord Eltham.'

'Issy.'

She was surprised by his informal use of her name. 'I take it Bentley is not to rejoin your staff?'

'Actually, he is!' He was unable to hide his smile and Issy grinned.

'I'm very pleased to hear it, but then, where is he?'

'He'll stay with his family in the next village for a few days – and when he returns here, he can claim there was some sort of family emergency he had to attend to.'

'I see. Then I'm very pleased for the two of you, for I feared the worst when I saw you were alone.'

She turned on her heel and made for the rear entrance to the hall, believing all that needed to be said between them had been said already.

'Issy! Please wait, I must speak with you.'

Of course, he must. He was about to end their engagement, and she could cry with the disappointment of it all. Here she was carrying a much wanted and much-loved child, and yet she had failed to secure a future for either him or his mother. She sighed and turned towards Lord Eltham, barely able to meet his eye.

'I think I have found a solution to our problems that may benefit us all, and that may also be to your liking.'

It was the very last thing Issy had expected to hear. She raised her eyes to his, and for once he was looking at her with warmth and what looked like genuine regard. 'Really?' She could scarcely believe that may be the case – she had been unable to think of any way out of their situation.

'Really... But first, we must fetch your grandmother.'

Once again they met in the library. Mama and Flora were with Lottie, Papa and Doctor Lisle were fishing, and Lady Eltham was seeing to her own matters in the village.

'So,' said Lady Brampton, 'you would still marry Isabelle, legally adopt my son as your own and raise him as such, provided she accepts your relationship with Bentley?'

'In a nutshell,' Lord Eltham confirmed. 'Though I believe we should remove ourselves from London and establish our married life at Worthington, where there is less cause for suspicion regarding the nature of my relationship with Bentley. We will be as husband and wife in matters of duty and estate, but our romantic lives will be our own affair. My mother can stay on at the home she loves with my sisters, and they may visit us as often as they wish. Ruben can take the name of Worthing-Eltham, given he is not truly of the Eltham line – though an outsider would see it as little more than the merging of our two old family names.'

'Yes,' said Lady Brampton, 'that suits nicely. Ruben was a Walker-Worthing you see, for Mr Walker had always aspired to be accepted as part of the landed gentry, not that society paid him much heed, much to his annoyance. In hindsight, that was likely to have been his main reason for marrying me to begin with.'

And as she nodded, satisfied with the arrangements, Issy was concerned for her. She had so desperately wanted to achieve a love match for her grandmother, and yet here she was resigning herself to a life devoid of it and she said as such.

'Nonsense, Issy,' said Lady Brampton. 'I am growing old. I have lived my life, and have been fortunate enough to share great love with Lord Brampton right up until his death. I am satisfied. But what I am not satisfied with, is how in doing so I never got to be the mother my son deserved, and this arrangement would grant me that greatest of blessings! Yes, I think it is an excellent arrangement – the best for all of us in the circumstances.'

'What does Bentley think about it?' Issy asked. 'Was it *his* idea?'

'No,' said Lord Eltham, 'but he approves, if you do...'

They were right, Issy supposed. They both were. 'I approve,' she said, eventually. It was not quite how she'd envisaged their relationship panning out, but it was far better than the alternative, for she shuddered to imagine what Mama and Papa would say if they were to break their engagement at this late stage – when all of society had been there to witness their betrothal. And it *was* a good arrangement – a way to navigate through the complexity of their situation – perhaps Lady Brampton could even look up Lord Brampton once again and involve him in their son's life.

Her grandmother had married once for love already, but she had never gotten to mother her son. Lord Eltham was not asking her to produce an heir of his own into the arrangement, he was simply happy to accept Ruben as such. This was a significant sacrifice on his part, in a time when continuation of the male line was everything, especially for a man who was the sole surviving son of his parents.

There was a knock at the door, and Lady Eltham walked in. 'I hope I'm not interrupting anything?' she asked warmly. 'For I believe the youngest Miss Worthing is asking for you, Miss Worthing.'

Issy summoned a smile. 'You are not, Lady Eltham, and everything is quite alright, as you see. I had better go up there and see what Lottie needs - please excuse me.'

On her way out, Lord Eltham extended a hand towards hers, and when he squeezed it, Issy squeezed right back. Lady Eltham and Lady Brampton looked fondly upon the exchange between the pair and, for their own reasons, smiled.

*

Issy hugged Lottie extra close that morning. It was the morning Lottie was finally permitted by Doctor Lisle to leave her bed, and as could be expected, she ignored all good advice and proceeded to sprint down the hallway on an ankle that had fortunately had ample time to heal. She ran all the way down the stairs, not anxious in the least, to indulge in a hearty final breakfast with the family, and with Lord Eltham's sisters in particular, with whom she chatted none-stop - before their planned return to London and the awaiting season, for Mama had no intention of sending the girls back home to the nursery when she had come so close to losing one of them. Only, though they didn't realise it yet – Issy and Lady Brampton would not be joining them.

'Are you sure you want to go?' Lady Brampton whispered whilst Lottie was holding the floor, as though reading her thoughts once again.

Issy regarded her surrogate family – Lottie, Flora, Mama and Papa, Lord Eltham and his mother and sisters - even old Doctor Lisle - and felt a surge of grief. But she knew that if everything turned out as she hoped, they would be getting the real Isabelle Worthing back, and Issy would be home with her own family where she truly belonged. The knowledge didn't make their parting any easier however - especially where Lottie was concerned - and Issy realised her real grandmother, Lucinda Worthing's motivation in having left her the key. If she was ever fortunate enough to have a daughter of her own, then she too would have her own great adventure, and with luck, they'd tell Issy all about it. The tales of her daughters and granddaughters would likely be as close as she'd ever get to travelling through time in her lifetime– and what an experience it had been.

'I'm sure,' she said.

As she observed Lottie, animated and with a healthy pink glow to her cheeks, her fiery hair hanging loose about her shoulders as it would remain until she came of age, Issy had a feeling that it was girls like her who would grow up to become the women who would pave the way for the females of her time to enjoy a new level of freedom, privilege, and equality that had historically always been denied them. Though there were still gains to be made, Issy hadn't previously understood how lucky she was to be able to take all that progress for granted – progress women had suffered for – and she decided that no matter what, when she got home, she would never again take it for granted.

'I'm ready,' she said, savouring every detail of their last breakfast together, for she couldn't face saying goodbye. Mama was excitedly plotting all the tea parties, balls, and events they would attend where she could show off her newly engaged daughter.

Beneath the table, Lady Brampton rested a warm hand on Issy's, and Lord Eltham peered across the table at them as though he knew exactly what they must be thinking, though he couldn't hear a word that was being said between them.

'Well, I must finish my packing for tomorrow. Mama, Papa, Lady Eltham, please excuse me,' said Issy, rising from the table, the layers of her beautiful coffee and cream-trimmed travelling suit falling against her legs, her posture as tall and poised as anyone of the era could ever hope it would be. Gosh, she would miss the gorgeous dresses – but definitely not the corsets - for she was of the firm view that if anything belonged in the past it was them, and she'd made her grandmother promise to wear hers loosely – or preferably not at all - until after her son was born.

'You mean you haven't packed?' Mama was aghast. 'When the carriage departs in less than an hour?'

Issy nodded, 'I'm sorry. I'll be quick!'

'Oh, never mind that,' said Lady Eltham. 'It seems that your son and my daughter are nothing but a distraction to one another, Lady Worthing, and that is exactly as it should be.'

To Issy's surprise, Mama didn't argue, she simply smiled.

*

Issy climbed into the trunk first, followed by a weary Lady Brampton who yelped in pain as she contorted her aching bones into position, assisted by Lord Eltham who did what he could to ensure her comfort – throwing in a couple of cushions off the bed and easing her in as gently as possible. They were top to tail, with Lady Brampton's feet up beneath Issy's debutante dress and resting against her hips. Issy thought that might be the best way to ensure they were both under the same dress, but not bound for the same destination – she could only hope that she was right, otherwise who knew what the consequences might be, or where they'd both end up.

'Are you ready?' Lord Eltham asked.

Issy looked into those astute violet eyes of Lady Brampton's and nodded. 'We are,' she said. 'Thomas... Thank you - for being a friend. I wish you and Isabelle and Bentley and little Ruben all the very best. Remember what I told you about those medications and supplies? How they work and when to give them? But the most important thing of all to remember, is that the woman Ruben must marry is a Miss Mary Day.'

'Oh!' Lady Brampton exclaimed with approval. 'I remember the Days. They were friends of Mama and Papa – a very good family. Old money.'

'I do,' said Lord Eltham. 'You take good care of yourself and your family, for you never know when one of your visiting ancestors may depend upon it. And your family is my family too now, remember.'

'I will,' Issy promised. 'And Grandmother,' she said, facing her, 'I love you. I'm so grateful I got to spend this time with you. Very soon you will be with Ruben.'

'Ahh,' Lady Brampton sighed as she slowly eased her head back inside the trunk, a wide smile upon her face that softened the lines and took years off her, 'I can hardly wait. Thank you, Issy. Thank you, my darling girl.'

The last thing Issy saw was Lord Eltham's earnest face and molten eyes as he closed the lid for the final time, and everything went black.

Before she even opened the lid, Issy knew she was alone, for she could no longer feel her grandmother's presence in the trunk alongside her. Just as she raised her arms to push back the lid, it was flung open from the other side, and there was her mum, with her tearstained face and arms outstretched, beckoning for Issy to step right inside them.

Minutes later, Issy remembered. 'The tapestry!' she said, removing herself from her mum's embrace and peeling off the debutante dress as quickly and carefully as she could.

Within moments they were there, and all of it was unchanged, except for Ruben Walker-Worthing having become Ruben Worthing-Eltham - the Eltham informally dropped as generations passed, and all the evidence Issy needed that dear little Lottie went on to live a very long life. Issy would never know why she'd been chosen to travel back in time, but she had the strongest feeling it was as much to secure her own future as it was to secure her family's past.

Epilogue

Issy had come home, and Susan didn't think anything could please her more than knowing her daughter was safe and not lost to her anymore. Even better, Issy's venture into the past had been entirely different from her own, and she had come through the experience remarkably unscathed. When Issy had offered to watch the girls for her, for a moment Susan was worried the real Issy had left her again and Mya had returned in her place, but no, it was still Issy, just a maturing version of the girl who had disappeared into the attic all those weeks ago. She had always been a proud mother, but never more so than she was now. Susan only hoped that Issy would always know how much she meant to her – that no matter what happened between them, Susan would be there for her always.

'Do you think she'll like it?' she bit her lip and Mrs Lamb smiled.

'You've done a remarkable job - she'll love it!'

Susan surveyed the ballroom, decked out with flowers cut by Mr Lamb from the manor's own walled garden, as well as paper garlands, bunting, and a ceiling studded with hundreds of tiny lights. She'd even been able to dig out one of her great-grandmother's ballgowns from the attic, and she'd laid it out on the bed for Issy as the perfect complement to her fair hair, creamy skin, and cornflower-blue eyes. She suspected a certain Georgie Stevens might notice it too.

Mrs Lamb glanced at the grandfather clock. 'We've still got a little time before the guests arrive, and everything is ready. How about I brew us a nice hot pot of tea and we can sit down and have a natter like old times?'

'Actually,' said Susan, 'I think I'll pop into the village and speak to the solicitor about all that paperwork he brought. I won't be long.'

'Then take your time. I can handle things here.'

But Susan knew she wouldn't miss that first look at Issy in her prom dress for the world, no matter how nice and engaging Mr Manning was, *no matter how kind his eyes, and no matter how impressive his paintings that were hung throughout the higgledy-piggledy rooms of his quaint country gallery. There would be plenty of other opportunities for them to get to know one another better, for Susan and the girls were going nowhere. She didn't know how she was going to make it all work, but they would be staying on at Worthington Manor with Mr and Mrs Lamb indefinitely, back home where they belonged.*

*

Mrs Lamb, aided by a team of willing assistants, had outdone herself, for Worthington Manor was scrubbed and polished to perfection, a veritable feast was laid out on trestle tables, and everywhere was a riot of colour from the balloon garlands framing the main entranceway, to the flowers and foliage Mr Lamb had carefully cut then festooned all about the ballroom and twisted along the balustrades of the grand staircase. The drapes had been pulled closed so that above them a thousand fairy lights twinkled, and in the corner a band played instrumental versions of all the latest hits. Issy's mum had overseen every last detail.

'Issy, they're coming!' Ella yelled excitedly. 'Hurry!' She was dressed in her best party dress and hopeful of being able to stay up almost as late as her sisters.

They could hear the crunching of cars upon gravel as parent after parent dropped off their eager sons and daughters from the village school, and Jasmine helped Mrs Lamb hand out berry mimosas upon arrival. The young men were dressed in their finest suits in beiges, blues and greys; the young ladies in beautiful dresses of aqua, peach and cerise - and everywhere they shimmered and sparkled from the intricate detailing of jewels and sequins.

Outside the sun still shone, so the guests milled about waiting for one another on the patio before steadily making their way into the ballroom, but Issy was nowhere to be seen. She was standing in front of her bedroom mirror studying her reflection from this angle and that, wondering and hoping that Georgie Stevens would come, and that he might one day come to like her as much as it sounded as though he had liked Mya.

'Hurry up, Issy, you're missing your own prom!'

Issy took a deep breath. She was ready.

She grasped the balustrade with one hand, and, remembering her lessons in deportment, held herself high with her chin up and back straight, poised and confident. Her dress was a vintage attic find, carefully restored to its former glory by Mrs Lamb. It was the same cornflower blue as her eyes, overlaid with a darker chiffon and a bodice of seed pearls. Her mother gasped when she saw her in it, and she was not the only one, for waiting for her at the bottom of the stairs, his forest-green eyes intent on hers the entire time, was Georgie.

He took her hand and led her to the dancefloor before pulling her into his strong embrace. They swayed together in rhythm to the music, Issy's skirts swishing about her legs and Georgie's broad chest against hers, her hands resting upon the taut muscles of his back. Her skin fizzed at his touch. His big hands upon the small of her back that made her feel delicate, and somehow in that moment – a moment which for all she knew she could have already lived before - she felt as if she'd truly come home.

'So,' she said, 'what was Mya *really* like?'

Georgie grinned. 'Beautiful. Like you. She was also intelligent, driven, and knew exactly what she wanted. She was training to become a sustainability consultant – apparently in 2068, every business has to get an assessment from one and implement their recommendations. She was specialising in flood management, so I'm guessing from the way things are going - she'll be kept pretty busy. And there was a guy on her course that she liked. But there was just one problem...'

'What?'

'She wasn't you.'

'But I thought-'

'I know! That's what I wanted you to think. I was attracted to you straight away, but you had that boyfriend of yours, and you didn't look as though you intended to stick around Worthington for long. What happened with him, anyway?'

'I don't know,' said Issy. 'He's most likely at his own prom with this other girl from school who was interested in him.' Stephanie Sutton.

Issy didn't feel it was the right time to tell him that after her experiences of Edwardian courtship, whilst she didn't exactly expect a marriage proposal, she did want more than to be pestered for nudes by a guy who barely knew her on any real level, which, from what a quick scan of Chad Connor's text messages had revealed, was about all he was interested in. She hoped Mila would fare better with his friend, and guessed she would find out when her mum brought her to stay with them for a couple of weeks over summer - something she was really looking forward to.

'I'm sorry to hear that,' said Georgie. 'Well, actually, I can't say I'm *that* sorry.'

'Me neither,' said Issy, and she dipped her head towards him, resting it against his chest as they moved, whilst with his other hand, Georgie toyed with a frond of her silken hair. Whilst Issy did not know what the future might hold for the two of them – she did know this was a pretty good place for it to start.

Issy was fortunate that Mya's revision had enabled her to confidently sit her A-Level examinations, and she'd even had time to apply to study nursing at a local university through clearing, inspired by her great, great, great aunt Lottie, whom she'd discovered had become a nurse during the First World War, before training as a midwife then getting married late in life to a man who shared the same degree of passion and commitment towards the rights of women and girls as she did. Together they'd established one of the first refuges for women in violent relationships and unmarried pregnant mothers, caring for their children and helping the women access the training they needed to secure future employment and independent means. Issy hoped she could one day become just like her - by embracing the opportunities that came her way to make a difference to those who needed it most.

Since Georgie would be studying landscape architecture at the same university and had already secured his first placement at Worthington Manor, Issy knew their paths would continue to cross for quite some time to come – not least because the moment the prospect of them staying on at the manor was mentioned to her sisters, there was no going back. They wanted nothing more than to stay, and it hadn't taken long for them to convince their mother, who was ready to put the past behind her once and for all and do justice to her own late mother's wishes for the manor. Issy only hoped their ancestors could forgive her mum's plan to monetise the estate – especially Lady Brampton.

'So,' said Mr Lamb to his wife, 'when are you gonna tell me about all these strange goin's on, then?'

'Ah, away with you and your superstitions! I don't know what you're talking about.'

Mrs Lamb affected an air of innocence, and smiled when she observed in her peripheral vision the arrival of Mr Manning, who made an immediate beeline towards Susan. She hoped Susan would forgive her presumption in inviting him – fortunately, she suspected she would.

'Don't you, indeed? By, if these old walls could talk...'

'They would say that whatever has happened within them, the good and the bad, it all turned out for the best. I'm sure you'd agree with me on that – as would the late Lady Worthing.' Mrs

Lamb knew her old mistress would have wanted nothing more than for her daughter and grandchildren to be happy, whether it was at Worthington Manor or elsewhere – and she could feel it in her old bones that they were going to be. She knew Lucinda Worthing would have loved nothing more for her family to have come home at last.

Mr Lamb raised his brow and walked away, making straight for the buffet. As the fairy lights twinkled above them and more and more couples slipped onto the dance floor; Susan, Jasmine and Ella watched on as Georgie dipped his head and covered the space between his mouth and Issy's and kissed her. Issy kissed him right back.

Somewhere, several months later in 1905, Lady Brampton pushed as hard as the midwife told her to and was grateful for the stronger medication Issy had slipped in for the purpose. Before long, she was rewarded with a gratifying cry, and in an instant her cheeks were wet with exhausted, happy tears as the midwife declared she'd had a baby boy and wrapped him in blankets before passing him over for her to hold. She marvelled at how light he was, at each of his tiny fingers and tiny toes, at the deep blue of his eyes and the lusty cry that his little form looked much too small to produce. He grasped her finger with his - his grip was surprisingly firm and strong - and she placed him to her breast and held him there tightly, filled with gratitude for this moment and for all the moments that they would now get to spend together.

Beside her, Lord Eltham looked at his son in wonder. 'Ruben,' he said. 'We'll call him Ruben.'

The End.

Acknowledgements

Dear Reader,

Thank you for reading *The Debutante*. Of all my novels, this one holds a special place in my heart as having been the most fun and most challenging (time travel does that!) to write.

I would like to thank, as always, my beautiful family for your enduring support and faith in me. Thanks also to Musrath Humaira Moon for capturing the magic of Issy's story with her beautiful cover design.

As always, your feedback is valued, and I would be delighted to hear from you via either my website, Facebook or Instagram. A review is one of most helpful ways to support an author and would be gratefully received and very much appreciated.

I hope to revisit the Worthing family once again in the future (or should that be, past!).

With very best wishes,

Gemma Frances

www.gemmafrances.com @gemma_frances

P.S. This book has been edited extensively. If there are any sneaky mistakes, they are my cat's contribution and therefore kind of cute, really – if you're a cat person.

About the author...

Gemma Frances is a married mum from Newcastle upon Tyne, UK currently living in Melbourne, Australia. She qualified as a Social Worker and has worked with children and families ever since. Her dream of travelling the world as cabin crew was never quite realised, as her interview was cancelled during the Global Financial Crisis, and she was left with an approved career break but nothing to do (which is probably for the best, as she now has a fear of flying!). Armed with a round-the-world flight and a suitcase (never a backpack), she travelled to Australia on a gap year, fell in love with her husband, and the rest is history.

Gemma's debut novel, *Meet Me at The Melbourne*, won Dick and Angel Strawbridge of the TV show *Escape to the Chateau's* Literature Competition in 2020 and was published through The Chateau Publishing Limited in 2021.

Ask the author...

What inspired The Debutante?

As a very young child, I often had a sense of having been born in the wrong century. If my mam asked me to point out clothing I liked at the shops, I would point out the most frilly, flouncy, lacy and velvety dresses they had; and she would tut and tell me *no way*. No matter the weather, I would refuse to get dressed for primary school unless I could wear a skirt or a dress. I didn't feel like a 'lady' otherwise. It's no surprise, then, that as I got older and developed a love of reading, I was drawn to historical fiction (Jane Austen's Pride and Prejudice is an enduring favourite). I always knew I wanted to write, and Issy's venture into the past provided the perfect opportunity for me to live out the alternate life that as a child I somehow believed I was meant to be living.

Why did you venture off genre with The Debutante?

Though Meet Me at The Melbourne and The Debutante are very different, they do have some threads in common – both heroines make a fresh start in new places, and both stories contain a hint of magic. I've always been drawn to stories with a magical element and have been inspired by movies such as Last Christmas, The Love Letter, Sliding Doors and Lake House (as a child, The Amazing Mr Blunden and The Canterville Ghost were firm favourites!). The Debutante gave me the freedom to incorporate those magical elements I enjoy watching so much on screen into my writing.

Who is your favourite character?

Aside from our heroine, Issy, I adore Lady Brampton's pragmatic approach to life and her ability to make allowances for a young woman raised on ideals very different to her own. It was heartening to see the developing of a bond between the two characters that crossed the boundaries of time. I find Susan's character intriguing and hope she's able to find happiness with Mr Manning, as well as a maturing peace in her relationship with her daughter.

Who is your favourite leading man?

That's a tough one. Probably Lord Eltham for his integrity and self-sacrifice, Mr Walker for his charm, and William Manning for his cheek and light-hearted sincerity. If you could combine all those traits, you'd have the perfect gentleman!

What challenges did you experience in writing this novel?

Unlike my earlier novels, this one flowed so easily it was written within a record 8 months! The biggest challenge was making sure Issy's family tree and key events lined up, given the complexity associated with the time travel aspect of the plot, especially when it came to tying up all the loose ends by the end of the novel. It also took time to research the Edwardian era and its associated etiquette and dress so I could convey a setting that, whilst fictional, was also plausible.

Will there be a sequel?

I hope so! I have some ideas floating about – I'm particularly interested in expanding on Lottie's work and her involvement in helping the disadvantaged young women of the era. If I can find a way to weave another time-travelling Worthing descendant into Lottie's life, I will!

Book Club Questions...

- Why do you think the first daughters of the Worthing line travel back in time?

- Which character did you sympathise with most?

- What advantages do young people have today that they didn't have in the Edwardian era?

- Were there any advantages to life in the Edwardian era?

- How do you feel about the treatment of the lower classes in the Edwardian era?

- Do feel that class is reflected differently in society today? How?

- Would you like the opportunity to travel back in time like Issy and Susan did? Why?

- If you could travel back in time, what era would you like to visit and for what purpose?

- Do you think society has carried any lessons from World War 2 into today? Discuss.

- What learnings can Susan and Issy take from their time travel experiences?

Also by Gemma Frances

The Melbourne Community Cafe
Meet Me at The Melbourne

Worthington Manor
The Debutante